Lady Merton: Colonist

Mrs. Humphry Ward

Illustrated by Albert Sterner

Esprios.com

"ELIZABETH ... COULD YET FIND TIME TO WALK AND CLIMB, PLUNGING SPIRIT AND SENSE IN THE BEAUTY OF THE ROCKIES"

LADY MERTON
COLONIST

BY

MRS. HUMPHRY WARD

FRONTISPIECE

BY ALBERT STERNER

1910

A FOREWORD

Towards the end of this story the readers of it will find an account of an "unknown lake" in the northern Rockies, together with a picture of its broad expanse, its glorious mountains, and of a white explorers' tent pitched beside it. Strictly speaking, "Lake Elizabeth" is a lake of dream. But it has an original on this real earth, which bears another and a real name, and was discovered two years ago by my friend Mrs. Schäffer, of Philadelphia, to whose enchanting narratives of travel and exploration in these untrodden regions I listened with delight at Field, British Columbia, in June, 1908. She has given me leave to use her own photograph of the "unknown lake," and some details from her record of it, for my own purposes; and I can only hope that in the summers to come she may unlock yet other secrets, unravel yet other mysteries, in that noble unvisited country which lies north and northeast of the Bow Valley and the Kicking Horse Pass.

MARY A. WARD.

Lady Merton: Colonist

CHAPTER I

"I call this part of the line beastly depressing."

The speaker tossed his cigarette-end away as he spoke. It fell on the railway line, and the tiny smoke from it curled up for a moment against the heavy background of spruce as the train receded.

"All the same, this is going to be one of the most exciting parts of Canada before long," said Lady Merton, looking up from her guide-book. "I can tell you all about it."

"For heaven's sake, don't!" said her companion hastily. "My dear Elizabeth, I really must warn you. You're losing your head."

"I lost it long ago. To-day I am a bore—to-morrow I shall be a nuisance. Make up your mind to it."

"I thought you were a reasonable person!—you used to be. Now look at that view, Elizabeth. We've seen the same thing for twelve hours, and if it wasn't soon going to be dark we should see the same thing for twelve hours more. What is there to go mad over in that?" Her brother waved his hand indignantly from right to left across the disappearing scene. "As for me, I am only sustained by the prospect of the good dinner that I know Yerkes means to give us in a quarter of an hour. I won't be a minute late for it! Go and get ready, Elizabeth—"

"Another lake!" cried Lady Merton, with a jump. "Oh, what a darling! That's the twentieth since tea. Look at the reflections—and that delicious island! And oh! what *are* those birds?"

She leant over the side of the observation platform, attached to the private car in which she and her brother were travelling, at the rear of the heavy Canadian Pacific train. To the left of the train a small blue lake had come into view, a lake much indented with small bays running up among the woods, and a couple of islands covered with scrub of beech and spruce, set sharply on the clear water. On one side of the lake, the forest was a hideous waste of burnt trunks, where the gaunt stems—charred or singed, snapped or twisted, or flayed—of the trees which remained standing rose dreadfully into the May sunshine, above a chaos of black ruin below. But except for this blemish—the only sign of man—the little lake was a gem of beauty. The spring green clothed its rocky sides; the white spring clouds floated above it, and within it; and small beaches of white pebbles seemed to invite the human feet which had scarcely yet come near them.

"What does it matter?" yawned her brother. "I don't want to shoot them. And why you make such a fuss about the lakes, when, as you say yourself, there are about two a mile, and none of them has got a name to its back, and they're all exactly alike, and all full of beastly mosquitoes in the summer—it beats me! I wish Yerkes would hurry up." He leant back sleepily against the door of the car and closed his eyes.

"It's *because* they haven't got a name—and they're so endless!—and the place is so big!—and the people so few!—and the chances are so many—and so queer!" said Elizabeth Merton laughing.

"What sort of chances?"

"Chances of the future."

"Hasn't got any chances!" said Philip Gaddesden, keeping his hands in his pockets.

"Hasn't it? Owl!" Lady Merton neatly pinched the arm nearest to her. "As I've explained to you many times before, this is the Hinterland of Ontario—and it's only been surveyed, except just along the railway, a few years ago—and it's as rich as rich—"

"I say, I wish you wouldn't reel out the guide-book like that!" grumbled the somnolent person beside her. "As if I didn't know all about the Cobalt mines, and that kind of stuff."

"Did you make any money out of them, Phil?"

"No—but the other fellows did. That's my luck."

"Never mind, there'll be heaps more directly—hundreds." She stretched out her hand vaguely towards an enchanting distance—hill beyond hill, wood beyond wood; everywhere the glimmer of water in the hollows; everywhere the sparkle of fresh leaf, the shining of the birch trunks among the firs, the greys and purples of limestone rock; everywhere, too, the disfiguring stain of fire, fire new or old, written, now on the mouldering stumps of trees felled thirty years ago when the railway was making, now on the young stems of yesterday.

"I want to see it all in a moment of time," Elizabeth continued, still above herself. "An air-ship, you know, Philip—and we should see it all in a day, from here to James Bay. A thousand miles of it—stretched below us—just waiting for man! And we'd drop down into an undiscovered lake, and give it a name—one of our names—and leave a letter under a stone. And then in a hundred years, when the settlers come, they'd find it, and your name—or mine—would live forever."

"I forbid you to take any liberties with my name, Elizabeth! I've something better to do with it than waste it on a lake in—what do you call it?—the 'Hinterland of Ontario.'" The young man mocked his sister's tone.

Elizabeth laughed and was silent.

The train sped on, at its steady pace of some thirty miles an hour. The spring day was alternately sunny and cloudy; the temperature was warm, and the leaves were rushing out. Elizabeth Merton felt the spring in her veins, an indefinable joyousness and expectancy; but she was conscious also of another intoxication—a heat of romantic perception kindled in her by this vast new country through which she was passing. She was a person of much travel, and many experiences; and had it been prophesied to her a year before this date that she could feel as she was now feeling, she would not have believed it. She was then in Rome, steeped in, ravished by the past—assisted by what is, in its way, the most agreeable society in Europe. Here she was absorbed in a rushing present; held by the vision of a colossal future; and society had dropped out of her ken. Quebec, Montreal and Ottawa had indeed made themselves pleasant to her; she had enjoyed them all. But it was in the wilderness that the spell had come upon her; in these vast spaces, some day to be the home of a new race; in these lakes, the playground of the Canada of the future; in these fur stations and scattered log cabins; above all in the great railway linking east and west, that she and her brother had come out to see.

For they had a peculiar relation to it. Their father had been one of its earliest and largest shareholders, might indeed be reckoned among its founders. He had been one, also, of a small group of very rich men who had stood by the line in one of the many crises of its early history, when there was often not enough money in the coffers of the company to pay the weekly wages of the navvies working on the great iron road. He was dead now, and his property in the line had been divided among his children. But his name and services were not forgotten at Montreal, and when his son and widowed daughter let it be known that they desired to cross from Quebec to Vancouver, and inquired what the cost of a private car might be for the journey, the authorities at Montreal insisted on placing one of the official cars at their disposal. So that they were now travelling as the guests of the C.P.R.; and the good will of one of the most powerful of modern corporations went with them.

They had left Toronto, on a May evening, when the orchards ran, one flush of white and pink, from the great lake to the gorge of Niagara, and all along the line northwards the white trilliums shone on the grassy banks in the shadow of the woods; while the pleasant Ontario farms flitted by, so mellowed and homelike already, midway between the old life of Quebec, and this new, raw West to which they were going. They had passed, also—but at night and under the moon—through the lake country which is the playground of Toronto, as well known, and as plentifully be-named as Westmoreland; and then at North Bay with the sunrise they had plunged into the wilderness,—into the thousand miles of forest and lake that lie between Old Ontario and Winnipeg.

And here it was that Elizabeth's enthusiasm had become in her brother's eyes a folly; that something wild had stirred in her blood, and sitting there in her shady hat at the rear of the train, her eyes pursuing the great track which her father had helped to bring into being, she shook Europe from her, and felt through her pulses the tremor of one who watches at a birth, and looks forward to a life to be—

"Dinner is ready, my lady."

"Thank Heaven!" cried Philip Gaddesden, springing up. "Get some champagne, please, Yerkes."

"Philip!" said his sister reprovingly, "it is not good for you to have champagne every night."

Philip threw back his curly head, and grinned.

"I'll see if I can do without it to-morrow. Come along, Elizabeth."

They passed through the outer saloon, with its chintz-covered sofas and chairs, past the two little bedrooms of the car, and the tiny kitchen to the dining-room at the further end. Here stood a man in steward's livery ready to serve, while from the door of the kitchen another older man, thin and tanned, in a cook's white cap and apron, looked benevolently out.

"Smells good, Yerkes!" said Gaddesden as he passed.

The cook nodded.

"If only her ladyship'll find something she likes," he said, not without a slight tone of reproach.

"You hear that, Elizabeth?" said her brother as they sat down to the well-spread board.

Elizabeth looked plaintive. It was one of her chief weaknesses to wish to be liked—adored, perhaps, is the better word—by her servants and she generally accomplished it. But the price of Yerkes's affections was too high.

"It seems to me that we have only just finished luncheon, not to speak of tea," she said, looking in dismay at the menu before her. "Phil, do you wish to see me return home like Mrs. Melhuish?"

Phil surveyed his sister. Mrs. Melhuish was the wife of their local clergyman in Hampshire; a poor lady plagued by abnormal weight, and a heart disease.

"You might borrow pounds from Mrs. Melhuish, and nobody would ever know. You really are too thin, Lisa—a perfect scarecrow. Of course Yerkes sees that he could do a lot for you. All the same, that's a pretty gown you've got on—an awfully pretty gown," he repeated with emphasis, adding immediately afterwards in another tone—"Lisa!—I say!—you're not going to wear black any more?"

"No"—said Lady Merton, "no—I am not going to wear black any more." The words came lingeringly out, and as the servant removed her plate, Elizabeth turned to look out of the window at the endless woods, a shadow on her beautiful eyes.

She was slenderly made, with a small face and head round which the abundant hair was very smoothly and closely wound. The hair was of a delicate brown, the complexion clear, but rather colourless. Among other young and handsome women, Elizabeth Merton made little effect; like a fine pencil drawing, she required an attentive eye. The modelling of the features, of the brow, the cheeks, the throat, was singularly refined, though without a touch of severity; her hands, with their very long and slender fingers, conveyed the same impression. Her dress, though dainty, was simple and inconspicuous, and her movements, light, graceful, self-controlled, seemed to show a person of equable temperament, without any strong emotions. In her light cheerfulness, her perpetual interest in the things about her, she might have reminded a spectator of some of the smaller sea-birds that flit endlessly from wave to wave, for whom the business of life appears to be summed up in flitting and poising.

The comparison would have been an inadequate one. But Elizabeth Merton's secrets were not easily known. She could rave of Canada; she rarely talked of herself. She had married, at the age of nineteen, a young Cavalry officer, Sir Francis Merton, who had died of fever within a year of their wedding, on a small West African expedition for which he had eagerly offered himself. Out of the ten months of their marriage, they had spent four together. Elizabeth was now twenty-seven, and her married life had become to her an insubstantial memory. She had been happy, but in the depths of the mind she knew that she might not have been happy very long. Her husband's piteous death had stamped upon her, indeed, a few sharp memories; she saw him always,—as the report of a brother officer, present at his funeral, had described him—wrapped in the Flag, and so lowered to his grave, in a desert land. This image effaced everything else; the weaknesses she knew, and those she had begun to guess at. But at the same time she had not been crushed by the tragedy; she had often scourged herself in secret for the rapidity with which, after it, life had once more become agreeable to her. She knew that many people thought her incapable of deep feeling. She supposed it must be true. And yet there were moments when a self within herself surprised and startled her; not so much, as yet, in connection with persons, as with ideas, causes—oppressions, injustices, helpless suffering; or, as now, with a new nation, visibly striking its "being into bounds."

During her widowhood she had lived much with her mother, and had devoted herself particularly to this only brother, a delicate lad—lovable, self-indulgent and provoking—for whom the unquestioning devotion of two women had not been the best of schools. An attack of rheumatic fever which had seized him on leaving Christchurch had scared both mother and sister. He had recovered, but his health was not yet what it had been; and as at home it was impossible to keep him from playing golf all day, and bridge all night, the family doctor, in despair, recommended travel, and Elizabeth had offered to take charge of him. It was not an easy task, for although Philip was extremely fond of his sister, as the male head of the family since his father's death he held strong convictions with regard to the natural supremacy of man, and would probably never "double Cape Turk." In another year's time, at the age of four and twenty, he would inherit the family estate, and his mother's guardianship would come to an end. He then intended to be done with petticoat government, and to show these two dear women a thing or two.

The dinner was good, as usual; in Elizabeth's eyes, monstrously good. There was to her something repellent in such luxurious fare enjoyed by strangers, on this tourist-flight through a country so eloquent of man's hard wrestle with rock and soil, with winter and the wilderness. The blinds of the car towards the next carriage were rigorously closed, that no one might interfere with the privacy of the rich; but Elizabeth had drawn up the blind beside her, and looked occasionally into the evening, and that endless medley of rock and forest and lake which lay there outside, under the sunset. Once she gazed out upon a great gorge, through which ran a noble river, bathed in crimson light; on its way, no doubt, to Lake Superior, the vast, crescent-shaped lake she had dreamed of in her school-room days, over her geography lessons, and was soon to see with her own eyes. She thought of the uncompanioned beauty of the streams, as it would be when the thunder of the train had gone by, of its distant sources in the wild, and the loneliness of its long, long journey. A little shiver stole upon her, the old tremor of man in presence of a nature not yet tamed to his needs, not yet identified with his feelings, still full therefore of stealthy and hostile powers, creeping unawares upon his life.

"This champagne is not nearly as good as last night," said Philip discontentedly. "Yerkes must really try for something better at Winnipeg. When do we arrive?"

"Oh, some time to-morrow evening."

"What a blessing we're going to bed!" said the boy, lighting his cigarette. "You won't be able to bother me about lakes, Lisa."

But he smiled at her as he spoke, and Elizabeth was so enchanted to notice the gradual passing away of the look of illness, the brightening of the eye, and slight filling out of the face, that he might tease her as he pleased.

Within an hour Philip Gaddesden was stretched on a comfortable bed sound asleep. The two servants had made up berths in the dining-room; Elizabeth's maid slept in the saloon. Elizabeth herself, wrapped in a large cloak, sat awhile outside, waiting for the first sight of Lake Superior.

It came at last. A gleam of silver on the left—a line of purple islands—frowning headlands in front—and out of the interminable shadow of the forests, they swept into a broad moonlight. Over high bridges and the roar of rivers, threading innumerable bays, burrowing through headlands and peninsulas, now hanging over the cold shining of the water, now lost again in the woods, the train sped on its wonderful way. Elizabeth on her platform at its rear was conscious of no other living creature. She seemed to be alone with the night and the vastness of the lake, the awfulness of its black and purple coast. As far as she could see, the trees on its shores were still bare; they had temporarily left the spring behind; the North seemed to have rushed upon her in its terror and desolation. She found herself imagining the storms that sweep the lake in winter, measuring her frail life against the loneliness and boundlessness around her. No sign of man, save in the few lights of these scattered stations; and yet, for long, her main impression was one of exultation in man's power and skill, which bore her on and on, safe, through the conquered wilderness.

Gradually, however, this note of feeling slid down into something much softer and sadder. She became conscious of herself, and her personal life; and little by little her exultation passed into yearning; her eyes grew wet. For she had no one beside her with whom to share these secret thoughts and passions—these fresh contacts with life and nature. Was it always to be so? There was in her a longing, a "sehnsucht," for she knew not what.

She could marry, of course, if she wished. There was a possibility in front of her, of which she sometimes thought. She thought of it now, wistfully and kindly; but it scarcely availed against the sudden melancholy, the passion of indefinite yearning which had assailed her.

The night began to cloud rapidly. The moonlight died from the lake and the coast. Soon a wind sprang up, lashing the young spruce and birch growing among the charred wreck of the older forest, through which the railway had been driven. Elizabeth went within, and she was no sooner in bed than the rain came pelting on her window.

Lady Merton: Colonist

She lay sleepless for a long time, thinking now, not of the world outside, or of herself, but of the long train in front of her, and its freight of lives; especially of the two emigrant cars, full, as she had seen at North Bay, of Galicians and Russian Poles. She remembered the women's faces, and the babies at their breasts. Were they all asleep, tired out perhaps by long journeying, and soothed by the noise of the train? Or were there hearts among them aching for some poor hovel left behind, for a dead child in a Carpathian graveyard?—for a lover?—a father?—some bowed and wrinkled Galician peasant whom the next winter would kill? And were the strong, swarthy men dreaming of wealth, of the broad land waiting, the free country, and the equal laws?

Elizabeth awoke. It was light in her little room. The train was at a standstill. Winnipeg?

A subtle sense of something wrong stole upon her. Why this murmur of voices round the train? She pushed aside a corner of the blind beside her. Outside a railway cutting, filled with misty rain— many persons walking up and down, and a babel of talk—

Bewildered, she rang for her maid, an elderly and precise person who had accompanied her on many wanderings.

"Simpson, what's the matter? Are we near Winnipeg?"

"We've been standing here for the last two hours, my lady. I've been expecting to hear you ring long ago."

Simpson's tone implied that her mistress had been somewhat crassly sleeping while more sensitive persons had been awake and suffering.

Elizabeth rubbed her eyes. "But what's wrong, Simpson, and where are we?"

"Goodness knows, my lady. We're hours away from Winnipeg— that's all I know—and we're likely to stay here, by what Yerkes says."

"Has there been an accident?"

Simpson replied—sombrely—that something had happened, she didn't know what—that Yerkes put it down to "the sink-hole," which according to him was "always doing it"—that there were two trains in front of them at a standstill, and trains coming up every minute behind them.

"My dear Simpson!—that must be an exaggeration. There aren't trains every minute on the C.P.R. Is Mr. Philip awake?"

"Not yet, my lady."

"And what on earth is a sink-hole?" asked Elizabeth.

CHAPTER II

Elizabeth had ample time during the ensuing sixteen hours for inquiry as to the nature of sink-holes.

When she emerged, dressed, into the saloon—she found Yerkes looking out of the window in a brown study. He was armed with a dusting brush and a white apron, but it did not seem to her that he had been making much use of them.

"Whatever is the matter, Yerkes? What is a sink-hole?"

Yerkes looked round.

"A sink-hole, my lady?" he said slowly—"A sink-hole, well, it's as you may say—a muskeg."

"A *what?*"

"A place where you can't find no bottom, my lady. This one's a vixen, she is! What she's cost the C.P.R.!"—he threw up his hands. "And there's no contenting her—the more you give her the more she wants. They give her ten trainloads of stuff a couple of months ago. No good! A bit of moist weather and there she is at it again. Let an engine and two carriages through last night—ten o'clock!"

"Gracious! Was anybody hurt? What—a kind of bog?—a quicksand?"

"Well," said Yerkes, resuming his dusting, and speaking with polite obstinacy, "muskegs is what they call 'em in these parts. They'll have to divert the line. I tell 'em so, scores of times. She was at this game last year. Held me up twenty-one hours last fall."

When Yerkes was travelling he spoke in a representative capacity. He *was* the line.

"How many trains ahead of us are there? Yerkes?"

"Two as I know on—may be more."

"And behind?"

"Three or four, my lady."

"And how long are we likely to be kept?"

"Can't say. They've been at her ten hours. She don't generally let anyone over her under a good twenty—or twenty-four."

"Yerkes!—what will Mr. Gaddesden say? And it's so damp and horrid."

Elizabeth looked at the outside prospect in dismay. The rain was drizzling down. The passengers walking up and down the line were in heavy overcoats with their collars turned up. To the left of the line there was a misty glimpse of water over a foreground of charred stumps. On the other side rose a bank of scrubby wood, broken by a patch of clearing, which held a rude log-cabin. What was she to do with Philip all day?

Suddenly a cow appeared on the patch of grass round the log hut. With a sound of jubilation, Yerkes threw down his dusting brush and rushed out of the car. Elizabeth watched him pursue the cow, and disappear round a corner. What on earth was he about?

Philip had apparently not yet been called. He was asleep, and Yerkes had let well alone. But he must soon awake to the situation, and the problem of his entertainment would begin. Elizabeth took up the guide-book and with difficulty made out that they were about a hundred miles from Winnipeg. Somewhere near Rainy Lake apparently. What a foolishly appropriate name!

"Hi!—hi!—"

The shout startled her. Looking out she saw a group of passengers grinning, and Yerkes running hard for the car, holding something in his hand, and pursued by a man in a slouch hat, who seemed to be swearing. Yerkes dashed into the car, deposited his booty in the kitchen, and standing in the doorway faced the enemy. A terrific babel arose.

Elizabeth appeared in the passage and demanded to know what had happened.

"All right, my lady," said Yerkes, mopping his forehead. "I've only been and milked his cow. No saying where I'd have got any milk this side of Winnipeg if I hadn't."

"But, Yerkes, he doesn't seem to like it."

"Oh, that's all right, my lady."

But the settler was now on the steps of the car gesticulating and scolding, in what Elizabeth guessed to be a Scandinavian tongue. He was indeed a gigantic Swede, furiously angry, and Elizabeth had thoughts of bearding him herself and restoring the milk, when some mysterious transaction involving coin passed suddenly between the two men. The Swede stopped short in the midst of a sentence, pocketed something, and made off sulkily for the log hut. Yerkes, with a smile, and a wink to the bystanders, retired triumphant on his prey.

Elizabeth, standing at the door of the kitchen, inquired if supplies were likely to run short.

"Not in this car," said Yerkes, with emphasis. "What *they'll* do"—a jerk of his thumb towards the rest of the train in front—"can't say."

"Of course we shall have to give them food!" cried Lady Merton, delighted at the thought of getting rid of some of their superfluities.

Yerkes showed a stolid face.

"The C.P.R.'ll have to feed 'em—must. That's the regulation. Accident—free meals. That hasn't nothing to do with me. They don't come poaching on my ground. I say, look out! Do yer call that bacon, or buffaler steaks?"

And Yerkes rushed upon his subordinate, Bettany, who was cutting the breakfast bacon with undue thickness, and took the thing in hand himself. The crushed Bettany, who was never allowed to finish anything, disappeared hastily in order to answer the electric bell which was ringing madly from Philip Gaddesden's berth.

"Conductor!" cried a voice from the inner platform outside the dining-room and next the train.

"And what might you be wanting, sir?" said Bettany jauntily, opening the door to the visitor. Bettany was a small man, with thin harrassed features and a fragment of beard, glib of speech towards everybody but Yerkes.

"Your conductor got some milk, I think, from that cabin."

"He did—but only enough for ourselves. Sorry we can't oblige you."

"All the same, I am going to beg some of it. May I speak to the gentleman?"

"Mr. Gaddesden, sir, is dressing. The steward will attend to you."

And Bettany retired ceremoniously in favour of Yerkes, who hearing voices had come out of his den.

"I have come to ask for some fresh milk for a baby in the emigrant car," said the stranger. "Looks sick, and the mother's been crying. They've only got tinned milk in the restaurant and the child won't touch it."

"Sorry it's that particular, sir. But I've got only what I want."

"Yerkes!" cried Elizabeth Merton, in the background. "Of course the baby must have it. Give it to the gentleman, please, at once."

The stranger removed his hat and stepped into the tiny dining-room where Elizabeth was standing. He was tall and fair-skinned, with a blonde moustache, and very blue eyes. He spoke—for an English ear—with the slight accent which on the Canadian side of the border still proclaims the neighbourhood of the States.

"I am sorry to trouble you, madam," he said, with deference. "But the child seems very weakly, and the mother herself has nothing to give it. It was the conductor of the restaurant car who sent me here."

"We shall be delighted," said Lady Merton, eagerly. "May I come with you, if you are going to take it? Perhaps I could do something for the mother."

The stranger hesitated a moment.

"An emigrant car full of Galicians is rather a rough sort of place—especially at this early hour in the morning. But if you don't mind—"

"I don't mind anything. Yerkes, is that *all* the milk?".

"All to speak of, my lady," said Yerkes, nimbly retreating to his den.

Elizabeth shook her head as she looked at the milk. But her visitor laughed.

"The baby won't get through that to-day. It's a regular little scarecrow. I shouldn't think the mother'll rear it."

They stepped out on to the line. The drizzle descended on Lady Merton's bare head and grey travelling dress.

"You ought to have an umbrella," said the Canadian, looking at her in some embarrassment. And he ran back to the car for one. Then, while she carried the milk carefully in both hands, he held the umbrella over her, and they passed through the groups of passengers who were strolling disconsolately up and down the line in spite of the wet, or exchanging lamentations with others from two more stranded trains, one drawn up alongside, the other behind.

Many glances were levelled at the slight Englishwoman, with the delicately pale face, and at the man escorting her. Elizabeth meanwhile was putting questions. How long would they be detained? Her brother with whom she was travelling was not at all strong. Unconsciously, perhaps, her voice took a note of complaint.

"Well, we can't any of us cross—can we?—till they come to some bottom in the sink-hole," said the Canadian, interrupting her a trifle bluntly.

Elizabeth laughed. "We may be here then till night."

"Possibly. But you'll be the first over."

"How? There are some trains in front."

"That doesn't matter. They'll move you up. They're very vexed it should have happened to you."

Elizabeth felt a trifle uncomfortable. Was the dear young man tilting at the idle rich—and the corrupt Old World? She stole a glance at him, but perceived only that in his own tanned and sunburnt way he was a remarkably handsome well-made fellow, built on a rather larger scale than the Canadians she had so far seen. A farmer? His manners were not countrified. But a farmer in Canada or the States may be of all social grades.

By this time they had reached the emigrant car, the conductor of which was standing on the steps. He was loth to allow Lady Merton to enter, but Elizabeth persisted. Her companion led the way, pushing through a smoking group of dark-faced men hanging round the entrance.

Inside, the car was thick, indeed, with smoke and the heavy exhalations of the night. Men and women were sitting on the wooden benches; some women were cooking in the tiny stove-room attached to the car; children, half naked and unwashed, were playing on the floor; here and there a man was still asleep; while one old man was painfully conning a paper of "Homestead Regulations" which had been given him at Montreal, a lad of eighteen helping him; and close by another lad was writing a letter, his eyes passing dreamily from the paper to the Canadian landscape outside, of which he was clearly not conscious. In a corner, surrounded by three or four other women, was the mother they had come to seek. She held a wailing baby of about a year old in her arms. At the sight of Elizabeth, the child stopped its wailing, and lay breathing fast and feebly, its large bright eyes fixed on the new-comer. The mother turned away abruptly. It was not unusual for persons from the parlour-cars to ask leave to walk through the emigrants'.

But Elizabeth's companion said a few words to her, apparently in Russian, and Elizabeth, stooping over her, held out the milk. Then a dark face reluctantly showed itself, and great black eyes, in deep, lined sockets; eyes rather of a race than a person, hardly conscious, hardly individualised, yet most poignant, expressing some feeling, remote and inarticulate, that roused Elizabeth's. She called to the conductor for a cup and a spoon; she made her way into the malodorous kitchen, and got some warm water and sugar; then kneeling by the child, she put a spoonful of the diluted and sweetened milk into the mother's hand.

"Was it foolish of me to offer her that money?" said Elizabeth with flushed cheeks as they walked back through the rain. "They looked so terribly poor."

The Canadian smiled.

"I daresay it didn't do any harm," he said indulgently. "But they are probably not poor at all. The Galicians generally bring in quite a fair sum. And after a year or two they begin to be rich. They never spend a farthing they can help. It costs money—or time—to be clean, so they remain dirty. Perhaps we shall teach them—after a bit."

His companion looked at him with a shy but friendly curiosity.

"How did you come to know Russian?"

"When I was a child there were some Russian Poles on the next farm to us. I used to play with the boys, and learnt a little. The conductor called me in this morning to interpret. These people come from the Russian side of the Carpathians."

"Then you are a Canadian yourself?—from the West?"

"I was born in Manitoba."

"I am quite in love with your country!"

Elizabeth paused beside the steps leading to their car. As she spoke, her brown eyes lit up, and all her small features ran over, suddenly, with life and charm.

"Yes, it's a good country," said the Canadian, rather drily. "It's going to be a great country. Is this your first visit?"

But the conversation was interrupted by a reproachful appeal from Yerkes.

"Breakfast, my lady, has been hotted twice."

The Canadian looked at Elizabeth curiously, lifted his hat, and went away.

"Well, if this doesn't take the cake!" said Philip Gaddesden, throwing himself disconsolately into an armchair. "I bet you, Elizabeth, we shall be here forty-eight hours. And this damp goes through one."

The young man shivered, as he looked petulantly out through the open doorway of the car to the wet woods beyond. Elizabeth surveyed him with some anxiety. Like herself he was small, and lightly built. But his features were much less regular than hers; the chin and nose were childishly tilted, the eyes too prominent. His bright colour, however—(mother and sister could well have dispensed with that touch of vivid red on the cheeks!)—his curly hair, and his boyish ways made him personally attractive; while in his moments of physical weakness, his evident resentment of Nature's treatment of him, and angry determination to get the best of her, had a touch of something that was pathetic—that appealed.

Elizabeth brought a rug and wrapped it round him. But she did not try to console him; she looked round for something or someone to amuse him.

On the line, just beyond the railed platform of the car, a group of men were lounging and smoking. One of them was her acquaintance of the morning. Elizabeth, standing on the platform waited till he turned in her direction—caught his eye, and beckoned. He came with alacrity. She stooped over the rail to speak to him.

"I'm afraid you'll think it very absurd"—her shy smile broke again—"but do you think there's anyone in this train who plays bridge?"

He laughed.

"Certainly. There is a game going on at this moment in the car behind you."

"Is it—is it anybody—we could ask to luncheon?—who'd come, I mean," she added, hurriedly.

"I should think they'd come—I should think they'd be glad. Your cook, Yerkes, is famous on the line. I know two of the people playing. They are Members of Parliament."

"Oh! then perhaps I know them too," cried Elizabeth, brightening.

He laughed again.

"The Dominion Parliament, I mean." He named two towns in Manitoba, while Lady Merton's pink flush showed her conscious of having betrayed her English insularity. "Shall I introduce you?"

"Please!—if you find an opportunity. It's for my brother. He's recovering from an illness."

"And you want to cheer him up. Of course. Well, he'll want it to-day." The young man looked round him, at the line strewn with unsightly débris, the ugly cutting which blocked the view, and the mists up-curling from the woods; then at the slight figure beside him. The corners of his mouth tried not to laugh. "I am afraid you are not going to like Canada, if it treats you like this."

"I've liked every minute of it up till now," said Elizabeth warmly. "Can you tell me—I should like to know—who all these people are?" She waved her hand towards the groups walking up and down.

"Well, you see," said the Canadian after a moment's hesitation, "Canada's a big place!"

He looked round on her with a smile so broad and sudden that Elizabeth felt a heat rising in her cheeks. Her question had no doubt been a little naïve.

But the young man hurried on, composing his face quickly.

"Some of them, of course, are tourists like yourselves. But I do know a few of them. That man in the clerical coat, and the round collar, is Father Henty—a Jesuit well known in Winnipeg—a great man among the Catholics here."

"But a disappointed one," said Lady Merton.

Lady Merton: Colonist

The Canadian looked surprised. Elizabeth, proud of her knowledge, went on:

"Isn't it true the Catholics hoped to conquer the Northwest—and so—with Quebec—to govern you all? And now the English and American immigration has spoilt all their chances—poor things!"

"That's about it. Did they tell you that in Toronto?"

Elizabeth stiffened. The slight persistent tone of mockery in the young man's voice was beginning to offend her.

"And the others?" she said, without noticing his question.

It was the Canadian's turn to redden. He changed his tone.

"—The man next him is a professor at the Manitoba University. The gentleman in the brown suit is going to Vancouver to look after some big lumber leases he took out last year. And that little man in the Panama hat has been keeping us all alive. He's been prospecting for silver in New Ontario—thinks he's going to make his fortune in a week."

"Oh, but that will do exactly for my brother!" cried Elizabeth, delighted. "Please introduce us."

And hurrying back into the car she burst upon the discontented gentleman within. Philip, who was just about to sally forth into the damp, against the entreaties of his servant, and take his turn at shying stones at a bottle on the line, was appeased by her report, and was soon seated, talking toy speculation, with a bronzed and brawny person, who watched the young Englishman, as they chatted, out of a pair of humorous eyes. Philip believed himself a great financier, but was not in truth either very shrewd or very daring, and his various coups or losses generally left his exchequer at the end of the year pretty much what it had been the year before. But the stranger, who seemed to have staked out claims at one time or another, across the whole face of the continent, from Klondyke to Nova Scotia, kept up a mining talk that held him enthralled; and Elizabeth breathed freely.

Lady Merton: Colonist

She returned to the platform. The scene was *triste*, but the rain had for the moment stopped. She hailed an official passing by, and asked if there was any chance of their soon going on. The man smiled and shook his head.

Her Canadian acquaintance, who was standing near, came up to the car as he heard her question.

"I have just seen a divisional superintendent. We may get on about nine o'clock to-night."

"And it is now eleven o'clock in the morning," sighed Lady Merton. "Well!—I think a little exercise would be a good thing."

And she descended the steps of the car. The Canadian hesitated.

"Would you allow me to walk with you?" he said, with formality. "I might perhaps be able to tell you a few things. I belong to the railway."

"I shall be greatly obliged," said Elizabeth, cordially. "Do you mean that you are an official?"

"I am an engineer—in charge of some construction work in the Rockies."

Lady Merton's face brightened.

"Indeed! I think that must be one of the most interesting things in the world to be."

The Canadian's eyebrows lifted a little.

"I don't know that I ever thought of it like that," he said, half smiling. "It's good work—but I've done things a good deal livelier in my time."

"You've not always been an engineer?"

"Very few people are always 'anything' in Canada," he said, laughing. "It's like the States. One tries a lot of things. Oh, I was trained as an engineer—at Montreal. But directly I had finished with that I went off to Klondyke. I made a bit of money—came back—and lost it all, in a milling business—over there"—he pointed eastwards—"on the Lake of the Woods. My partner cheated me. Then I went exploring to the north, and took a Government job at the same time—paying treaty money to the Indians. Then, five years ago, I got work for the C.P.R. But I shall cut it before long. I've saved some money again. I shall take up land, and go into politics."

"Politics?" repeated Elizabeth, wishing she might some day know what politics meant in Canada. "You're not married?" she added pleasantly.

"I am not married."

"And may I ask your name?"

His name, it seemed, was George Anderson, and presently as they walked up and down he became somewhat communicative about himself, though always within the limits, as it seemed to her, of a natural dignity, which developed indeed as their acquaintance progressed. He told her tales, especially, of his Indian journeys through the wilds about the Athabasca and Mackenzie rivers, in search of remote Indian settlements—that the word of England to the red man might be kept; and his graphic talk called up before her the vision of a northern wilderness, even wilder and remoter than that she had just passed through, where yet the earth teemed with lakes and timber and trout-bearing streams, and where—"we shall grow corn some day," as he presently informed her. "In twenty years they will have developed seed that will ripen three weeks earlier than wheat does now in Manitoba. Then we shall settle that country—right away!—to the far north." His tone stirred and deepened. A little while before, it had seemed to her that her tourist enthusiasm amused him. Yet by flashes, she began to feel in him something, beside which her own raptures fell silent. Had she, after all, hit upon a man—a practical man—who was yet conscious of the romance of Canada?

Presently she asked him if there was no one dependent on him—no mother?—or sisters?

"I have two brothers—in the Government service at Ottawa. I had four sisters."

"Are they married?"

"They are dead," he said, slowly. "They and my mother were burnt to death."

She exclaimed. Her brown eyes turned upon him—all sudden horror and compassion.

"It was a farmhouse where we were living—and it took fire. Mother and sisters had no time to escape. It was early morning. I was a boy of eighteen, and was out on the farm doing my chores. When I saw smoke and came back, the house was a burning mass, and—it was all over."

"Where was your father?"

"My father is dead."

"But he was there—at the time of the fire?"

"Yes. He was there."

He had suddenly ceased to be communicative, and she instinctively asked no more questions, except as to the cause of the conflagration.

"Probably an explosion of coal-oil. It was sometimes used to light the fire with in the morning."

"How very, very terrible!" she said gently, after a moment, as though she felt it. "Did you stay on at the farm?"

"I brought up my two brothers. They were on a visit to some neighbours at the time of the fire. We stayed on three years."

"With your father?"

"No; we three alone."

She felt vaguely puzzled; but before she could turn to another subject, he had added—

"There was nothing else for us to do. We had no money and no relations—nothing but the land. So we had to work it—and we managed. But after three years we'd saved a little money, and we wanted to get a bit more education. So we sold the land and moved up to Montreal."

"How old were the brothers when you took on the farm?"

"Thirteen—and fifteen."

"Wonderful!" she exclaimed. "You must be proud."

He laughed out.

"Why, that kind of thing's done every day in this country! You can't idle in Canada."

They had turned back towards the train. In the doorway of the car sat Philip Gaddesden lounging and smoking, enveloped in a fur coat, his knees covered with a magnificent fur rug. A whisky and soda had just been placed at his right hand. Elizabeth thought—"He said that because he had seen Philip." But when she looked at him, she withdrew her supposition. His eyes were not on the car, and he was evidently thinking of something else.

"I hope your brother will take no harm," he said to her, as they approached the car. "Can I be of any service to you in Winnipeg?"

"Oh, thank you. We have some introductions—"

"Of course. But if I can—let me know."

An official came along the line, with a packet in his hand. At sight of Elizabeth he stopped and raised his hat.

"Am I speaking to Lady Merton? I have some letters here, that have been waiting for you at Winnipeg, and they've sent them out to you."

He placed the packet in her hand. The Canadian moved away, but not before Elizabeth had seen again the veiled amusement in his eyes. It seemed to him comic, no doubt, that the idlers of the world should be so royally treated. But after all—she drew herself up—her father had been no idler.

She hastened to her brother; and they fell upon their letters.

"Oh, Philip!"—she said presently, looking up—"Philip! Arthur Delaine meets us at Winnipeg."

"Does he? *Does he?*" repeated the young man, laughing. "I say, Lisa!—"

Elizabeth took no notice of her brother's teasing tone. Nor did her voice, as she proceeded to read him the letter she held in her hand, throw any light upon her own feelings with regard to it.

The weary day passed. The emigrants were consoled by free meals; and the delicate baby throve on the Swede's ravished milk. For the rest, the people in the various trains made rapid acquaintance with each other; bridge went merrily in more than one car, and the general inconvenience was borne with much philosophy, even by Gaddesden. At last, when darkness had long fallen, the train to which the private car was attached moved slowly forward amid cheers of the bystanders.

Elizabeth and her brother were on the observation platform, with the Canadian, whom with some difficulty they had persuaded to share their dinner.

"I told you"—said Anderson—"that you would be passed over first." He pointed to two other trains in front that had been shunted to make room for them.

Elizabeth turned to him a little proudly.

"But I should like to say—it's not for our own sakes—not in the least!—it is for my father, that they are so polite to us."

"I know—of course I know!" was the quick response. "I have been talking to some of our staff," he went on, smiling. "They would do anything for you. Perhaps you don't understand. You are the guests of the railway. And I too belong to the railway. I am a very humble person, but—"

"You also would do anything for us?" asked Elizabeth, with her soft laugh. "How kind you all are!"

She looked charming as she said it—her face and head lit up by the line of flaring lights through which they were slowly passing. The line was crowded with dark-faced navvies, watching the passage of the train as it crept forward.

One of the officials in command leapt up on the platform of the car, and introduced himself. He was worn out with the day's labour, but triumphant. "It's all right now—but, my word! the stuff we've thrown in!—"

He and Anderson began some rapid technical talk. Slowly, they passed over the quicksand which in the morning had engulfed half a train; amid the flare of torches, and the murmur of strange speech, from the Galician and Italian labourers, who rested on their picks and stared and laughed, as they went safely by.

"How I love adventures!" cried Elizabeth, clasping her hands.

"Even little ones?" said the Canadian, smiling. But this time she was not conscious of any note of irony in his manner, rather of a kind protectingness—more pronounced, perhaps, than it would have been in an Englishman, at the same stage of acquaintance. But Elizabeth liked it; she liked, too, the fine bare head that the torchlight revealed; and the general impression of varied life that the man's personality produced upon her. Her sympathies, her imagination were all trembling towards the Canadians, no less than towards their country.

CHAPTER III

"Mr. Delaine, sir?"

The gentleman so addressed turned to see the substantial form of Simpson at his elbow. They were both standing in the spacious hall of the C.P.R. Hotel adjoining the station at Winnipeg.

"Her ladyship, sir, asked me to tell you she would be down directly. And would you please wait for her, and take her to see the place where the emigrants come. She doesn't think Mr. Gaddesden will be down till luncheon-time."

Arthur Delaine thanked the speaker for her information, and then sat down in a comfortable corner, *Times* in hand, to wait for Lady Merton.

She and her brother had arrived, he understood, in the early hours at Winnipeg, after the agitations and perils of the sink-hole. Philip had gone at once to bed and to slumber. Lady Merton would soon, it seemed, be ready for anything that Winnipeg might have to show her.

The new-comer had time, however, to realise and enjoy a pleasant expectancy before she appeared. He was apparently occupied with the *Times*, but in reality he was very conscious all the time of his own affairs and of a certain crisis to which, in his own belief, he had now brought them. In the first place, he could not get over his astonishment at finding himself where he was. The very aspect of the Winnipeg hotel, as he looked curiously round it, seemed to prove to him both the seriousness of certain plans and intentions of his own, and the unusual decision with which he had been pursuing them.

For undoubtedly, of his own accord, and for mere travellers' reasons, he would not at this moment be travelling in Canada. The old world was enough for him; and neither in the States nor in Canada had he so far seen anything which would of itself have drawn him away from his Cumberland house, his classical library, his pets, his friends and correspondents, his old servants and all the other items in a comely and dignified way of life.

He was just forty and unmarried, a man of old family, easy disposition, and classical tastes. He had been for a time Member of Parliament for one of the old Universities, and he was now engaged on a verse translation of certain books of the Odyssey. That this particular labour had been undertaken before did not trouble him. It was in fact his delight to feel himself a link in the chain of tradition—at once the successor and progenitor of scholars. Not that his scholarship was anything illustrious or profound. Neither as poet nor Hellenist would he ever leave any great mark behind him; but where other men talk of "the household of faith," he might have talked rather of "the household of letters," and would have seen himself as a warm and familiar sitter by its hearth. A new edition of some favourite classic; his weekly *Athenæum*; occasional correspondence with a French or Italian scholar—(he did not read German, and disliked the race)—these were his pleasures. For the rest he was the landlord of a considerable estate, as much of a sportsman as his position required, and his Conservative politics did not include any sympathy for the more revolutionary doctrines—economic or social—which seemed to him to be corrupting his party. In his youth, before the death of an elder brother, he had been trained as a doctor, and had spent some time in a London hospital. In no case would he ever have practised. Before his training was over he had revolted against the profession, and against the "ugliness," as it seemed to him, of the matters and topics with which a doctor must perforce be connected. His elder brother's death, which, however, he sincerely regretted, had in truth solved many difficulties.

In person he was moderately tall, with dark grizzled hair, agreeable features and a moustache. Among his aristocratic relations whom he met in London, the men thought him a little dishevelled and old-fashioned; the women pronounced him interesting and "a dear." His manners were generally admired, except by captious persons who held that such a fact was of itself enough to condemn them; and he was welcome in many English and some foreign circles. For he travelled every spring, and was well acquainted with the famous places of Europe. It need only be added that he had a somewhat severe taste in music, and could render both Bach and Handel on the piano with success.

His property was only some six miles distant from Martindale Park, the Gaddesdens' home. During the preceding winter he had become a frequent visitor at Martindale, while Elizabeth Merton was staying with her mother and brother, and a little ripple of talk had begun to flow through the district. Delaine, very fastidious where personal dignity was concerned, could not make up his mind either to be watched or laughed at. He would have liked to woo—always supposing that wooing there was to be—with a maximum of dignity and privacy, surrounded by a friendly but not a forcing atmosphere. But Elizabeth Merton was a great favourite in her own neighbourhood, and people became impatient. Was it to be a marriage or was it not?

As soon as he felt this enquiry in the air, Mr. Delaine went abroad— abruptly—about a month before Elizabeth and her brother started for Canada. It was said that he had gone to Italy; but some few persons knew that it was his intention to start from Genoa for the United States, in order that he might attend a celebration at Harvard University in honour of a famous French Hellenist, who had covered himself with glory in Delaine's eyes by identifying a number of real sites with places mentioned in the Odyssey. Nobody, however, knew but himself, that, when that was done, he meant to join the brother and sister on part of their Canadian journey, and that he hoped thereby to become better acquainted with Elizabeth Merton than was possible—for a man at least of his sensitiveness—under the eyes of an inquisitive neighbourhood.

For this step Lady Merton's consent was of course necessary. He had accordingly written from Boston to ask if it would be agreeable to them that he should go with them through the Rockies. The proposal was most natural. The Delaines and Gaddesdens had been friends for many years, and Arthur Delaine enjoyed a special fame as a travelling companion—easy, accomplished and well-informed.

Nevertheless, he waited at Boston in some anxiety for Elizabeth's answer. When it came, it was all cordiality. By all means let him go with them to the Rockies. They could not unfortunately offer him sleeping room in the car. But by day Lady Merton hoped he would be their guest, and share all their facilities and splendours. "I shall be so glad of a companion for Philip, who is rapidly getting strong enough to give me a great deal of trouble."

That was how she put it—how she must put it, of course. He perfectly understood her.

And now here he was, sitting in the C.P.R. Hotel at Winnipeg, at a time of year when he was generally in Paris or Rome, investigating the latest Greek acquisitions of the Louvre, or the last excavation in the Forum; picnicking in the Campagna; making expeditions to Assisi or Subiaco; and in the evenings frequenting the drawing-rooms of ministers and ambassadors.

He looked up presently from the *Times*, and at the street outside; the new and raw street, with its large commercial buildings of the American type, its tramcars and crowded sidewalks. The muddy roadway, the gaps and irregularities in the street façade, the windows of a great store opposite, displeased his eye. The whole scene seemed to him to have no atmosphere. As far as he was concerned, it said nothing, it touched nothing.

What was it he was to be taken to see? Emigration offices? He resigned himself, with a smile. The prospect made him all the more pleasantly conscious that one feeling, and one feeling only, could possibly have brought him here.

"Ah! there you are."

A light figure hurried toward him, and he rose in haste.

But Lady Merton was intercepted midway by a tall man, quite unknown to Delaine.

"I have arranged everything for three o'clock," said the interloper. "You are sure that will suit you?"

"Perfectly! And the guests?"

"Half a dozen, about, are coming." George Anderson ran through the list, and Elizabeth laughed merrily, while extending her hand to Delaine.

"How amusing! A party—and I don't know a soul in Winnipeg. Arrived this morning—and going this evening! So glad to see you, Mr. Arthur. You are coming, of course?"

"Where?" said Delaine, bewildered.

"To my tea, this afternoon. Mr. Anderson—Mr. Delaine. Mr. Anderson has most kindly arranged a perfectly delightful party!—in our car this afternoon. We are to go and see a great farm belonging to some friend of his, about twenty miles out—prize cattle and horses—that kind of thing. Isn't it good of him?"

"Charming!" murmured Delaine. "Charming!" His gaze ran over the figure of the Canadian.

"Yerkes of course will give us tea," said Elizabeth. "His cakes are a strong point"; she turned to Anderson. "And we may really have an engine?"

"Certainly. We shall run you out in forty minutes. You still wish to go on to-night?"

"Philip does. Can we?"

"You can do anything you wish," said Anderson, smiling.

Elizabeth thanked him, and they chatted a little more about the arrangements and guests for the afternoon, while Delaine listened. Who on earth was this new acquaintance of Lady Merton's? Some person she had met in the train apparently, and connected with the C.P.R. A good-looking fellow, a little too sure of himself; but that of course was the Colonial fault.

"One of the persons coming this afternoon is an old Montreal fellow-student of mine," the Canadian was saying. "He is going to be a great man some day. But if you get him to talk, you won't like his opinions—I thought I'd better warn you."

"How very interesting!" put in Delaine, with perhaps excessive politeness. "What sort of opinions? Do you grow any Socialists here?"

Anderson examined the speaker, as it were for the first time.

"The man I was speaking of is a French-Canadian," he said, rather shortly, "and a Catholic."

"The very man I want to see," cried Elizabeth. "I suppose he hates us?"

"Who?—England? Not at all. He loves England—or says he does—and hates the Empire."

"'Love me, love my Empire!'" said Elizabeth. "But, I see—I am not to talk to him about the Boer War, or contributing to the Navy?"

"Better not," laughed Anderson. "I am sure he will want to behave himself; but he sometimes loses his head."

Elizabeth sincerely hoped he might lose it at her party.

"We want as much Canada as possible, don't we?" She appealed to Delaine.

"To see, in fact, the 'young barbarians—all at play!'" said Anderson. The note of sarcasm had returned to his clear voice. He stood, one hand on his hip, looking down on Lady Merton.

"Oh!" exclaimed Elizabeth, protesting; while Delaine was conscious of surprise that anyone in the New World should quote anything.

Anderson hastily resumed: "No, no. I know you are most kind, in wishing to see everything you can."

"Why else should one come to the Colonies?" put in Delaine. Again his smile, as he spoke, was a little overdone.

"Oh, we mustn't talk of Colonies," cried Elizabeth, looking at Anderson; "Canada, Mr. Arthur, doesn't like to be called a colony."

"What is she, then?" asked Delaine, with an amused shrug of the shoulders.

"She is a nation!" said the Canadian, abruptly. Then, turning to Lady Merton, he rapidly went through some other business arrangements with her.

"Three o'clock then for the car. For this morning you are provided?" He glanced at Delaine.

Lady Merton replied that Mr. Delaine would take her round; and Anderson bowed and departed.

"Who is he, and how did you come across him?" asked Delaine, as they stepped into the street.

Elizabeth explained, dwelling with enthusiasm on the kindness and ability with which the young man, since their acquaintance began, had made himself their courier. "Philip, you know, is no use at all. But Mr. Anderson seems to know everybody—gets everything done. Instead of sending my letters round this morning he telephoned to everybody for me. And everybody is coming. Isn't it too kind? You know it is for Papa's sake"—she explained eagerly—"because Canada thinks she owes him something."

Delaine suggested that perhaps life in Winnipeg was monotonous, and its inhabitants might be glad of distractions. He also begged—with a slight touch of acerbity—that now that he had joined them he too might be made use of.

"Ah! but you don't know the country," said Lady Merton gently. "Don't you feel that we must get the natives to guide us—to put us in the way? It is only they who can really feel the poetry of it all."

Her face kindled. Arthur Delaine, who thought that her remark was one of the foolish exaggerations of nice women, was none the less conscious as she made it, that her appearance was charming—all indeed that a man could desire in a wife. Her simple dress of white linen, her black hat, her lovely eyes, and little pointed chin, the bunch of white trilliums at her belt, which a child in the emigrant car had gathered and given her the day before—all her personal possessions and accessories seemed to him perfection. Yes!—but he meant to go slowly, for both their sakes. It seemed fitting and right, however, at this point that he should express his great pleasure and gratitude in being allowed to join them. Elizabeth replied simply, without any embarrassment that could be seen. Yet secretly both were conscious that something was on its trial, and that more was in front of them than a mere journey through the Rockies. He was an old friend both of herself and her family. She believed him to be honourable, upright, affectionate. He was of the same world and tradition as herself, well endowed, a scholar and a gentleman. He would make a good brother for Philip. And heretofore she had seen him on ground which had shown him to advantage; either at home or abroad, during a winter at Rome—a spring at Florence.

Indeed, as they strolled about Winnipeg, he talked to her incessantly about persons and incidents connected with the spring of the year before, when they had both been in Rome.

"You remember that delicious day at Castel Gandolfo?—on the terrace of the Villa Barberini? And the expedition to Horace's farm? You recollect the little girl there—the daughter of the Dutch Minister? She's married an American—a very good fellow. They've bought an old villa on Monte Mario."

And so on, and so on. The dear Italian names rolled out, and the speaker grew more and more animated and agreeable.

Only, unfortunately, Elizabeth's attention failed him. A motor car had been lent them in the hospitable Canadian way; and as they sped through and about the city, up the business streets, round the park, and the residential suburb rising along the Assiniboine, as they plunged through seas of black mud to look at the little old-fashioned Cathedral of St. John, with its graveyard recalling the earliest days of the settlement, Lady Merton gradually ceased even to pretend to listen to her companion.

"They have found some extremely jolly things lately at Porto D'Anzio—a fine torso—quite Greek."

"Have they?" said Elizabeth, absently—"Have they?—And to think that in 1870, just a year or two before my father and mother married, there was nothing here but an outpost in the wilderness!—a few scores of people! One just *hears* this country grow." She turned pensively away from the tombstone of an old Scottish settler in the shady graveyard of St. John.

"Ah! but what will it grow to?" said Delaine, drily. "Is Winnipeg going to be interesting? — is it going to *matter*?"

"Come and look at the Emigration Offices," laughed Elizabeth for answer.

And he found himself dragged through room after room of the great building, and standing by while Elizabeth, guided by an official who seemed to hide a more than Franciscan brotherliness under the aspects of a canny Scot, and helped by an interpreter, made her way into the groups of home-seekers crowding round the clerks and counters of the lower room — English, Americans, Swedes, Dutchmen, Galicians, French Canadians. Some men, indeed, who were actually hanging over maps, listening to the directions and information of the officials, were far too busy to talk to tourists, but there were others who had finished their business, or were still waiting their turn, and among them, as also among the women, the little English lady found many willing to talk to her.

And what courage, what vivacity she threw into the business! Delaine, who had seen her till now as a person whose natural reserve was rather displayed than concealed by her light agreeable manner, who had often indeed had cause to wonder where and what might be the real woman, followed her from group to group in a silent astonishment. Between these people — belonging to the primitive earth-life — and herself, there seemed to be some sudden intuitive sympathy which bewildered him; whether she talked to some Yankee farmer from the Dakotas, long-limbed, lantern-jawed, all the moisture dried out of him by hot summers, hard winters, and long toil, who had come over the border with a pocket full of money, the proceeds of prairie-farming in a republic, to sink it all joyfully in a new venture under another flag; or to some broad-shouldered English youth from her own north country; or to some hunted Russian from the Steppes, in whose eyes had begun to dawn the first lights of liberty; or to the dark-faced Italians and Frenchmen, to whom she chattered in their own tongues.

An Indian reserve of good land had just been thrown open to settlers. The room was thronged. But Elizabeth was afraid of no one; and no one repulsed her. The high official who took them through, lingered over the process, busy as the morning was, all for the *beaux yeux* of Elizabeth; and they left him pondering by what legerdemain he could possibly so manipulate his engagements that afternoon as to join Lady Merton's tea-party.

"Well, that was quite interesting!" said Delaine as they emerged.

Elizabeth, however, would certainly have detected the perfunctoriness of the tone, and the hypocrisy of the speech, had she had any thoughts to spare.

But her face showed her absorbed.

"Isn't it *amazing*!" Her tone was quiet, her eyes on the ground.

"Yet, after all, the world has seen a good many emigrations in its day!" remarked Delaine, not without irritation.

She lifted her eyes.

"Ah—but nothing like this! One hears of how the young nations came down and peopled the Roman Empire. But that lasted so long. One person—with one life—could only see a bit of it. And here one sees it *all*—all, at once!—as a great march—the march of a new people to its home. Fifty years ago, wolves and bears, and buffaloes—twelve years ago even, the great movement had not begun—and now, every week, a new town!—the new nation spreading, spreading over the open land, irresistibly, silently; no one setting bounds to it, no one knowing what will come of it!"

She checked herself. Her voice had been subdued, but there was a tremor in it. Delaine caught her up, rather helplessly.

"Ah! isn't that the point? What will come of it? Numbers and size aren't everything. Where is it all tending?"

She looked up at him, still exalted, still flushed, and said softly, as though she could not help it, "'On to the bound of the waste—on to the City of God!'"

He gazed at her in discomfort. Here was an Elizabeth Merton he had yet to know. No trace of her in the ordinary life of an English country house!

"You *are* Canadian!" he said with a smile.

"No, no!" said Elizabeth eagerly, recovering herself, "I am only a spectator. *We* see the drama—we feel it—much more than they can who are in it. At least"—she wavered—"Well!—I have met one man who seems to feel it!"

"Your Canadian friend?"

Elizabeth nodded.

"He sees the vision—he dreams the dream!" she said brightly. "So few do. But I think he does. Oh, dear—*dear!*—how time flies! I must go and see what Philip is after."

Delaine was left discontented. He had come to press his suit, and he found a lady preoccupied. Canada, it seemed, was to be his rival! Would he ever be allowed to get in a word edgewise?

Was there ever anything so absurd, so disconcerting? He looked forward gloomily to a dull afternoon, in quest of fat cattle, with a car-full of unknown Canadians.

CHAPTER IV

At three o'clock, in the wide Winnipeg station, there gathered on the platform beside Lady Merton's car a merry and motley group of people. A Chief Justice from Alberta, one of the Senators for Manitoba, a rich lumberman from British Columbia, a Toronto manufacturer—owner of the model farm which the party was to inspect, two or three ladies, among them a little English girl with fine eyes, whom Philip Gaddesden at once marked for approval; and a tall, dark-complexioned man with hollow cheeks, large ears, and a long chin, who was introduced, with particular emphasis, to Elizabeth by Anderson, as "Mr. Félix Mariette"—Member of Parliament, apparently, for some constituency in the Province of Quebec.

The small crowd of persons collected, all eminent in the Canadian world, and some beyond it, examined their hostess of the afternoon with a kindly amusement. Elizabeth had sent round letters; Anderson, who was well known, it appeared, in Winnipeg, had done a good deal of telephoning. And by the letters and the telephoning this group of busy people had allowed itself to be gathered; simply because Elizabeth was her father's daughter, and it was worth while to put such people in the right way, and to send them home with some rational notions of the country they had come to see.

And she, who at home never went out of her way to make a new acquaintance, was here the centre of the situation, grasping the identities of all these strangers with wonderful quickness, flitting about from one to another, making friends with them all, and constraining Philip to do the same. Anderson followed her closely, evidently feeling a responsibility for the party only second to her own.

He found time, however, to whisper to Mariette, as they were all about to mount the car:

"Eh bien?"

"Mais oui—très gracieuse!" said the other, but without a smile, and with a shrug of the shoulders. *He* was only there to please Anderson. What did the aristocratic Englishwoman on tour—with all her little Jingoisms and Imperialisms about her—matter to him, or he to her?

While the stream of guests was slowly making its way into the car, while Yerkes at the further end, resplendent in a buttonhole and a white cap and apron, was watching the scene, and the special engine, like an impatient horse, was puffing and hissing to be off, a man, who had entered the cloak-room of the station to deposit a bundle just as the car-party arrived, approached the cloak-room door from the inside, and looked through the glazed upper half. His stealthy movements and his strange appearance passed unnoticed. There was a noisy emigrant party in the cloak-room, taking out luggage deposited the night before; they were absorbed in their own affairs, and in some wrangle with the officials which involved a good deal of lost temper on both sides.

The man was old and grey. His face, large-featured and originally comely in outline, wore the unmistakable look of the outcast. His eyes were bloodshot, his mouth trembled, so did his limbs as he stood peering by the door. His clothes were squalid, and both they and his person diffused the odours of the drinking bar from which he had just come. The porter in charge of the cloak-room had run a hostile eye over him as he deposited his bundle. But now no one observed him; while he, gathered up and concentrated, like some old wolf upon a trail, followed every movement of the party entering the Gaddesden car.

George Anderson and his French Canadian friend left the platform last. As Anderson reached the door of the car he turned back to speak to Mariette, and his face and figure were clearly visible to the watcher behind the barred cloak-room door. A gleam of savage excitement passed over the old man's face; his limbs trembled more violently.

Through the side windows of the car the party could be seen distributing themselves over the comfortable seats, laughing and talking in groups. In the dining-room, the white tablecloth spread for tea, with the china and silver upon it, made a pleasant show. And now two high officials of the railway came hurrying up, one to shake hands with Lady Merton and see that all was right, the other to accompany the party.

Elizabeth Merton came out in her white dress, and leant over the railing, talking, with smiles, to the official left behind. He raised his hat, the car moved slowly off, and in the group immediately behind Lady Merton the handsome face and thick fair hair of George Anderson showed conspicuous as long as the special train remained in sight.

The old man raised himself and noiselessly went out upon the platform. Outside the station he fell in with a younger man, who had been apparently waiting for him; a strong, picturesque fellow, with the skin and countenance of a half-breed.

"Well?" said the younger, impatiently. "Thought you was goin' to take a bunk there."

"Couldn't get out before. It's all right."

"Don't care if it is," said the other sulkily. "Don't care a damn button not for you nor anythin' you're after! But you give me my two dollars sharp, and don't keep me another half-hour waitin'. That's what I reckoned for, an' I'm goin' to have it." He held out his hand.

The old man fumbled slowly in an inner pocket of his filthy overcoat.

"You say the car's going on to-night?"

"It is, old bloke, and Mr. George Anderson same train—number ninety-seven—as ever is. Car shunted at Calgary to-morrow night. So none of your nonsense—fork out! I had a lot o' trouble gettin' you the tip."

The old man put some silver into his palm with shaking fingers. The youth, who was a bartender from a small saloon in the neighbourhood of the station, looked at him with contempt.

"Wonder when you was sober last? Think you'd better clean yourself a bit, or they'll not let you on the train."

"Who told you I wanted to go on the train?" said the old man sharply. "I'm staying at Winnipeg."

"Oh! you are, are you?" said the other mockingly. "We shouldn't cry our eyes out if you *was* sayin' good-bye. Ta-ta!" And with the dollars in his hand, head downwards, he went off like the wind.

The old man waited till the lad was out of sight, then went back into the station and bought an emigrant ticket to Calgary for the night train. He emerged again, and walked up the main street of Winnipeg, which on this bright afternoon was crowded with people and traffic. He passed the door of a solicitor's office, where a small sum of money, the proceeds of a legacy, had been paid him the day before, and he finally made his way into the free library of Winnipeg, and took down a file of the *Winnipeg Chronicle*.

He turned some pages laboriously, yet not vaguely. His eyes were dim and his hands palsied, but he knew what he was looking for. He found it at last, and sat pondering it—the paragraph which, when he had hit upon it by chance in the same place twenty-four hours earlier, had changed the whole current of his thoughts.

"Donaldminster, Sask., May 6th.—We are delighted to hear from this prosperous and go-ahead town that, with regard to the vacant seat the Liberals of the city have secured as a candidate Mr. George Anderson, who achieved such an important success last year for the C.P.R. by his settlement on their behalf of the dangerous strike which had arisen in the Rocky Mountains section of the line, and which threatened not only to affect all the construction camps in the district but to spread to the railway workers proper and to the whole Winnipeg section. Mr. Anderson seems to have a remarkable hold on the railway men, and he is besides a speaker of great force. He is said to have addressed twenty-three meetings, and to have scarcely eaten or slept for a fortnight. He was shrewd and fair in negotiation, as well as eloquent in speech. The result was an amicable settlement, satisfactory to all parties. And the farmers of the West owe Mr. Anderson a good deal. So does the C.P.R. For if the strike had broken out last October, just as the movement of the fall crops eastward was at its height, the farmers and the railway, and Canada in general would have been at its mercy. We wish Mr. Anderson a prosperous election (it is said, indeed, that he is not to be opposed) and every success in his political career. He is, we believe, Canadian born—sprung from a farm in Manitoba—so that he has grown up with the Northwest, and shares all its hopes and ambitions."

The old man, with both elbows on the table, crouched over the newspaper, incoherent pictures of the past coursing through his mind, which was still dazed and stupid from the drink of the night before.

Meanwhile, the special train sped along the noble Red River and out into the country. All over the prairie the wheat was up in a smooth green carpet, broken here and there by the fields of timothy and clover, or the patches of summer fallow, or the white homestead buildings. The June sun shone down upon the teeming earth, and a mirage, born of sun and moisture, spread along the edge of the horizon, so that Elizabeth, the lake-lover, could only imagine in her bewilderment that Lake Winnipeg or Lake Manitoba had come dancing south and east to meet her, so clearly did the houses and trees, far away behind them, and on either side, seem to be standing at the edge of blue water, in which the white clouds overhead were mirrored, and reed-beds stretched along the shore. But as the train receded, the mirage followed them; the dream-water lapped up the trees and the fields, and even the line they had just passed over seemed to be standing in water.

How foreign to an English eye was the flat, hedgeless landscape! with its vast satin-smooth fields of bluish-green wheat; its farmhouses with their ploughed fireguards and shelter-belts of young trees; its rare villages, each stretching in one long straggling line of wooden houses along the level earth; its scattered, treeless lakes, from which the duck rose as the train passed! Was it this mere foreignness, this likeness in difference, that made it strike so sharply, with such a pleasant pungency on Elizabeth's senses? Or was it something else—some perception of an opening future, not only for Canada but for herself, mingling with the broad light, the keen air, the lovely strangeness of the scene?

Yet she scarcely spoke to Arthur Delaine, with whom one might have supposed this hidden feeling connected. She was indeed aware of him all the time. She watched him secretly; watching herself, too, in the characteristic modern way. But outwardly she was absorbed in talking with the guests.

The Chief Justice, roundly modelled, with a pink ball of a face set in white hair, had been half a century in Canada, and had watched the Northwest grow from babyhood. He had passed his seventieth year, but Elizabeth noticed in the old men of Canada a strained expectancy, a buoyant hope, scarcely inferior to that of the younger generation. There was in Sir Michael's talk no hint of a Nunc Dimittis; rather a passionate regret that life was ebbing, and the veil falling over a national spectacle so enthralling, so dramatic.

"Before this century is out we shall be a people of eighty millions, and within measurable time this plain of a thousand miles from here to the Rockies will be as thickly peopled as the plain of Lombardy."

"Well, and what then?" said a harsh voice in a French accent, interrupting the Chief Justice.

Arthur Delaine's face, turning towards the speaker, suddenly lightened, as though its owner said, "Ah! precisely."

"The plain of Lombardy is not a Paradise," continued Mariette, with a laugh that had in it a touch of impatience.

"Not far off it," murmured Delaine, as he looked out on the vast field of wheat they were passing—a field two miles long, flat and green and bare as a billiard-table—and remembered the chestnuts and the looping vines, the patches of silky corn and spiky maize, and all the interlacing richness and broidering of the Italian plain. His soul rebelled against this naked new earth, and its bare new fortunes. All very well for those who must live in it and make it. "Yet is there better than it!"—lands steeped in a magic that has been woven for them by the mere life of immemorial generations.

He murmured this to Elizabeth, who smiled.

"Their shroud?" she said, to tease him. "But Canada has on her wedding garment!"

Again he asked himself what had come to her. She looked years younger than when he had parted from her in England. The delicious thought shot through him that his advent might have something to do with it.

He stooped towards her.

"Willy-nilly, your friends must like Canada!" he said, in her ear; "if it makes you so happy."

He had no art of compliment, but the words were simple and sincere, and Elizabeth grew suddenly rosy, to her own great annoyance. Before she could reply, however, the Chief Justice had insisted on bringing her back into the general conversation.

"Come and keep the peace, Lady Merton! Here is my friend Mariette playing the devil's advocate as usual. Anderson tells me you are inclined to think well of us; so perhaps you ought to hear it."

Mariette smiled and bowed a trifle sombrely. He was plain and gaunt, but he had the air of a *grand seigneur*, and was in fact a member of one of the old seigneurial families of Quebec.

"I have been enquiring of Sir Michael, madam, whether he is quite happy in his mind as to these Yankees that are now pouring into the new provinces. He, like everyone else, prophesies great things for Canada; but suppose it is an American Canada?"

"Let them come," said Anderson, with a touch of scorn. "Excellent stuff! We can absorb them. We are doing it fast."

"Can you? They are pouring all over the new districts as fast as the survey is completed and the railways planned. They bring capital, which your Englishman doesn't. They bring knowledge of the prairie and the climate, which your Englishmen haven't got. As for capital, America is doing everything; financing the railways, the mines, buying up the lands, and leasing the forests. British Columbia is only nominally yours; American capital and business have got their grip firm on the very vitals of the province."

"Perfectly true!"—put in the lumberman from Vancouver—"They have three-fourths of the forests in their hands."

"No matter!" said Anderson, kindling. "There was a moment of danger—twenty years ago. It is gone. Canada will no more be American than she will be Catholic—with apologies to Mariette. These Yankees come in—they turn Englishmen in six months—they celebrate Dominion Day on the first of July, and Independence Day, for old sake's sake, on the fourth; and their children will be as loyal as Toronto."

"Aye, and as dull!" said Mariette fiercely.

The conversation dissolved in protesting laughter. The Chief Justice, Anderson, and the lumberman fell upon another subject. Philip and the pretty English girl were flirting on the platform outside, Mariette dropped into a seat beside Elizabeth.

"You know my friend, Mr. Anderson, madam?"

"I made acquaintance with him on the journey yesterday. He has been most kind to us."

"He is a very remarkable man. When he gets into the House, he will be heard of. He will perhaps make his mark on Canada."

"You and he are old friends?"

"Since our student days. I was of course at the French College—and he at McGill. But we saw a great deal of each other. He used to come home with me in his holidays."

"He told me something of his early life."

"Did he? It is a sad history, and I fear we—my family, that is, who are so attached to him—have only made it sadder. Three years ago he was engaged to my sister. Then the Archbishop forbade mixed marriages. My sister broke it off, and now she is a nun in the Ursuline Convent at Quebec."

"Oh, poor things!" cried Elizabeth, her eye on Anderson's distant face.

"My sister is quite happy," said Mariette sharply. "She did her duty. But my poor friend suffered. However, now he has got over it. And I hope he will marry. He is very dear to me, though we have not a single opinion in the world in common."

Elizabeth kept him talking. The picture of Anderson drawn for her by the admiring but always critical affection of his friend, touched and stirred her. His influence at college, the efforts by which he had placed his brothers in the world, the sensitive and generous temperament which had won him friends among the French Canadian students, he remaining all the time English of the English; the tendency to melancholy—a personal and private melancholy—which mingled in him with a passionate enthusiasm for Canada, and Canada's future; Mariette drew these things for her, in a stately yet pungent French that affected her strangely, as though the French of Saint Simon—or something like it—breathed again from a Canadian mouth. Anderson meanwhile was standing outside with the Chief Justice. She threw a glance at him now and then, wondering about his love affair. Had he really got over it?—or was that M. Mariette's delusion? She liked, on the contrary, to think of him as constant and broken-hearted!

The car stopped, as it seemed, on the green prairie, thirty miles from Winnipeg. Elizabeth was given up to the owner of the great farm—one of the rich men of Canada for whom experiment in the public interest becomes a passion; and Anderson walked on her other hand.

Delaine endured a wearisome half-hour. He got no speech with Elizabeth, and prize cattle were his abomination. When the half-hour was done, he slipped away, unnoticed, from the party. He had marked a small lake or "slough" at the rear of the house, with wide reed-beds and a clump of cottonwood. He betook himself to the cottonwood, took out his pocket Homer and a notebook, and fell to his task. He was in the thirteenth book:

[Greek: ôs d hot anêr dorpoio lilaietai, ô te pauêmar neion an helkêton boe oinope pêkton arotron]

"As when a man longeth for supper, for whom, the livelong day, two wine-coloured oxen have dragged the fitted plough through the fallow, and joyful to such an one is the going down of the sun that sends him to his meal, for his knees tremble as he goes—so welcome to Odysseus was the setting of the sun": ...

He lost himself in familiar joy—the joy of the Greek itself, of the images of the Greek life. He walked with the Greek ploughman, he smelt the Greek earth, his thoughts caressed the dark oxen under the yoke. These for him had savour and delight; the wide Canadian fields had none.

Philip Gaddesden meanwhile could not be induced to leave the car. While the others were going through the splendid stables and cowsheds, kept like a queen's parlour, he and the pretty girl were playing at bob-cherry in the saloon, to the scandal of Yerkes, who, with the honour of the car and the C.P.R. and Canada itself on his shoulders, could not bear that any of his charges should shuffle out of the main item in the official programme.

But Elizabeth, as before, saw everything transfigured; the splendid Shire horses; the famous bull, progenitor of a coming race; the sheds full of glistening cows and mottled calves. These smooth, sleek creatures, housed there for the profit of Canada and her farm life, seemed to Elizabeth no less poetic than the cattle of Helios to Delaine. She loved the horses, and the patient, sweet-breathed kine; she found even a sympathetic mind for the pigs.

Presently when her host, the owner, left her to explain some of his experiments to the rest of the party, she fell to Anderson alone. And as she strolled at his side, Anderson found the June afternoon pass with extraordinary rapidity. Yet he was not really as forthcoming or as frank as he had been the day before. The more he liked his companion, the more he was conscious of differences between them which his pride exaggerated. He himself had never crossed the Atlantic; but he understood that she and her people were "swells"—well-born in the English sense, and rich. Secretly he credited them with those defects of English society of which the New World talks—its vulgar standards and prejudices. There was not a sign of them certainly in Lady Merton's conversation. But it is easy to be gracious in a new country; and the brother was sometimes inclined to give himself airs. Anderson drew in his tentacles a little; ready indeed to be wroth with himself that he had talked so much of his own affairs to this little lady the day before. What possible interest could she have taken in them!

All the same, he could not tear himself from her side. Whenever Delaine left his seat by the lake, and strolled round the corner of the wood to reconnoitre, the result was always the same. If Anderson and Lady Merton were in sight at all, near or far, they were together. He returned, disconsolate, to Homer and the reeds.

As they went back to Winnipeg, some chance word revealed to Elizabeth that Anderson also was taking the night train for Calgary.

"Oh! then to-morrow you will come and talk to us!" cried Elizabeth, delighted.

Her cordial look, the pretty gesture of her head, evoked in Anderson a start of pleasure. He was not, however, the only spectator of them. Arthur Delaine, standing by, thought for the first time in his life that Elizabeth's manner was really a little excessive.

The car left Winnipeg that night for the Rockies. An old man, in a crowded emigrant car, with a bundle under his arm, watched the arrival of the Gaddesden party. He saw Anderson accost them on the platform, and then make his way to his own coach just ahead of them.

The train sped westwards through the Manitoba farms and villages. Anderson slept intermittently, haunted by various important affairs that were on his mind, and by recollections of the afternoon. Meanwhile, in the front of the train, the paragraph from the *Winnipeg Chronicle* lay carefully folded in an old tramp's waistcoat pocket.

CHAPTER V

"I say, Elizabeth, you're not going to sit out there all day, and get your death of cold? Why don't you come in and read a novel like a sensible woman?"

"Because I can read a novel at home—and I can't see Canada."

"See Canada! What is there to see?" The youth with the scornful voice came to lean against the doorway beside her. "A patch of corn—miles and miles of some withered stuff that calls itself grass, all of it as flat as your hand—oh! and, by Jove! a little brown fellow—gopher, is that their silly name?—scootling along the line. Go it, young 'un!" Philip shied the round end of a biscuit tin after the disappearing brown thing. "A boggy lake with a kind of salt fringe—unhealthy and horrid and beastly—a wretched farm building—et cetera, et cetera!"

"Oh! look there, Philip—here is a school!"

Elizabeth bent forward eagerly. On the bare prairie stood a small white house, like the house that children draw on their slates: a chimney in the middle, a door, a window on either side. Outside, about twenty children playing and dancing. Inside, through the wide-open doorway a vision of desks and a few bending heads.

Philip's patience was put to it. Had she supposed that children went without schools in Canada?

But she took no heed of him.

"Look how lovely the children are, and how happy! What'll Canada be when they are old? And not another sign of habitation anywhere—nothing—but the little house—on the bare wide earth! And there they dance, as though the world belonged to them. So it does!"

"And my sister to a lunatic asylum!" said Philip, exasperated. "I say, why doesn't that man Anderson come and see us?"

"He promised to come in and lunch."

"He's an awfully decent kind of fellow," said the boy warmly.

Elizabeth opened her eyes.

"I didn't know you had taken any notice of him, Philip."

"No more I did," was the candid reply. "But did you see what he brought me this morning?" He pointed to the seat behind him, littered with novels, which Elizabeth recognized as new additions to their travelling store. "He begged or borrowed them somewhere from his friends or people in the hotel; told me frankly he knew I should be bored to-day, and might want them. Rather 'cute of him, wasn't it?"

Elizabeth was touched. Philip had certainly shown rather scant civility to Mr. Anderson, and this trait of thoughtfulness for a sickly and capricious traveller appealed to her.

"I suppose Delaine will be here directly?" Philip went on.

"I suppose so."

Philip let himself down into the seat beside her.

"Look here, Elizabeth," lowering his voice; "I don't think Delaine is any more excited about Canada than I am. He told me last night he thought the country about Winnipeg perfectly hideous."

"*Oh!*" cried Elizabeth, as though someone had flipped her.

"You'll have to pay him for this journey, Elizabeth. Why did you ask him to come?"

"I *didn't* ask him, Philip. He asked himself."

"Ah! but you let him come," said the youth shrewdly. "I think, Elizabeth, you're not behaving quite nicely."

"How am I not behaving nicely?"

"Well, you don't pay any attention to him. Do you know what he was doing while you were looking at the cows yesterday?"

Elizabeth reluctantly confessed that she had no idea.

"Well, he was sitting by a lake—a kind of swamp—at the back of the house, reading a book." Philip went off into a fit of laughter.

"Poor Mr. Delaine!" cried Elizabeth, though she too laughed. "It was probably Greek," she added pensively.

"Well, that's funnier still. You know, Elizabeth, he could read Greek at home. It's because you were neglecting him."

"Don't rub it in, Philip," said Elizabeth, flushing. Then she moved up to him and laid a coaxing hand on his arm. "Do you know that I have been awake half the night?"

"All along of Delaine? Shall I tell him?"

"Philip, I just want you to be a dear, and hold your tongue," said Lady Merton entreatingly. "When there's anything to tell, I'll tell you. And if I have—"

"Have what?"

"Behaved like a fool, you'll have to stand by me." An expression of pain passed over her face.

"Oh, I'll stand by you. I don't know that I want Mr. Arthur for an extra bear-leader, if that's what you mean. You and mother are quite enough. Hullo! Here he is."

A little later Delaine and Elizabeth were sitting side by side on the garden chairs, four of which could just be fitted into the little railed platform at the rear of the car. Elizabeth was making herself agreeable, and doing it, for a time, with energy. Nothing also could have been more energetic than Delaine's attempts to meet her. He had been studying Baedeker, and he made intelligent travellers' remarks on the subject of Southern Saskatchewan. He discussed the American "trek" into the province from the adjoining States. He understood the new public buildings of Regina were to be really fine, only to be surpassed by those at Edmonton. He admired the effects of light and shadow on the wide expanse; and noticed the peculiarities of the alkaline lakes.

Meanwhile, as he became more expansive, Elizabeth contracted. One would have thought soon that Canada had ceased to interest her at all. She led him slyly on to other topics, and presently the real Arthur Delaine emerged. Had she heard of the most recent Etruscan excavations at Grosseto? Wonderful! A whole host of new clues! Boni—Lanciani—the whole learned world in commotion. A fragment of what might very possibly turn out to be a bi-lingual inscription was the last find. Were we at last on the brink of solving the old, the eternal enigma?

He threw himself back in his chair, transformed once more into the talkative, agreeable person that Europe knew. His black and grizzled hair, falling perpetually forward in strong waves, made a fine frame for his grey eyes and large, well-cut features. He had a slight stammer, which increased when he was animated, and a trick of forever pushing back the troublesome front locks of hair.

Elizabeth listened for a long, long time, and at last—could have cried like a baby because she was missing so much! There was a chance, she knew, all along this portion of the line, of seeing antelope and coyotes, if only one kept one's eyes open; not to speak of the gophers—enchanting little fellows, quite new to such travellers as she—who seemed to choose the very railway line itself, by preference, for their burrowings and their social gatherings. Then, as she saw, the wheat country was nearly done; a great change was in progress; her curiosity sprang to meet it. Droves of horses and cattle began to appear at rare intervals on the vast expanse. No white, tree-sheltered farms here, like the farms in Manitoba; but scattered at long distances, near the railway or on the horizon, the first primitive dwellings of the new settlers—the rude "shack" of the first year—beginnings of villages—sketches of towns.

"I have always thought the Etruscan problem the most fascinating in the whole world," cried Delaine, with pleasant enthusiasm. "When you consider all its bearings, linguistic and historical—"

"Oh! *do* you see," exclaimed Elizabeth, pointing—"*do* you see all those lines and posts, far out to the horizon? Do you know that all these lonely farms are connected with each other and the railway by *telephones*? Mr. Anderson told me so; that some farmers actually make their fences into telephone lines, and that from that little hut over there you can speak to Montreal when you please? And just before I left London I was staying in a big country house, thirty miles from Hyde Park Corner, and you couldn't telephone to London except by driving five miles to the nearest town!"

"I wonder why that should strike you so much—the telephones, I mean?"

Delaine's tone was stiff. He had thrown himself back in his chair with folded arms, and a slight look of patience. "After all, you know, it may only be one dull person telephoning to another dull person—on subjects that don't matter!"

Elizabeth laughed and coloured.

"Oh! it isn't telephones in themselves. It's—" She hesitated, and began again, trying to express herself. "When one thinks of all the haphazard of history—how nations have tumbled up, or been dragged up, through centuries of blind horror and mistake, how wonderful to see a nation made consciously!—before your eyes—by science and intelligence—everything thought of, everything foreseen! First of all, this wonderful railway, driven across these deserts, against opposition, against unbelief, by a handful of men, who risked everything, and have—perhaps—changed the face of the world!"

She stopped smiling. In truth, her new capacity for dithyramb was no less surprising to herself than to Delaine.

"I return to my point"—he made it not without tartness—"will the new men be adequate to the new state?"

"Won't they?" He fancied a certain pride in her bearing. "They explained to me the other day at Winnipeg what the Government do for the emigrants—how they guide and help them—take care of them in sickness and in trouble, through the first years—protect them, really, even from themselves. And one thinks how Governments have taxed, and tortured, and robbed, and fleeced—Oh, surely, surely, the world improves!" She clasped her hands tightly on her knee, as though trying by the physical action to restrain the feeling within. "And to see here the actual foundations of a great state laid under your eyes, deep and strong, by men who know what it is they are doing—to see history begun on a blank page, by men who know what they are writing—isn't it wonderful, *wonderful!*"

"Dear lady!" said Delaine, smiling, "America has been dealing with emigrants for generations; and there are people who say that corruption is rife in Canada."

But Elizabeth would not be quenched.

"We come after America—we climb on her great shoulders to see the way. But is there anything in America to equal the suddenness of this? Twelve years ago even—in all this Northwest—practically nothing. And then God said: 'Let there be a nation!'—and there was a nation—in a night and a morning." She waved her hand towards the great expanse of prairie. "And as for corruption—"

"Well?" He waited maliciously.

"There is no great brew without a scum," she said laughing. "But find me a brew anywhere in the world, of such power, with so little."

"Mr. Anderson would, I think, be pleased with you," said Delaine, drily.

Elizabeth frowned a little.

"Do you think I learnt it from him? I assure you he never rhapsodises."

"No; but he gives you the material for rhapsodies."

"And why not?" said Elizabeth indignantly. "If he didn't love the country and believe in it he wouldn't be going into its public life. You can feel that he is Canadian through and through."

"A farmer's son, I think, from Manitoba?"

"Yes." Elizabeth's tone was a little defensive.

"Will you not sometimes—if you watch his career—regret that, with his ability, he has not the environment—and the audience—of the Old World?"

"No, never! He will be one of the shapers of the new."

Delaine looked at her with a certain passion.

"All very well, but *you* don't belong to it. We can't spare you from the old."

"Oh, as for me, I'm full of vicious and corrupt habits!" put in Elizabeth hurriedly. "I am not nearly good enough for the new!"

"Thank goodness for that!" said Delaine fervently, and, bending forward, he tried to see her face. But Elizabeth did not allow it. She could not help flushing; but as she bent over the side of the platform looking ahead, she announced in her gayest voice that there was a town to be seen, and it was probably Regina.

The station at Regina, when they steamed into it, was crowded with folk, and gay with flags. Anderson, after a conversation with the station-master, came to the car to say that the Governor-General, Lord Wrekin, who had been addressing a meeting at Regina, was expected immediately, to take the East-bound train; which was indeed already lying, with its steam up, on the further side of the station, the Viceregal car in its rear.

"But there are complications. Look there!"

He pointed to a procession coming along the platform. Six men bore a coffin covered with white flowers. Behind it came persons in black, a group of men, and one woman; then others, mostly young men, also in mourning, and bare-headed.

As the procession passed the car, Anderson and Delaine uncovered.

Elizabeth turned a questioning look on Anderson.

"A young man from Ontario," he explained, "quite a lad. He had come here out West to a farm—to work his way—a good, harmless little fellow—the son of a widow. A week ago a vicious horse kicked him in the stable. He died yesterday morning. They are taking him back to Ontario to be buried. The friends of his chapel subscribed to do it, and they brought his mother here to nurse him. She arrived just in time. That is she."

He pointed to the bowed figure, hidden in a long crape veil. Elizabeth's eyes filled.

"But it comes awkwardly," Anderson went on, looking back along the platform—"for the Governor-General is expected this very moment. The funeral ought to have been here half an hour ago. They seem to have been delayed. Ah! here he is!"

"Elizabeth!—his Excellency!" cried Philip, emerging from the car.

"Hush!" Elizabeth put her finger to her lip. The young man looked at the funeral procession in astonishment, which was just reaching the side of the empty van on the East-bound train which was waiting, with wide-open doors, to receive the body. The bearers let down the coffin gently to the ground, and stood waiting in hesitation. But there were no railway employés to help them. A flurried stationmaster and his staff were receiving the official party. Suddenly someone started the revival hymn, "Shall We Gather at the River?" It was taken up vigorously by the thirty or forty young men who had followed the coffin, and their voices, rising and falling in a familiar lilting melody, filled the station:

/P Yes, we'll gather at the river, The beautiful, beautiful river— Gather with the saints at the river, That flows by the throne of God! P/

Elizabeth looked towards the entrance of the station. A tall and slender man had just stepped on to the platform. It was the Governor-General, with a small staff behind him. The staff and the station officials stood hat in hand. A few English tourists from the West-bound train hurried up; the men uncovered, the ladies curtsied. A group of settlers' wives newly arrived from Minnesota, who were standing near the entrance, watched the arrival with curiosity. Lord Wrekin, seeing women in his path, saluted them; and they replied with a friendly and democratic nod. Then suddenly the

Governor-General heard the singing, and perceived the black distant crowd. He inquired of the persons near him, and then passed on through the groups which had begun to gather round himself, raising his hand for silence. The passengers of the West-bound train had by now mostly descended, and pressed after him. Bare-headed, he stood behind the mourners while the hymn proceeded, and the coffin was lifted and placed in the car with the wreaths round it. The mother clung a moment to the side of the door, unconsciously resisting those who tried to lead her away. The kind grey eyes of the Governor-General rested upon her, but he made no effort to approach or speak to her. Only his stillness kept the crowd still.

Elizabeth at her window watched the scene—the tall figure of his Excellency—the bowed woman—the throng of officials and of mourners. Over the head of the Governor-General a couple of flags swelled in a light breeze—the Union Jack and the Maple Leaf; beyond the heads of the crowd there was a distant glimpse of the barracks of the Mounted Police; and then boundless prairie and floating cloud.

At last the mother yielded, and was led to the carriage behind the coffin. Gently, with bent head, Lord Wrekin made his way to her. But no one heard what passed between them. Then, silently, the funeral crowd dispersed, and another crowd—of officials and business men—claimed the Governor-General. Standing in its midst, he turned for a moment to scan the West-bound train.

"Ah, Lady Merton!" He had perceived the car and Elizabeth's face at the window, and he hastened across to speak to her. They were old friends in England, and they had already met in Ottawa.

"So I find you on your travels! Well?"

His look, gay and vivacious as a boy's, interrogated hers. Elizabeth stammered a few words in praise of Canada. But her eyes were still wet, and the Governor-General perceived it.

"That was touching?" he said. "To die in your teens in this country!—just as the curtain is up and the play begins—hard! Hullo, Anderson!"

The great man extended a cordial hand, chaffed Philip a little, gave Lady Merton some hurried but very precise directions as to what she was to see—and whom—at Vancouver and Pretoria. "You must see So-and-so and So-and-so—great friends of mine. D——'ll tell you all about the lumbering. Get somebody to show you the Chinese quarter. And there's a splendid old fellow—a C.P.R. man—did some of the prospecting for the railway up North, toward the Yellowhead. Never heard such tales; I could have sat up all night." He hastily scribbled a name on a card and gave it to Elizabeth. "Good-bye—good-bye!"

He hastened off, but they saw him standing a few moments longer on the platform, the centre of a group of provincial politicians, farmers, railway superintendents, and others—his hat on the back of his head, his pleasant laugh ringing every now and then above the clatter of talk. Then came departure, and at the last moment he jumped into his carriage, talking and talked to, almost till it had left the platform.

Anderson hailed a farming acquaintance.

"Well? What has the Governor-General been doing?"

"Speaking at a Farmers' Conference. Awful shindy yesterday!—between the farmers and the millers. Row about the elevators. The farmers want the Dominion to own 'em—vow they're cheated and bullied, and all the rest of it. Row about the railway, too. Shortage of cars; you know the old story. A regular wasp's nest, the whole thing! Well, the Governor-General came this morning, and everything's blown over! Can't remember what he said, but we're all sure somebody's going to do something. Hope you know how he does it!—I don't."

Anderson laughed as he sat down beside Elizabeth, and the train began to move.

"We seem to send you the right men!" she said, smiling—with a little English conceit that became her.

The train left the station. As it did so, an old man in the first emigrant car, who, during the wait at Regina, had appeared to be asleep in a corner, with a battered slouch hat drawn down over his eyes and face, stealthily moved to the window, and looked back upon the now empty platform.

Some hours later Anderson was still sitting beside Elizabeth. They were in Southern Alberta. The June day had darkened. And for the first time Elizabeth felt the chill and loneliness of the prairies, where as yet she had only felt their exhilaration. A fierce wind was sweeping over the boundless land, with showers in its train. The signs of habitation became scantier, the farms fewer. Bunches of horses and herds of cattle widely scattered over the endless grassy plains—the brown lines of the ploughed fire-guards running beside the railway—the bents of winter grass, white in the storm-light, bleaching the rolling surface of the ground, till the darkness of some cloud-shadow absorbed them; these things breathed—of a sudden—wildness and desolation. It seemed as though man could no longer cope with the mere vastness of the earth—an earth without rivers or trees, too visibly naked and measureless.

"At last I am afraid of it!" said Elizabeth, shivering in her fur coat, with a little motion of her hand toward the plain. "And what must it be in winter!"

Anderson laughed.

"The winter is much milder here than in Manitoba! Radiant sunshine day after day—and the warm chinook-wind. And it is precisely here that the railway lands are selling at a higher price for the moment than anywhere else, and that settlers are rushing in. Look there!"

Elizabeth peered through the gloom, and saw the gleam of water. The train ran along beside it for a minute or two, then the gathering darkness seemed to swallow it up.

"A river?"

"No, a canal, fed from the Bow River—far ahead of us. We are in the irrigation belt—and in the next few years thousands of people will settle here. Give the land water—the wheat follows! South and North, even now, the wheat is spreading and driving out the ranchers. Irrigation is the secret. We are mastering it! And you thought"—he looked at her with amusement and a kind of triumph—"that the country had mastered us?"

There was something in his voice and eyes, as though not he spoke, but a nation through him. "Splendid!" was the word that rose in Elizabeth's mind; and a thrill ran with it.

The gloom of the afternoon deepened. The showers increased. But Elizabeth could not be prevailed upon to go in. In the car Delaine and Philip were playing dominoes, in despair of anything more amusing. Yerkes was giving his great mind to the dinner which was to be the consolation of Philip's day.

Meanwhile Elizabeth kept Anderson talking. That was her great gift. She was the best of listeners. Thus led on he could not help himself, any more than he had been able to help himself on the afternoon of the sink-hole. He had meant to hold himself strictly in hand with this too attractive Englishwoman. On the contrary, he had never yet poured out so frankly to mortal ear the inmost dreams and hopes which fill the ablest minds of Canada—dreams half imagination, half science; and hopes which, yesterday romance, become reality to-morrow.

He showed her, for instance, the great Government farms as they passed them, standing white and trim upon the prairie, and bade her think of the busy brains at work there—magicians conjuring new wheats that will ripen before the earliest frosts, and so draw onward the warm tide of human life over vast regions now desolate; or trees that will stand firm against the prairie winds, and in the centuries to come turn this bare and boundless earth, this sea-floor of a primeval ocean, which is now Western Canada, into a garden of the Lord. Or from the epic of the soil, he would slip on to the human epic bound up with it—tale after tale of life in the ranching country, and of the emigration now pouring into Alberta—witched out of him by this delicately eager face, these lovely listening eyes. And here, in spite of his blunt, simple speech, came out the deeper notes of feeling, feeling richly steeped in those "mortal things"—earthy, tender, humorous, or terrible—which make up human fate.

Had he talked like this to the Catholic girl in Quebec? And yet she had renounced him? She had never loved him, of course! To love this man would be to cleave to him.

Once, in a lifting of the shadows of the prairie, Elizabeth saw a group of antelope standing only a few hundred yards from the train, tranquilly indifferent, their branching horns clear in a pallid ray of light; and once a prairie-wolf, solitary and motionless; and once, as the train moved off after a stoppage, an old badger leisurely shambling off the line itself. And once, too, amid a driving storm-shower, and what seemed to her unbroken formless solitudes, suddenly, a tent by the railway side, and the blaze of a fire; and as the train slowly passed, three men—lads rather—emerging to laugh and beckon to it. The tent, the fire, the gay challenge of the young faces and the English voices, ringed by darkness and wild weather, brought the tears back to Elizabeth's eyes, she scarcely knew why.

"Settlers, in their first year," said Anderson, smiling, as he waved back again.

But, to Elizabeth, it seemed a parable of the new Canada.

An hour later, amid a lightening of the clouds over the West, that spread a watery gold over the prairie, Anderson sprang to his feet.

"The Rockies!"

And there, a hundred miles away, peering over the edge of the land, ran from north to south a vast chain of snow peaks, and Elizabeth saw at last that even the prairies have an end.

The car was shunted at Calgary, in order that its occupants might enjoy a peaceful night. When she found herself alone in her tiny room, Elizabeth stood for a while before her reflection in the glass. Her eyes were frowning and distressed; her cheeks glowed. Arthur Delaine, her old friend, had bade her a cold good night, and she knew well enough that—from him—she deserved it. "Yet I gave him the whole morning," she pleaded with herself. "I did my best. But oh, why, why did I ever let him come!"

And even in the comparative quiet of the car at rest, she could not sleep; so quickened were all her pulses, and so vivid the memories of the day.

CHAPTER VI

Arthur Delaine was strolling and smoking on the broad wooden balcony, which in the rear of the hotel at Banff overlooks a wide scene of alp and water. The splendid Bow River comes swirling past the hotel, on its rush from the high mountains to the plains of Saskatchewan. Craggy mountains drop almost to the river's edge on one side; on the other, pine woods mask the railway and the hills; while in the distance shine the snow-peaks of the Rockies. It is the gateway of the mountains, fair and widely spaced, as becomes their dignity.

Delaine, however, was not observing the scenery. He was entirely absorbed by reflection on his own affairs. The party had now been stationary for three or four days at Banff, enjoying the comforts of hotel life. The travelling companion on whom Delaine had not calculated in joining Lady Merton and her brother—Mr. George Anderson—had taken his leave, temporarily, at Calgary. In thirty-six hours, however, he had reappeared. It seemed that the construction work in which he was engaged in the C—— valley did not urgently require his presence; that his position towards the railway, with which he was about to sever his official connection, was one of great freedom and influence, owing, no doubt, to the services he had been able to render it the year before. He was, in fact, master of his time, and meant to spend it apparently in making Lady Merton's tour agreeable.

For himself, Delaine could only feel that the advent of this stranger had spoilt the whole situation. It seemed now as though Elizabeth and her brother could not get on without him. As he leant over the railing of the balcony, Delaine could see far below, in the wood, the flutter of a white dress. It belonged to Lady Merton, and the man beside her was George Anderson. He had been arranging their walks and expeditions for the last four days, and was now about to accompany the English travellers on a special journey with a special engine through the Kicking Horse Pass and back, a pleasure suggested by the kindness of the railway authorities.

It was true that he had at one time been actively engaged on the important engineering work now in progress in the pass; and Lady Merton could not, therefore, have found a better showman. But why any showman at all? What did she know about this man who had sprung so rapidly into intimacy with herself and her brother? Yet Delaine could not honestly accuse him of presuming on a chance acquaintance, since it was not to be denied that it was Philip Gaddesden himself, who had taken an invalid's capricious liking to the tall, fair-haired fellow, and had urgently requested—almost forced him to come back to them.

Delaine was not a little bruised in spirit, and beginning to be angry. During the solitary day he had been alone with them Elizabeth had been kindness and complaisance itself. But instead of that closer acquaintance, that opportunity for a gradual and delightful courtship on which he had reckoned, when the restraint of watching eyes and neighbourly tongues should be removed, he was conscious that he had never been so remote from her during the preceding winter at home, as he was now that he had journeyed six thousand miles simply and solely on the chance of proposing to her. He could not understand how anything so disastrous, and apparently so final, could have happened to him in one short week! Lady Merton—he saw quite plainly—did not mean him to propose to her, if she could possibly avoid it. She kept Philip with her, and gave no opportunities. And always, as before, she was possessed and bewitched by Canada! Moreover, the Chief Justice and the French Canadian, Mariette, had turned up at the hotel two days before, on their way to Vancouver. Elizabeth had been sitting, figuratively, at the feet of both of them ever since; and both had accepted an invitation to join in the Kicking Horse party, and were delaying their journey West accordingly.

Instead of solitude, therefore, Delaine was aware of a most troublesome amount of society. Aware also, deep down, that some test he resented but could not escape had been applied to him on this journey, by fortune—and Elizabeth!—and that he was not standing it well. And the worst of it was that as his discouragement in the matter of Lady Merton increased, so also did his distaste for this raw, new country, without associations, without art, without antiquities, in which he should never, never have chosen to spend one of his summers of this short life, but for the charms of Elizabeth! And the more boredom he was conscious of, the less congenial and sympathetic, naturally, did he become as a companion for Lady Merton. Of this he was dismally aware. Well! he hoped, bitterly, that she knew what she was about, and could take care of herself. This man she had made friends with was good-looking and, by his record, possessed ability. He had fairly gentlemanly manners, also; though, in Delaine's opinion, he was too self-confident on his own account, and too boastful on Canada's, But he was a man of humble origin, son of a farmer who seemed, by the way, to be dead; and grandson, so Delaine had heard him say, through his mother, of one of the Selkirk settlers of 1812—no doubt of some Scotch gillie or shepherd. Such a person, in England, would have no claim whatever to the intimate society of Elizabeth Merton. Yet here she was alone, really without protection—for what use was this young, scatter-brained brother?—herself only twenty-seven, and so charming? so much prettier than she had ever seemed to be at home. It was a dangerous situation—a situation to which she ought not to have been exposed. Delaine had always believed her sensitive and fastidious; and in his belief all women should be sensitive and fastidious, especially as to who are, and who are not, their social equals. But it was clear he had not quite understood her. And this man whom they had picked up was undoubtedly handsome, strong and masterful, of the kind that the natural woman admires. But then he—Delaine—had never thought of Elizabeth Merton as the natural woman. There lay the disappointment.

What was his own course to be? He believed himself defeated, but to show any angry consciousness of it would be to make life very uncomfortable in future, seeing that he and the Gaddesdens were inevitably neighbours and old friends. After all, he had not committed himself beyond repair. Why not resume the friendly relation which had meant so much to him before other ideas had entered in? Ah! it was no longer easy. The distress of which he was conscious had some deep roots. He must marry—the estate demanded it. But his temperament was invincibly cautious; his mind moved slowly. How was he to begin upon any fresh quest? His quiet pursuit of Elizabeth had come about naturally and by degrees.

Propinquity had done it. And now that his hopes were dashed, he could not imagine how he was to find any other chance; for, as a rule, he was timid and hesitating with women. As he hung, in his depression, over the river, this man of forty envisaged—suddenly and not so far away—old age and loneliness. A keen and peevish resentment took possession of him.

Lady Merton and Anderson began to ascend a long flight of steps leading from the garden path below to the balcony where Delaine stood. Elizabeth waved to him with smiles, and he must perforce watch her as she mounted side by side with the fair-haired Canadian.

"Oh! such delightful plans!" she said, as she sank out of breath into a seat. "We have ordered the engine for two o'clock. Please observe, Mr. Arthur. Never again in this mortal life shall I be able to 'order' an engine for two o'clock!—and one of these C.P.R. engines, too, great splendid fellows! We go down the pass, and take tea at Field; and come up the pass again this evening, to dine and sleep at Laggan. As we descend, the engine goes in front to hold us back; and when we ascend, it goes behind to push us up; and I understand that the hill is even steeper"—she bent forward, laughing, to Delaine, appealing to their common North Country recollections—"than the Shap incline!"

"Too steep, I gather," said Delaine, "to be altogether safe." His tone was sharp. He stood with his back to the view, looking from Elizabeth to her companion.

Anderson turned.

"As we manage it, it is perfectly safe! But it costs us too much to make it safe. That's the reason for the new bit of line."

Elizabeth turned away uncomfortably, conscious again, as she had often been before, of the jarring between the two men.

At two o'clock the car and the engine were ready, and Yerkes received them at the station beaming with smiles. According to him, the privilege allowed them was all his doing, and he was exceedingly jealous of any claim of Anderson's in the matter.

"You come to *me*, my lady, if you want anything. Last year I ran a Russian princess through—official. 'You take care of the Grand Duchess, Yerkes,' they says to me at Montreal; for they know there isn't anybody on the line they can trust with a lady as they can me. Of course, I couldn't help her faintin' at the high bridges, going up Rogers Pass; that wasn't none of my fault!"

"Faint—at bridges!" said Elizabeth with scorn. "I never heard of anybody doing such a thing, Yerkes."

"Ah! you wait till you see 'em, my lady," said Yerkes, grinning.

The day was radiant, and even Philip, as they started from Banff station, was in a Canadian mood. So far he had been quite cheerful and good-tempered, though not, to Elizabeth's anxious eye, much more robust yet than when they had left England. He smoked far too much, and Elizabeth wished devoutly that Yerkes would not supply him so liberally with whisky and champagne. But Philip was not easily controlled. The very decided fancy, however, which he had lately taken for George Anderson had enabled Elizabeth, in one or two instances, to manage him more effectively. The night they arrived at Calgary, the lad had had a wild desire to go off on a moonlight drive across the prairies to a ranch worked by an old Cambridge friend of his. The night was cold, and he was evidently tired by the long journey from Winnipeg. Elizabeth was in despair, but could not move him at all. Then Anderson had intervened; had found somehow and somewhere a trapper just in from the mountains with a wonderful "catch" of fox and marten; and in the amusement of turning over a bundle of magnificent furs, and of buying something straight from the hunter for his mother, the youth had forgotten his waywardness. Behind his back, Elizabeth had warmly thanked her lieutenant.

"He only wanted a little distraction," Anderson had said, with a shy smile, as though he both liked and disliked her thanks. And then, impulsively, she had told him a good deal about Philip and his illness, and their mother, and the old house in Cumberland. She, of all persons, to be so communicative about the family affairs to a stranger! Was it that two days in a private car in Canada went as far as a month's acquaintance elsewhere?

Lady Merton: Colonist

Another passenger had been introduced to Lady Merton by Anderson, an hour before the departure of the car, and had made such a pleasant impression on her that he also had been asked to join the party, and had very gladly consented. This was the American, Mr. Val Morton, now the official receiver, so Elizabeth understood, of a great railway system in the middle west of the United States. The railway had been handed over to him in a bankrupt condition. His energy and probity were engaged in pulling it through. More connections between it and the Albertan railways were required; and he was in Canada looking round and negotiating. He was already known to the Chief Justice and Mariette, and Elizabeth fell quickly in love with his white hair, his black eyes, his rapier-like slenderness and keenness, and that pleasant mingling in him—so common in the men of his race—of the dry shrewdness of the financier with a kind of headlong courtesy to women.

On sped the car through the gate of the Rockies. The mountains grew deeper, the snows deeper against the blue, the air more dazzling, the forests closer, breathing balm into the sunshine.

Suddenly the car slackened and stopped. No sign of a station. Only a rustic archway, on which was written "The Great Divide," and beneath the archway two small brooklets issuing, one flowing to the right, the other to the left.

They all left the car and stood round the tiny streams. They were on the watershed. The water in the one streamlet flowed to the Atlantic, that in its fellow to the Pacific.

Eternal parable of small beginnings and vast fates! But in this setting of untrodden mountains, and beside this railway which now for a few short years had been running its parlour and dining cars, its telegraphs and electric lights and hotels, a winding thread of life and civilisation, through the lonely and savage splendours of snow-peak and rock, transforming day by day the destinies of Canada—the parable became a truth, proved upon the pulses of men.

The party sat down on the grass beside the bright, rippling water, and Yerkes brought them coffee. While they were taking it, the two engine-drivers descended from the cab of the engine and began to gather a few flowers and twigs from spring bushes that grew near. They put them together and offered them to Lady Merton. She, going to speak to them, found that they were English and North Country.

"Philip!—Mr. Arthur!—they come from our side of Carlisle!"

Philip looked up with a careless nod and smile. Delaine rose and went to join her. A lively conversation sprang up between her and the two men. They were, it seemed, a stalwart pair of friends, kinsmen indeed, who generally worked together, and were now entrusted with some of the most important work on the most difficult sections of the line. But they were not going to spend all their days on the line—not they! Like everybody in the West, they had their eyes on the land. Upon a particular district of it, moreover, in Northern Alberta, not yet surveyed or settled. But they were watching it, and as soon as the "steel gang" of a projected railway came within measurable distance they meant to claim their sections and work their land together.

When the conversation came to an end and Elizabeth, who with her companions had been strolling along the line a little in front of the train, turned back towards her party, Delaine looked down upon her, at once anxious to strike the right note, and moodily despondent of doing it.

"Evidently, two very good fellows!" he said in his rich, ponderous voice. "You gave them a great pleasure by going to talk to them."

"I?" cried Elizabeth. "They are a perfect pair of gentlemen!—and it is very kind of them to drive us!"

Delaine laughed uneasily.

"The gradations here are bewildering—or rather the absence of gradations."

"One gets down to the real thing," said Elizabeth, rather hotly.

Delaine laughed again, with a touch of bitterness.

"The real thing? What kind of reality? There are all sorts."

Elizabeth was suddenly conscious of a soreness in his tone. She tried to walk warily.

"I was only thinking," she protested, "of the chances a man gets in this country of showing what is in him."

"Remember, too," said Delaine, with spirit, "the chances that he misses!"

"The chances that belong only to the old countries? I am rather bored with them!" said Elizabeth flippantly.

Delaine forced a smile.

"Poor Old World! I wonder if you will ever be fair to it again, or — or to the people bound up with it!"

She looked at him, a little discomposed, and said, smiling:

"Wait till you meet me next in Rome!"

"Shall I ever meet you again in Rome?" he replied, under his breath, as though involuntarily.

As he spoke he made a determined pause, a stone's throw from the rippling stream that marks the watershed; and Elizabeth must needs pause with him. Beyond the stream, Philip sat lounging among rugs and cushions brought from the car, Anderson and the American beside him. Anderson's fair, uncovered head and broad shoulders were strongly thrown out against the glistening snows of the background. Upon the three typical figures — the frail English boy — the Canadian — the spare New Yorker — there shone an indescribable brilliance of light. The energy of the mountain sunshine and the mountain air seemed to throb and quiver through the persons talking — through Anderson's face, and his eyes fixed upon Elizabeth — through the sunlit water — the sparkling grasses — the shimmering spectacle of mountain and summer cloud that begirt them.

"Dear Mr. Arthur, of course we shall meet again in Rome!" said Elizabeth, rosy, and not knowing in truth what to say. "This place has turned my head a little!" — she looked round her, raising her hand to the spectacle as though in pretty appeal to him to share her own exhilaration—"but it will be all over so soon—and you *know* I don't forget old friends—or old pleasures."

Her voice wavered a little. He looked at her, with parted lips, and a rather hostile, heated expression; then drew back, alarmed at his own temerity.

"Of course I know it! You must forgive a bookworm his grumble. Shall I help you over the stream?"

But she stepped across the tiny streamlet without giving him her hand.

As they later rejoined the party, Morton, the Chief Justice, and Mariette returned from a saunter in the course of which they too had been chatting to the engine-drivers.

"I know the part of the country those men want," the American was saying. "I was all over Alberta last fall—part of it in a motor car. We jumped about those stubble-fields in a way to make a leopard jealous! Every bone in my body was sore for weeks afterwards. But it was worth while. That's a country!"—he threw up his hands. "I was at Edmonton on the day when the last Government lands, the odd numbers, were thrown open. I saw the siege of the land offices, the rush of the new population. Ah, well, of course, we're used to such scenes in the States. There's a great trek going on now in our own Southwest. But when that's over, our free land is done. Canada will have the handling of the last batch on this planet."

"If Canada by that time is not America," said Mariette, drily.

The American digested the remark.

"Well," he said, at last, with a smile, "if I were a Canadian, perhaps I should be a bit nervous."

Thereupon, Mariette with great animation developed his theme of the "American invasion." Winnipeg was one danger spot, British Columbia another. The "peaceful penetration," both of men and capital, was going on so rapidly that a movement for annexation, were it once started in certain districts of Canada, might be irresistible. The harsh and powerful face of the speaker became transfigured; one divined in him some hidden motive which was driving him to contest and belittle the main currents and sympathies about him. He spoke as a prophet, but the faith which envenomed the prophecy lay far out of sight.

Anderson took it quietly. The Chief Justice smiled.

"It might have been," he said, "it might have been! This railroad has made the difference." He stretched out his hand towards the line and the pass. "Twenty years ago, I came over this ground with the first party that ever pushed through Rogers Pass and down the Illecillewaet Valley to the Pacific. We camped just about here for the night. And in the evening I was sitting by myself on the slopes of that mountain opposite"—he raised his hand—"looking at the railway camps below me, and the first rough line that had been cut through the forests. And I thought of the day when the trains would be going backwards and forwards, and these nameless valleys and peaks would become the playground of Canada and America. But what I didn't see was the shade of England looking on!—England, whose greater destiny was being decided by those gangs of workmen below me, and the thousands of workmen behind me, busy night and day in bridging the gap between east and west. Traffic from north and south"—he turned towards the American—"that meant, for *your* Northwest, fusion with *our* Northwest; traffic from east to west—that meant England, and the English Sisterhood of States! And that, for the moment, I didn't see."

"Shall I quote you something I found in an Edmonton paper the other day?" said Anderson, raising his head from where he lay, looking down into the grass. And with his smiling, intent gaze fixed on the American, he recited:

> Land of the sweeping eagle, your goal is not our goal!
> For the ages have taught that the North and the South breed difference of soul.
> We toiled for years in the snow and the night, because we believed in the spring,
> And the mother who cheered us first, shall be first at the

> banquetting!
> The grey old mother, the dear old mother, who taught us the note we sing!

The American laughed.

"A bit raw, like some of your prairie towns; but it hits the nail. I dare say we have missed our bargain. What matter! Our own chunk is as big as we can chew."

There was a moment's silence. Elizabeth's eyes were shining; even Philip sat open-mouthed and dumb, staring at Anderson.

In the background Delaine waited, grudgingly expectant, for the turn of Elizabeth's head, and the spark of consciousness passing between the two faces which he had learnt to watch. It came—a flash of some high sympathy—involuntary, lasting but a moment. Then Mariette threw out:

"And in the end, what are you going to make of it? A replica of Europe, or America?—a money-grubbing civilisation with no faith but the dollar? If so, we shall have had the great chance of history—and lost it!"

"We shan't lose it," said Anderson, "unless the gods mock us."

"Why not?" said Mariette sombrely. "Nations have gone mad before now."

"Ah!—prophesy, prophesy!" said the Chief Justice sadly. "All very well for you young men, but for us, who are passing away! Here we are at the birth. Shall we never, in any state of being, know the end? I have never felt so bitterly as I do now the limitations of our knowledge and our life."

No one answered him. But Elizabeth looking up saw the aspect of Mariette—the aspect of a thinker and a mystic—slowly relax. Its harshness became serenity, its bitterness peace. And with her quick feeling she guessed that the lament of the Chief Justice had only awakened in the religious mind the typical religious cry, "*Thou, Lord, art the Eternal, and Thy years shall not fail.*"

At Field, where a most friendly inn shelters under the great shoulders of Mount Stephen, they left the car a while, took tea in the hotel, and wandered through the woods below it. All the afternoon, Elizabeth had shown a most delicate and friendly consideration for Delaine. She had turned the conversation often in his direction and on his subjects, had placed him by her side at tea, and in general had more than done her duty by him. To no purpose. Delaine saw himself as the condemned man to whom indulgences are granted before execution. She would probably have done none of these things if there had been any real chance for him.

But in the walk after tea, Anderson and Lady Merton drifted together. There had been so far a curious effort on both their parts to avoid each other's company. But now the Chief Justice and Delaine had foregathered; Philip was lounging and smoking on the balcony of the hotel with a visitor there, an old Etonian fishing and climbing in the Rockies for health, whom they had chanced upon at tea. Mariette, after one glance at the company, especially at Elizabeth and Anderson, had turned aside into the woods by himself.

They crossed the river and strolled up the road to Emerald Lake. Over the superb valley to their left hung the great snowy mass, glistening and sunlit, of Mount Stephen; far to the West the jagged peaks of the Van Home range shot up into the golden air; on the flat beside the river vivid patches of some crimson flower, new to Elizabeth's eyes, caught the sloping light; and the voice of a swollen river pursued them.

They began to talk, this time of England. Anderson asked many questions as to English politics and personalities. And she, to please him, chattered of great people and events, of scenes and leaders in Parliament, of diplomats and royalties; all the gossip of the moment, in fact, fluttering round the principal figures of English and European politics. It was the talk most natural to her; the talk of the world she knew best; and as Elizabeth was full of shrewdness and natural salt, without a trace of malice, no more at least than a woman should have—to borrow the saying about Wilkes and his squint—her chatter was generally in request, and she knew it.

But Anderson, though he had led up to it, did not apparently enjoy it; on the contrary, she felt him gradually withdrawing and cooling, becoming a little dry and caustic, even satirical, as on the first afternoon of their acquaintance. So that after a while her gossip flagged; since the game wants two to play it. Then Anderson walked on with a furrowed brow, and raised colour; and she could not imagine what had been done or said to annoy him.

She could only try to lead him back to Canada. But she got little or no response.

"Our politics must seem to you splashes in a water-butt," he said impatiently, "after London and Europe."

"A pretty big water-butt!"

"Size makes no difference." Elizabeth's lips twitched as she remembered Arthur Delaine's similar protests; but she kept her countenance, and merely worked the harder to pull her companion out of this odd pit of ill-humour into which he had fallen. And in the end she succeeded; he repented, and let her manage him as she would. And whether it was the influence of this hidden action and reaction between their minds, or of the perfumed June day breathing on them from the pines, or of the giant splendour of Mount Burgess, rising sheer in front of them out of the dark avenue of the forest, cannot be told; but, at least, they became more intimate than they had yet been, more deeply interesting each to the other. In his thoughts and ideals she found increasing fascination; her curiosity, her friendly and womanly curiosity, grew with satisfaction. His view of life was often harsh or melancholy; but there was never a false nor a mean note.

Yet before the walk was done he had startled her. As they turned back towards Field, and were in the shadows of the pines, he said, with abrupt decision:

"Will you forgive me if I say something?"

She looked up surprised.

"Don't let your brother drink so much champagne!"

The colour rushed into Elizabeth's face. She drew herself up, conscious of sharp pain, but also of anger. A stranger, who had not yet known them ten days! But she met an expression on his face, timid and yet passionately resolved, which arrested her.

"I really don't know what you mean, Mr. Anderson!" she said proudly.

"I thought I had seen you anxious. I should be anxious if I were you," he went on hurriedly. "He has been ill, and is not quite master of himself. That is always the critical moment. He is a charming fellow—you must be devoted to him. For God's sake, don't let him ruin himself body and soul!"

Elizabeth was dumbfounded. The tears rushed into her eyes, her voice choked in her throat. She must, she would defend her brother. Then she thought of the dinner of the night before, and the night before that—of the wine bill at Winnipeg and Toronto. Her colour faded away; her heart sank; but it still seemed to her an outrage that he should have dared to speak of it. He spoke, however, before she could.

"Forgive me," he said, recovering his self-control. "I know it must seem mere insolence on my part. But I can't help it—I can't look on at such a thing, silently. May I explain? Please permit me! I told you"—his voice changed—"my mother and sisters had been burnt to death. I adored my mother. She was everything to me. She brought us up with infinite courage, though she was a very frail woman. In those days a farm in Manitoba was a much harder struggle than it is now. Yet she never complained; she was always cheerful; always at work. But—my father drank! It came upon him as a young man—after an illness. It got worse as he grew older. Every bit of prosperity that came to us, he drank away; he would have ruined us again and again, but for my mother. And at last he murdered her—her and my poor sisters!"

Elizabeth made a sound of horror.

"Oh, there was no intention to murder," said Anderson bitterly. "He merely sat up drinking one winter night with a couple of whisky bottles beside him. Then in the morning he was awakened by the cold; the fire had gone out. He stumbled out to get the can of coal-oil from the stable, still dazed with drink, brought it in and poured some on the wood. Some more wood was wanted. He went out to fetch it, leaving his candle alight, a broken end in a rickety candlestick, on the floor beside the coal-oil. When he got to the stable it was warm and comfortable; he forgot what he had come for, fell down on a bundle of straw, and went into a dead sleep. The candle must have fallen over into the oil, the oil exploded, and in a few seconds the wooden house was in flames. By the time I came rushing back from the slough where I had been breaking the ice for water, the roof had already fallen in. My poor mother and two of the children had evidently tried to escape by the stairway and had perished there; the two others were burnt in their beds."

"And your father?" murmured Elizabeth, unable to take her eyes from the speaker.

"I woke him in the stable, and told him what had happened. Bit by bit I got out of him what he'd done. And then I said to him, 'Now choose!—either you go, or we. After the funeral, the boys and I have done with you. You can't force us to go on living with you. We will kill ourselves first. Either you stay here, and we go into Winnipeg; or you can sell the stock, take the money, and go. We'll work the farm.' He swore at me, but I told him he'd find we'd made up our minds. And a week later, he disappeared. He had sold the stock, and left us the burnt walls and the land."

"And you've never seen him since?"

"Never."

"You believe him dead?"

"I know that he died—in the first Yukon rush of ten years ago. I tracked him there, shortly afterwards. He was probably killed in a scuffle with some miners as drunken as himself."

There was a silence, which he broke very humbly.

"Do you forgive me? I know I am not sane on this point. I believe I have spoilt your day."

She looked up, her eyes swimming in tears, and held out her hand.

"It's nothing, you know," she said, trying to smile—"in our case. Philip is such a baby."

"I know; but look after him!" he said earnestly, as he grasped it.

The trees thinned, and voices approached. They emerged from the forest, and found themselves hailed by the Chief Justice.

The journey up the pass was even more wonderful than the journey down. Sunset lights lay on the forests, on the glorious lonely mountains, and on the valley of the Yoho, roadless and houseless now, but soon to be as famous through the world as Grindelwald or Chamounix. They dismounted and explored the great camps of workmen in the pass; they watched the boiling of the stream, which had carved the path of the railway; they gathered white dogwood, and yellow snow-lilies, and red painter's-brush.

Elizabeth and Anderson hardly spoke to each other. She talked a great deal with Delaine, and Mariette held a somewhat acid dispute with her on modern French books—Loti, Anatole France, Zola—authors whom his soul loathed.

But the day had forged a lasting bond between Anderson and Elizabeth, and they knew it.

The night rose clear and cold, with stars shining on the snow. Delaine, who with Anderson had found quarters in one of Laggan's handful of houses, went out to stroll and smoke alone, before turning into bed. He walked along the railway line towards Banff, in bitterness of soul, debating with himself whether he could possibly leave the party at once.

When he was well out of sight of the station and the houses, he became aware of a man persistently following him, and not without a hasty grip on the stout stick he carried, he turned at last to confront him.

"What do you want with me? You seem to be following me."

"Are you Mr. Arthur Delaine?" said a thick voice.

"That is my name. What do you want?"

"And you be lodging to-night in the same house with Mr. George Anderson?"

"I am. What's that to you?"

"Well, I want twenty minutes' talk with you," said the voice, after a pause. The accent was Scotch. In the darkness Delaine dimly perceived an old and bent man standing before him, who seemed to sway and totter as he leant upon his stick.

"I cannot imagine, sir, why you should want anything of the kind." And he turned to pursue his walk. The old man kept up with him, and presently said something which brought Delaine to a sudden stop of astonishment. He stood there listening for a few minutes, transfixed, and finally, turning round, he allowed his strange companion to walk slowly beside him back to Laggan.

Lady Merton: Colonist

CHAPTER VII

Oh! the freshness of the morning on Lake Louise!

It was barely eight o'clock, yet Elizabeth Merton had already taken her coffee on the hotel verandah, and was out wandering by herself. The hotel, which is nearly six thousand feet above the sea, had only just been opened for its summer guests, and Elizabeth and her party were its first inmates. Anderson indeed had arranged their coming, and was to have brought them hither himself. But on the night of the party's return to Laggan he had been hastily summoned by telegraph to a consultation of engineers on a difficult matter of railway grading in the Kootenay district. Delaine, knocking at his door in the morning, had found him flown. A note for Lady Merton explained his flight, gave all directions for the drive to Lake Louise, and expressed his hope to be with them again as expeditiously as possible. Three days had now elapsed since he had left them. Delaine, rather to Elizabeth's astonishment, had once or twice inquired when he might be expected to return.

Elizabeth found a little path by the lake shore, and pursued it a short way; but presently the splendour and the beauty overpowered her; her feet paused of themselves. She sat down on a jutting promontory of rock, and lost herself in the forms and hues of the morning. In front of her rose a wall of glacier sheer out of the water and thousands of feet above the lake, into the clear brilliance of the sky. On either side of its dazzling whiteness, mountains of rose-coloured rock, fledged with pine, fell steeply to the water's edge, enclosing and holding up the glacier; and vast rock pinnacles of a paler rose, melting into gold, broke, here and there, the gleaming splendour of the ice. The sun, just topping the great basin, kindled the ice surfaces, and all the glistening pinks and yellows, the pale purples and blood-crimsons of the rocks, to flame and splendour; while the shadows of the coolest azure still held the hollows and caves of the glacier. Deep in the motionless lake, the shining snows repeated themselves, so also the rose-red rocks, the blue shadows, the dark buttressing crags with their pines. Height beyond height, glory beyond glory—from the reality above, the eye descended to its lovelier image below, which lay there, enchanted and insubstantial, Nature's dream of itself.

The sky was pure light; the air pure fragrance. Heavy dews dripped from the pines and the moss, and sparkled in the sun. Beside Elizabeth, under a group of pines, lay a bed of snow-lilies, their golden heads dew-drenched, waiting for the touch of the morning, waiting, too—so she thought—for that Canadian poet who will yet place them in English verse beside the daffodils of Westmoreland.

She could hardly breathe for delight. The Alps, whether in their Swiss or Italian aspects, were dear and familiar to her. She climbed nimbly and well; and her senses knew the magic of high places. But never surely had even travelled eyes beheld a nobler fantasy of Nature than that composed by these snows and forests of Lake Louise; such rocks of opal and pearl; such dark gradations of splendour in calm water; such balanced intricacy and harmony in the building of this ice-palace that reared its majesty above the lake; such a beauty of subordinate and converging outline in the supporting mountains on either hand; as though the Earth Spirit had lingered on his work, finishing and caressing it in conscious joy.

And in Elizabeth's heart, too, there was a freshness of spring; an overflow of something elemental and irresistible.

Yet, strangely enough, it was at that moment expressing itself in regret and compunction. Since the dawn, that morning, she had been unable to sleep. The strong light, the pricking air, had kept her wakeful; and she had been employing her time in writing to her mother, who was also her friend.

"... Dear little mother—You will say I have been unkind—I say it to myself. But would it really have been fairer if I had forbidden him to join us? There was just a chance—it seems ridiculous now—but there was—I confess it! And by my letter from Toronto—though really my little note might have been written to anybody—I as good as said so to him, 'Come and throw the dice and—let us see what falls out!' Practically, that is what it amounted to—I admit it in sackcloth and ashes. Well!—we have thrown the dice—and it won't do! No, it won't, it won't do! And it is somehow all my fault—which is abominable. But I see now, what I never saw at home or in Italy, that he is a thousand years older than I—that I should weary and jar upon him at every turn, were I to marry him. Also I have discovered—out here—I believe, darling, you have known it all along!—that there is at the very root of me a kind of savage—a creature that hates fish-knives and finger-glasses and dressing for dinner—the things I have done all my life, and Arthur Delaine will go on doing all his. Also that I never want to see a museum again—at least, not for a long time; and that I don't care twopence whether Herculaneum is excavated or not!

"Isn't it shocking? I can't explain myself; and poor Mr. Arthur evidently can't make head or tail of me, and thinks me a little mad. So I am, in a sense. I am suffering from a new kind of *folie des grandeurs*. The world has suddenly grown so big; everything in the human story—all its simple fundamental things at least—is writ so large here. Hope and ambition—love and courage—the man wrestling with the earth—the woman who bears and brings up children—it is as though I had never felt, never seen them before. They rise out of the dust and mist of our modern life—great shapes warm from the breast of Nature—and I hold my breath. Behind them, for landscape, all the dumb age-long past of these plains and mountains; and in front, the future on the loom, and the young radiant nation, shuttle in hand, moving to and fro at her unfolding task!

"How unfair to Mr. Arthur that this queer intoxication of mine should have altered him so in my foolish eyes—as though one had scrubbed all the golden varnish from an old picture, and left it crude and charmless. It is not his fault—is mine. In Europe we loved the same things; his pleasure kindled mine. But here he enjoys nothing that I enjoy; he is longing for a tiresome day to end, when my heart is just singing for delight. For it is not only Canada in the large that holds me, but all its dear, human, dusty, incoherent detail—all its clatter of new towns and spreading farms—of pushing railways and young parliaments—of roadmaking and bridgemaking—of saw-mills and lumber camps—detail so different from anything I have ever discussed with Arthur Delaine before. Some of it is ugly, I know—I don't care! It is like a Rembrandt ugliness—that only helps and ministers to a stronger beauty, the beauty of prairie and sky, and the beauty of the human battle, the battle of blood and brain, with the earth and her forces.

"'Enter these enchanted woods, ye who dare!'"

"There is a man here—a Mr. George Anderson, of whom I told you something in my last letter—who seems to embody the very life of this country, to be the prairie, and the railway, and the forest—their very spirit and avatar. Personally, he is often sad; his own life has been hard; and yet the heart of him is all hope and courage, all delight too in the daily planning and wrestling, the contrivance and the cleverness, the rifling and outwitting of Nature—that makes a Canadian—at any rate a Western Canadian. I suppose he doesn't know anything about art. Mr. Arthur seems to have nothing in common with him; but there is in him that rush and energy of life, from which, surely, art and poetry spring, when the time is ripe.

"Don't of course imagine anything absurd! He is just a young Scotch engineer, who seems to have made some money as people do make money here—quickly and honestly—and is shortly going into Parliament. They say that he is sure to be a great man. To us—to Philip and me, he has been extremely kind. I only meant that he seems to be in place here—or anywhere, indeed, where the world is moving; while Mr. Arthur, in Canada, is a walking anachronism. He is out of perspective; he doesn't fit.

"You will say, that if I married him, it would not be to live in Canada, and once at home again, the old estimates and 'values' would reassert themselves. But in a sense—don't be alarmed—I shall always live in Canada. Or, rather, I shall never be quite the same again; and Mr. Arthur would find me a restless, impracticable, discontented woman.

"Would it not really be kinder if I suggested to him to go home by California, while we come back again through the Rockies? Don't you think it would? I feel that I have begun to get on his nerves—as he on mine. If you were only here! But, I assure you, he doesn't *look* miserable; and I think he will bear up very well. And if it will be any comfort to you to be told that I know what is meant by the gnawing of the little worm, Compunction, then be comforted, dearest; for it gnaws horribly, and out of all proportion—I vow—to my crimes.

"Philip is better on the whole, and has taken an enormous fancy to Mr. Anderson. But, as I have told you all along, he is not so much better as you and I hoped he would be. I take every care of him that I can, but you know that he is not wax, when it comes to managing. However, Mr. Anderson has been a great help."

Recollections of this letter, and other thoughts besides, coming from much deeper strata of the mind than she had been willing to reveal to her mother, kept slipping at intervals through Elizabeth's consciousness, as she sat beside the lake.

A step beside her startled her, and she looked up to see Delaine approaching.

"Out already, Mr. Arthur! But *I* have had breakfast!"

"So have I. What a place!"

Elizabeth did not answer, but her smiling eyes swept the glorious circle of the lake.

"How soon will it all be spoilt and vulgarised?" said Delaine, with a shrug. "Next year, I suppose, a funicular, to the top of the glacier."

Elizabeth cried out.

"Why not?" he asked her, as he rather coolly and deliberately took his seat beside her. "You applaud telephones on the prairies; why not funiculars here?"

"The one serves, the other spoils," said Elizabeth eagerly.

"Serves whom? Spoils what?" The voice was cold. "All travellers are not like yourself."

"I am not afraid. The Canadians will guard their heritage."

"How dull England will seem to you when you go back to it!" he said to her, after a moment. His tone had an under-note of bitterness which Elizabeth uncomfortably recognised.

"Oh! I have a way of liking what I must like," she said, hurriedly. "Just now, certainly, I am in love with deserts—flat or mountainous—tempered by a private car."

He laughed perfunctorily. And suddenly it seemed to her that he had come out to seek her with a purpose, and that a critical moment might be approaching. Her cheeks flushed, and to hide them she leant over the water's edge and began to trail her finger in its clear wave.

He, however, sat in hesitation, looking at her, the prey of thoughts to which she had no clue. He could not make up his mind, though he had just spent an almost sleepless night on the attempt to do it.

The silence became embarrassing. Then, if he still groped, she seemed to see her way, and took it.

"It was very good of you to come out and join our wanderings," she said suddenly. Her voice was clear and kind. He started.

"You know I could ask for nothing better," was his slow reply, not without dignity. "It has been an immense privilege to see you like this, day by day."

Elizabeth's pulse quickened.

"How can I manage it?" she desperately thought. "But I must—"

"That's very sweet of you," she said aloud, "when I have bored you so with my raptures. And now it's coming to an end, like all nice things. Philip and I think of staying a little in Vancouver. And the Governor has asked us to go over to Victoria for a few days. You, I suppose, will be doing the proper round, and going back by Seattle and San Francisco?"

Delaine received the blow—and understood it. There had been no definite plans ahead. Tacitly, it had been assumed, he thought, that he was to return with them to Montreal and England. This gentle question, then, was Elizabeth's way of telling him that his hopes were vain and his journey fruitless.

He had not often been crossed in his life, and a flood of resentment surged up in a very perplexed mind.

"Thank you. Yes—I shall go home by San Francisco."

The touch of haughtiness in his manner, the manner of one accustomed all his life to be a prominent and considered person in the world, did not disguise from Elizabeth the soreness underneath. It was hard to hurt her old friend. But she could only sit as though she felt nothing—meant nothing—of any importance.

And she achieved it to perfection. Delaine, through all his tumult of feeling, was sharply conscious of her grace, her reticence, her soft dignity. They were exactly what he coveted in a wife—what he hoped he had captured in Elizabeth. How was it they had been snatched from him? He turned blindly on the obstacle that had risen in his path, and the secret he had not yet decided how to handle began to run away with him.

He bent forward, with a slightly heightened colour.

"Lady Merton—we might not have another opportunity—will you allow me a few frank words with you—the privilege of an old friend?"

Elizabeth turned her face to him, and a pair of startled eyes that tried not to waver.

"Of course, Mr. Arthur," she said smiling. "Have I been doing anything dreadful?"

"May I ask what you personally know of this Mr. Anderson?"

He saw—or thought he saw—her brace herself under the sudden surprise of the name, and her momentary discomfiture pleased him.

"What I know of Mr. Anderson?" she repeated wondering. "Why, no more than we all know. What do you mean, Mr. Arthur? Ah, yes, I remember, you first met him in Winnipeg; *we* made acquaintance with him the day before."

"For the first time? But you are now seeing a great deal of him. Are you quite sure—forgive me if I seem impertinent—that he is—quite the person to be admitted to your daily companionship?"

He spoke slowly and harshly. The effort required before a naturally amiable and nervous man could bring himself to put such an uncomfortable question made it appear particularly offensive.

"Our daily companionship?" repeated Elizabeth in bewilderment. "What can you mean, Mr. Arthur? What is wrong with Mr. Anderson? You saw that everybody at Winnipeg seemed to know him and respect him; people like the Chief Justice, and the Senator—what was his name?—and Monsieur Mariette. I don't understand why you ask me such a thing. Why should we suppose there are any mysteries about Mr. Anderson?"

Unconsciously her slight figure had stiffened, her voice had changed.

Delaine felt an admonitory qualm. He would have drawn back; but it was too late. He went on doggedly—

"Were not all these persons you named acquainted with Mr. Anderson in his public capacity? His success in the strike of last year brought him a great notoriety. But his private history—his family and antecedents—have you gathered anything at all about them?"

Something that he could not decipher flashed through Elizabeth's expression. It was a strange and thrilling sense that what she had gathered she would not reveal for—a kingdom!

"Monsieur Mariette told me all that anyone need want to know!" she cried, breathing quick. "Ask him what he thinks—what he feels! But if you ask *me*, I think Mr. Anderson carries his history in his face."

Delaine pondered a moment, while Elizabeth waited, challenging, expectant, her brown eyes all vivacity.

"Well—some facts have come to my knowledge," he said, at last, "which have made me ask you these questions. My only object—you must, you will admit that!—is to save you possible pain—a possible shock."

"Mr. Arthur!" the voice was peremptory—"If you have learned anything about Mr. Anderson's private history—by chance—without his knowledge—that perhaps he would rather we did not know—I beg you will not tell me—indeed—please—I forbid you to tell me. We owe him much kindness these last few weeks. I cannot gossip about him behind his back."

All her fine slenderness of form, her small delicacy of feature, seemed to him tense and vibrating, like some precise and perfect instrument strained to express a human feeling or intention. But what feeling? While he divined it, was she herself unconscious of it? His bitterness grew.

"Dear Lady Merton—can you not trust an old friend?"

She did not soften.

"I do trust him. But"—her smile flashed—"even new acquaintances have their rights."

"You will not understand," he said, earnestly. "What is in my mind came to me, through no wish or will of mine. You cannot suppose that I have been prying into Mr. Anderson's affairs! But now that the information is mine, I feel a great responsibility towards you."

"Don't feel it. I am a wilful woman."

"A rather perplexing one! May I at least be sure that"—he hesitated—"that you will be on your guard?"

"On my guard?" she lifted her eyebrows proudly—"and against what?"

"That is precisely what you won't let me tell you."

She laughed—a little fiercely.

"There we are; no forrarder. But please remember, Mr. Arthur, how soon we shall all be separating. Nothing very dreadful can happen in these few days—can it?"

For the first time there was a touch of malice in her smile.

Delaine rose, took one or two turns along the path in front of her, and then suddenly stopped beside her.

"I think"—he said, with emphasis, "that Mr. Anderson will probably find himself summoned away—immediately—before you get to Vancouver. But that I will discuss with him. You could give me no address, so I have not yet been able to communicate with him."

Again Elizabeth's eyebrows went up. She rose.

"Of course you will do what you think best. Shall we go back to the hotel?"

They walked along in silence. He saw that she was excited, and that he had completely missed his stroke; but he did not see how to mend the situation.

"Oh! there is Philip, going to fish," said Elizabeth at last, as though nothing had happened. "I wondered what could possibly have got him up so early."

Philip waved to her as she spoke, shouting something which the mountain echoes absorbed. He was accompanied by a young man, who seemed to be attached to the hotel as guide, fisherman, hunter—at the pleasure of visitors. But Elizabeth had already discovered that he had the speech of a gentleman, and attended the University of Manitoba during the winter. In the absence of Anderson, Philip had no doubt annexed him for the morning.

There was a pile of logs lying on the lake side. Philip, rod in hand, began to scramble over them to a point where several large trunks overhung deep water. His companion meanwhile was seated on the moss, busy with some preparations.

"I hope Philip will be careful," said Delaine, suddenly. "There is nothing so slippery as logs."

Elizabeth, who had been dreaming, looked up anxiously. As she did so Philip, high perched on the furthest logs, turned again to shout to his sister, his light figure clear against the sunlit distance. Then the figure wavered, there was a sound of crashing wood, and Philip fell head-foremost into the lake before him.

The young man on the bank looked up, threw away his rod and his coat, and was just plunging into the lake when he was anticipated by another man who had come running down the bank of the hotel, and was already in the water. Elizabeth, as she rushed along the edge, recognized Anderson. Philip seemed to have disappeared; but Anderson dived, and presently emerged with a limp burden. The guide was now aiding him, and between them they brought young Gaddesden to land. The whole thing passed so rapidly that Delaine and Elizabeth, running at full speed, had hardly reached the spot before Anderson was on the shore, bearing the lad in his arms.

Elizabeth bent over him with a moan of anguish. He seemed to her dead.

"He has only fainted," said Anderson peremptorily. "We must get him in." And he hurried on, refusing Delaine's help, carrying the thin body apparently with ease along the path and up the steps to the hotel. The guide had already been sent flying ahead to warn the household.

Thus, by one of the commonplace accidents of travel, the whole scene was changed for this group of travellers. Philip Gaddesden would have taken small harm from his tumble into the lake, but for the fact that the effects of rheumatic fever were still upon him. As it was, a certain amount of fever, and some heart-symptoms that it was thought had been overcome, reappeared, and within a few hours of the accident it became plain that, although he was in no danger, they would be detained at least ten days, perhaps a fortnight, at Lake Louise. Elizabeth sat down in deep despondency to write to her mother, and then lingered awhile with the letter before her, her head in her hands, pondering with emotion what she and Philip owed to George Anderson, who had, it seemed, arrived by a night train, and walked up to the hotel, in the very nick of time. As to the accident itself, no doubt the guide, a fine swimmer and *coureur de bois*, would have been sufficient, unaided, to save her brother. But after all, it was Anderson's strong arms that had drawn him from the icy depths of the lake, and carried him to safety! And since? Never had telephone and railway, and general knowledge of the resources at command, been worked more skilfully than by him, and the kind people of the hotel. "Don't be the least anxious"—she had written to her mother—"we have a capital doctor—all the chemist's stuff we want—and we could have a nurse at any moment. Mr. Anderson has only to order one up from the camp hospital in the pass. But for the present, Simpson and I are enough for the nursing."

She heard voices in the next room; a faint question from Philip, Anderson replying. What an influence this man of strong character had already obtained over her wilful, self-indulgent brother! She saw the signs of it in many directions; and she was passionately grateful for it. Her thoughts went wandering back over the past three weeks—over the whole gradual unveiling of Anderson's personality. She recalled her first impressions of him the day of the "sink-hole." An ordinary, strong, capable, ambitious young man, full of practical interests, with brusque manners, and a visible lack of some of the outer wrappings to which she was accustomed—it was so that she had first envisaged him. Then at Winnipeg—through Mariette and others—she had seen him as other men saw him, his seniors and contemporaries, the men engaged with him in the making of this vast country. She had appreciated his character in what might be hereafter, apparently, its public aspects; the character of one for whom the world surrounding him was eagerly prophesying a future and a career. His profound loyalty to Canada, and to certain unspoken ideals behind, which were really the source of the loyalty; the atmosphere at once democratic and imperial in which his thoughts and desires moved, which had more than once communicated its passion to her; a touch of poetry, of melancholy, of greatness even—all this she had gradually perceived. Winnipeg and the prairie journey had developed him thus before her.

So much for the second stage in her knowledge of him. There was a third; she was in the midst of it. Her face flooded with colour against her will. "Out of the strong shall come forth sweetness." The words rushed into her mind. She hoped, as one who wished him well, that he would marry soon and happily. And the woman who married him would find it no tame future.

Suddenly Delaine's warnings occurred to her. She laughed, a little hysterically.

Could anyone have shown himself more helpless, useless, incompetent, than Arthur Delaine since the accident? Yet he was still on the spot. She realised, indeed, that it was hardly possible for their old friend to desert them under the circumstances. But he merely represented an additional burden.

A knock at the sitting-room door disturbed her. Anderson appeared.

"I am off to Banff, Lady Merton," he said from the threshold. "I think I have all your commissions. Is your letter ready?"

She sealed it and gave it to him. Then she looked up at him; and for the first time he saw her tremulous and shaken; not for her brother, but for himself.

"I don't know how to thank you." She offered her hand; and one of those beautiful looks—generous, friendly, sincere—of which she had the secret.

He, too, flushed, his eyes held a moment by hers. Then he, somewhat brusquely, disengaged himself.

"Why, I did nothing! He was in no danger; the guide would have had him out in a twinkle. I wish"—he frowned—"you wouldn't look so done up over it."

"Oh! I am all right."

"I brought you a book this morning. Mercifully I left it in the drawing-room, so it hasn't been in the lake."

He drew it from his pocket. It was a French novel she had expressed a wish to read.

She exclaimed,

"How did you get it?"

"I found Mariette had it with him. He sends it me from Vancouver. Will you promise to read it—and rest?"

He drew a sofa towards the window. The June sunset was blazing on the glacier without. Would he next offer to put a shawl over her, and tuck her up? She retreated hastily to the writing-table, one hand upon it. He saw the lines of her gray dress, her small neck and head; the Quakerish smoothness of her brown hair, against the light. The little figure was grace, refinement, embodied. But it was a grace that implied an environment—the cosmopolitan, luxurious environment, in which such women naturally move.

His look clouded. He said a hasty good-bye and departed. Elizabeth was left breathing quick, one hand on her breast. It was as though she had escaped something—or missed something.

As he left the hotel, Anderson found himself intercepted by Delaine in the garden, and paused at once to give him the latest news.

"The report is really good, everything considered," he said, with a cordiality born of their common anxiety; and he repeated the doctor's last words to himself.

"Excellent!" said Delaine; then, clearing his throat, "Mr. Anderson, may I have some conversation with you?"

Anderson looked surprised, threw him a keen glance, and invited him to accompany him part of the way to Laggan. They turned into a solitary road, running between the woods. It was late evening, and the sun was striking through the Laggan valley beneath them in low shafts of gold and purple.

"I am afraid what I have to say will be disagreeable to you," began Delaine, abruptly. "And on this particular day—when we owe you so much—it is more than disagreeable to myself. But I have no choice. By some extraordinary chance, with which I beg you to believe my own will has had nothing to do, I have become acquainted with something—something that concerns you privately—something that I fear will be a great shock to you."

Anderson stood still.

"What can you possibly mean?" he said, in growing amazement.

"I was accosted the night before last, as I was strolling along the railway line, by a man I had never seen before, a man who—pardon me, it is most painful to me to seem to be interfering with anyone's private affairs—who announced himself as"—the speaker's nervous stammer intervened before he jerked out the words—"as your father!"

"As my father? Somebody must be mad!" said Anderson quietly. "My father has been dead ten years."

"I am afraid there is a mistake. The man who spoke to me is aware that you suppose him dead—he had his own reasons, he declares, for allowing you to remain under a misconception; he now wishes to reopen communications with you, and to my great regret, to my indignation, I may say he chose me—an entire stranger—as his intermediary. He seems to have watched our party all the way from Winnipeg, where he first saw you, casually, in the street. Naturally I tried to escape from him—to refer him to you. But I could not possibly escape from him, at night, with no road for either of us but the railway line. I was at his mercy."

"What was his reason for not coming direct to me?"

They were still pausing in the road. Delaine could see in the failing light that Anderson had grown pale. But he perceived also an expression of scornful impatience in the blue eyes fixed upon him.

"He has professed to be afraid—"

"That I should murder him?" said Anderson with a laugh. "And he told you some sort of a story?"

"A long one, I regret to say."

"And not to my credit?"

"The tone of it was certainly hostile. I would rather not repeat it."

"I should not dream of asking you to do so. And where is this precious individual to be found?"

Delaine named the address which had been given him—of a lodging mainly for railway men near Laggan.

"I will look him up," said Anderson briefly. "The whole story of course is a mere attempt to get money—for what reason I do not know; but I will look into it."

Delaine was silent. Anderson divined from his manner that he believed the story true. In the minds of both the thought of Lady Merton emerged. Anderson scorned to ask, "Have you said anything to them?" and Delaine was conscious of a nervous fear lest he should ask it. In the light of the countenance beside him, no less than of the event of the day, his behaviour of the morning began to seem to him more than disputable. In the morning he had seemed to himself the defender of Elizabeth and the class to which they both belonged against low-born adventurers with disreputable pasts. But as he stood there, confronting the "adventurer," his conscience as a gentleman—which was his main and typical conscience—pricked him.

The inward qualm, however, only stiffened his manner. And Anderson asked nothing. He turned towards Laggan.

"Good night. I will let you know the result of my investigations." And, with the shortest of nods, he went off at a swinging pace down the road.

"I have only done my duty," argued Delaine with himself as he returned to the hotel. "It was uncommonly difficult to do it at such a moment! But to him I have no obligations whatever; my obligations are to Lady Merton and her family."

CHAPTER VIII

It was dark when Anderson reached Laggan, if that can be called darkness which was rather a starry twilight, interfused with the whiteness of snow-field and glacier. He first of all despatched a message to Banff for Elizabeth's commissions. Then he made straight for the ugly frame house of which Delaine had given him the address. It was kept by a couple well known to him, an Irishman and his wife who made their living partly by odd jobs on the railway, partly by lodging men in search of work in the various construction camps of the line. To all such persons Anderson was a familiar figure, especially since the great strike of the year before.

The house stood by itself in a plot of cleared ground, some two or three hundred yards from the railway station. A rough road through the pine wood led up to it.

Anderson knocked, and Mrs. Ginnell came to the door, a tired, and apparently sulky woman.

"I hear you have a lodger here, Mrs. Ginnell," said Anderson, standing in the doorway, "a man called McEwen; and that he wants to see me on some business or other."

Mrs. Ginnell's countenance darkened.

"We have an old man here, Mr. Anderson, as answers to that name, but you'll get no business out of him—and I don't believe he *have* any business with any decent crater. When he arrived two days ago he was worse for liquor, took on at Calgary. I made my husband look after him that night to see he didn't get at nothing, but yesterday he slipped us both, an' I believe he's now in that there outhouse, a-sleeping it off. Old men like him should be sent somewhere safe, an' kep' there."

"I'll go and see if he's awake, Mrs. Ginnell. Don't you trouble to come. Any other lodgers?"

"No, sir. There was a bunch of 'em left this morning—got work on the Crow's Nest."

Anderson made his way to the little "shack," Ginnell's house of the first year, now used as a kind of general receptacle for tools, rubbish and stores.

He looked in. On a heap of straw in the corner lay a huddled figure, a kind of human rag. Anderson paused a moment, then entered, hung the lamp he had brought with him on a peg, and closed the door behind him.

He stood looking down at the sleeper, who was in the restless stage before waking. McEwen threw himself from side to side, muttered, and stretched.

Slowly a deep colour flooded Anderson's cheeks and brow; his hands hanging beside him clenched; he checked a groan that was also a shudder. The abjectness of the figure, the terrible identification proceeding in his mind, the memories it evoked, were rending and blinding him. The winter morning on the snow-strewn prairie, the smell of smoke blown towards him on the wind, the flames of the burning house, the horror of the search among the ruins, his father's confession, and his own rage and despair—deep in the tissues of life these images were stamped. The anguish of them ran once more through his being.

How had he been deceived? And what was to be done? He sat down on a heap of rubbish beside the straw, looking at his father. He had last seen him as a man of fifty, vigorous, red-haired, coarsely handsome, though already undermined by drink. The man lying on the straw was approaching seventy, and might have been much older. His matted hair was nearly white, face blotched and cavernous; and the relaxation of sleep emphasised the mean cunning of the mouth. His clothing was torn and filthy, the hands repulsive.

Anderson could only bear a few minutes of this spectacle. A natural shame intervened. He bent over his father and called him.

"Robert Anderson!"

A sudden shock passed through the sleeper. He started up, and Anderson saw his hand dart for something lying beside him, no doubt a revolver.

But Anderson grasped the arm.

"Don't be afraid; you're quite safe."

McEwen, still bewildered by sleep and drink, tried to shake off the grasp, to see who it was standing over him. Anderson released him, and moved so that the lamplight fell upon himself.

Slowly McEwen's faculties came together, began to work. The lamplight showed him his son George—the fair-haired, broad-shouldered fellow he had been tracking all these days—and he understood.

He straightened himself, with an attempt at dignity.

"So it's you, George? You might have given me notice."

"Where have you been all these years?" said Anderson, indistinctly. "And why did you let me believe you dead?"

"Well, I had my reasons, George. But I don't mean to go into 'em. All that's dead and gone. There was a pack of fellows then on my shoulders—I was plumb tired of 'em. I had to get rid of—I did get rid of 'em—and you, too. I knew you were inquiring after me, and I didn't want inquiries. They didn't suit me. You may conclude what you like. I tell you those times are dead and gone. But it seemed to me that Robert Anderson was best put away for a bit. So I took measures according."

"You knew I was deceived."

"Yes, I knew," said the other composedly. "Couldn't be helped."

"And where have you been since?"

"In Nevada, George—Comstock—silver-mining. Rough lot, but you get a stroke of luck sometimes. I've got a chance on now—me and a friend of mine—that's first-rate."

"What brought you back to Canada?"

"Well, it was your aunt, Mrs. Harriet Sykes. Ever hear of her, George?"

Anderson shook his head.

"You must have heard of her when you were a little chap. When I left Ayrshire in 1840 she was a lass of sixteen; never saw her since. But she married a man well-to-do, and was left a widder with no children. And when she died t'other day, she'd left me something in her will, and told the lawyers to advertise over here, in Canada and the States—both. And I happened on the advertisement in a Chicago paper. Told yer to call on Smith & Dawkins, Winnipeg. So that was how I came to see Winnipeg again."

"When were you there?"

"Just when you was," said the old man, with a triumphant look, which for the moment effaced the squalor of his aspect. "I was coming out of Smith & Dawkins's with the money in my pocket, when I saw you opposite, just going into a shop. You could ha' knocked me down easy, I warrant ye. Didn't expect to come on yer tracks as fast as all that. But there you were, and when you came out and went down t' street, I just followed you at a safe distance, and saw you go into the hotel. Afterwards, I went into the Free Library to think a bit, and then I saw the piece in the paper about you and that Saskatchewan place; and I got hold of a young man in a saloon who found out all about you and those English swells you've been hanging round with; and that same night, when you boarded the train, I boarded it, too. See? Only I am not a swell like you. And here we are. See?"

The last speech was delivered with a mixture of bravado, cunning, and sinister triumph. Anderson sat with his head in his hands, his eyes on the mud floor, listening. When it was over he looked up.

"Why didn't you come and speak to me at once?"

The other hesitated.

"Well, I wasn't a beauty to look at. Not much of a credit to you, am I? Didn't think you'd own me. And I don't like towns—too many people about. Thought I'd catch you somewhere on the quiet. Heard you was going to the Rockies. Thought I might as well go round by Seattle home. See?"

"You have had plenty of chances since Winnipeg of making yourself known to me," said Anderson sombrely. "Why did you speak to a stranger instead of coming direct to me?"

McEwen hesitated a moment.

"Well, I wasn't sure of you. I didn't know how you'd take it. And I'd lost my nerve, damn it! the last few years. Thought you might just kick me out, or set the police on me."

Anderson studied the speaker. His fair skin was deeply flushed; his brow frowned unconsciously, reflecting the travail of thought behind it.

"What did you say to that gentleman the other night?"

McEwen smiled a shifty smile, and began to pluck some pieces of straw from his sleeve.

"Don't remember just what I did say. Nothing to do you no harm, anyway. I might have said you were never an easy chap to get on with. I might have said that, or I mightn't. Think I did. Don't remember."

The eyes of the two men met for a moment, Anderson's bright and fixed. He divined perfectly what had been said to the Englishman, Lady Merton's friend and travelling companion. A father overborne by misfortunes and poverty, disowned by a prosperous and Pharisaical son—admitting a few peccadilloes, such as most men forgive, in order to weigh them against virtues, such as all men hate. Old age and infirmity on the one hand; mean hardness and cruelty on the other. Was Elizabeth already contemplating the picture?

And yet—No! unless perhaps under the shelter of darkness, it could never have been possible for this figure before him to play the part of innocent misfortune, at all events. Could debauch, could ruin of body and soul be put more plainly? Could they express themselves more clearly than through this face and form?

A shudder ran through Anderson, a cry against fate, a sick wondering as to his own past responsibility, a horror of the future.

Then his will strengthened, and he set himself quietly to see what could be done.

"We can't talk here," he said to his father. "Come back into the house. There are some rooms vacant. I'll take them for you."

McEwen rose with difficulty, groaning as he put his right foot to the ground. Anderson then perceived that the right foot and ankle were wrapped round with a bloodstained rag, and was told that the night before their owner had stumbled over a jug in Mrs. Ginnell's kitchen, breaking the jug and inflicting some deep cuts on his own foot and ankle. McEwen, indeed, could only limp along, with mingled curses and lamentations, supported by Anderson. In the excitement of his son's appearance he had forgotten his injury. The pain and annoyance of it returned upon him now with added sharpness, and Anderson realised that here was yet another complication as they moved across the yard.

A few words to the astonished Mrs. Ginnell sufficed to secure all her vacant rooms, four in number. Anderson put his father in one on the ground floor, then shut the door on him and went back to the woman of the house. She stood looking at him, flushed, in a bewildered silence. But she and her husband owed various kindnesses to Anderson, and he quickly made up his mind.

In a very few words he quietly told her the real facts, confiding them both to her self-interest and her humanity. McEwen was to be her only lodger till the next step could be determined. She was to wait on him, to keep drink from him, to get him clothes. Her husband was to go out with him, if he should insist on going out; but Anderson thought his injury would keep him quiet for a day or two. Meanwhile, no babbling to anybody. And, of course, generous payment for all that was asked of them.

But Mrs. Ginnell understood that she was being appealed to not only commercially, but as a woman with a heart in her body and a good share of Irish wit. That moved and secured her. She threw herself nobly into the business. Anderson might command her as he pleased, and she answered for her man. Renewed groans from the room next door disturbed them. Mrs. Ginnell went in to answer them, and came out demanding a doctor. The patient was in much pain, the wounds looked bad, and she suspected fever.

"Yo can't especk places to heal with such as him," she said, grimly.

With doggedness, Anderson resigned himself. He went to the station and sent a wire to Field for a doctor. What would happen when he arrived he did not know. He had made no compact with his father. If the old man chose to announce himself, so be it. Anderson did not mean to bargain or sue. Other men have had to bear such burdens in the face of the world. Should it fall to him to be forced to take his up in like manner, let him set his teeth and shoulder it, sore and shaken as he was. He felt a fierce confidence that could still make the world respect him.

An hour passed away. An answer came from Field to the effect that a doctor would be sent up on a freight train just starting, and might be expected shortly.

While Mrs. Ginnell was still attending on her lodger, Anderson went out into the starlight to try and think out the situation. The night was clear and balmy. The high snows glimmered through the lingering twilight, and in the air there was at last a promise of "midsummer pomps." Pine woods and streams breathed freshness, and when in his walk along the railway line—since there is no other road through the Kicking Horse Pass—he reached a point whence the great Yoho valley became visible to the right, he checked the rapid movement which had brought him a kind of physical comfort, and set himself— in face of that far-stretching and splendid solitude—to wrestle with calamity.

First of all there was the Englishman—Delaine—and the letter that must be written him. But there, also, no evasions, no suppliancy. Delaine must be told that the story was true, and would no doubt think himself entitled to act upon it. The protest on behalf of Lady Merton implied already in his manner that afternoon was humiliating enough. The smart of it was still tingling through Anderson's being. He had till now felt a kind of instinctive contempt for Delaine as a fine gentleman with a useless education, inclined to patronise "colonists." The two men had jarred from the beginning, and at Banff, Anderson had both divined in him the possible suitor of Lady Merton, and had also become aware that Delaine resented his own intrusion upon the party, and the rapid intimacy which had grown up between him and the brother and sister. Well, let him use his chance! if it so pleased him. No promise whatever should be asked of him; there should be no suggestion even of a line of action. The bare fact which he had become possessed of should be admitted, and he should be left to deal with it. Upon his next step would depend Anderson's; that was all.

But Lady Merton?

Anderson stared across the near valley, up the darkness beyond, where lay the forests of the Yoho, and to those ethereal summits whence a man might behold on one side the smoke-wreaths of the great railway, and on the other side the still virgin peaks of the northern Rockies, untamed, untrodden. But his eyes were holden; he saw neither snow, nor forests, and the roar of the stream dashing at his feet was unheard.

Three weeks, was it, since he had first seen that delicately oval face, and those clear eyes? The strong man—accustomed to hold himself in check, to guard his own strength as the instrument, firm and indispensable, of an iron will—recoiled from the truth he was at last compelled to recognise. In this daily companionship with a sensitive and charming woman, endowed beneath her light reserve with all the sweetness of unspoilt feeling, while yet commanding through her long training in an old society a thousand delicacies and subtleties, which played on Anderson's fresh senses like the breeze on young leaves—whither had he been drifting—to the brink of what precipice had he brought himself, unknowing?

He stood there indefinitely, among the charred tree-trunks that bordered the line, his arms folded, looking straight before him, motionless.

Supposing to-day had been yesterday, need he—together with this sting of passion—have felt also this impotent and angry despair? Before his eyes had seen that figure lying on the straw of Mrs.

Ginnell's outhouse, could he ever have dreamed it possible that Elizabeth Merton should marry him?

Yes! He thought, trembling from head to foot, of that expression in her eyes he had seen that very afternoon. Again and again he had checked his feeling by the harsh reminder of her social advantages. But, at this moment of crisis, the man in him stood up, confident and rebellious. He knew himself sound, intellectually and morally. There was a career before him, to which a cool and reasonable ambition looked forward without any paralysing doubts. In this growing Canada, measuring himself against the other men of the moment, he calmly foresaw his own growing place. As to money, he would make it; he was in process of making it, honourably and sufficiently.

He was well aware indeed that in the case of many women sprung from the English governing class, the ties that bind them to their own world, its traditions, and its outlook, are so strong that to try and break them would be merely to invite disaster. But then from such women his own pride—his pride in his country—would have warned his passion. It was to Elizabeth's lovely sympathy, her generous detachment, her free kindling mind—that his life had gone out. *She* would, surely, never be deterred from marrying a Canadian—if he pleased her—because it would cut her off from London and Paris, and all the ripe antiquities and traditions of English or European life? Even in the sparsely peopled Northwest, with which his own future was bound up, how many English women are there—fresh, some of them, from luxurious and fastidious homes—on ranches, on prairie farms, in the Okanagan valley! "This Northwest is no longer a wilderness!" he proudly thought; "it is no longer a leap in the dark to bring a woman of delicate nurture and cultivation to the prairies."

So, only a few hours before, he might have flattered the tyranny of longing and desire which had taken hold upon him.

But now! All his life seemed besmirched. His passion had been no sooner born than, like a wounded bird, it fluttered to the ground. Bring upon such a woman as Elizabeth Merton the most distant responsibility for such a being as he had left behind him in the log-hut at Laggan? Link her life in however remote a fashion with that life? Treachery and sacrilege, indeed! No need for Delaine to tell him that! His father as a grim memory of the past—that Lady Merton knew. His own origins—his own story—as to that she had nothing to discover. But the man who might have dared to love her, up to that moment in the hut, was now a slave, bound to a corpse—

Finis!

And then as the anguish of the thought swept through him, and by a natural transmission of ideas, there rose in Anderson the sore and sudden memory of old, unhappy things, of the tender voices and faces of his first youth. The ugly vision of his degraded father had brought back upon him, through a thousand channels of association, the recollection of his mother. He saw her now—the worn, roughened face, the sweet swimming eyes; he felt her arms around him, the tears of her long agony on his face. She had endured—he too must endure. Close, close—he pressed her to his heart. As the radiant image of Elizabeth vanished from him in the darkness, his mother—broken, despairing, murdered in her youth—came to him and strengthened him. Let him do his duty to this poor outcast, as she would have done it—and put high thoughts from him.

He tore himself resolutely from his trance of thought, and began to walk back along the line. All the same, he would go up to Lake Louise, as he had promised, on the following morning. As far as his own intention was concerned, he would not cease to look after Lady Merton and her brother; Philip Gaddesden would soon have to be moved, and he meant to escort them to Vancouver.

Sounds approached, from the distance—the "freight," with the doctor, climbing the steep pass. He stepped on briskly to a signal-man's cabin and made arrangements to stop the train.

It was towards midnight when he and the doctor emerged from the Ginnell's cabin.

"Oh, I daresay we'll heal those cuts," said the doctor. "I've told Mrs. Ginnell what to do; but the old fellow's in a pretty cranky state. I doubt whether he'll trouble the world very long."

Anderson started. With his eyes on the ground and his hands in his pockets, he inquired the reason for this opinion.

"Arteries—first and foremost. It's a wonder they've held out so long, and then—a score of other things. What can you expect?"

The speaker went into some details, discussing the case with gusto. A miner from Nevada? Queer hells often, those mining camps, whether on the Canadian or the American side of the border.

"You were acquainted with his family? Canadian, to begin with, I understand?"

"Yes. He applied to me for help. Did he tell you much about himself?"

"No. He boasted a lot about some mine in the Comstock district which is to make his fortune, if he can raise the money to buy it up. If he can raise fifteen thousand dollars, he says, he wouldn't care to call Rockefeller his uncle!"

"That's what he wants, is it?" said Anderson, absently, "fifteen thousand dollars?"

"Apparently. Wish he may get it!" laughed the doctor. "Well, keep him from drink, if you can. But I doubt if you'll cheat the undertaker very long. Good night. There'll be a train along soon that'll pick me up."

Anderson went back to the cabin, found that his father had dropped asleep, left money and directions with Mrs. Ginnell, and then returned to his own lodgings.

He sat down to write to Delaine. It was clear that, so far, that gentleman and Mrs. Ginnell were the only other participants in the secret of McEwen's identity. The old man had not revealed himself to the doctor. Did that mean that—in spite of his first reckless interview with the Englishman—he had still some notion of a bargain with his son, on the basis of the fifteen thousand dollars?

Possibly. But that son had still to determine his own line of action. When at last he began to write, he wrote steadily and without a pause. Nor was the letter long.

CHAPTER IX

On the morning following his conversation with Anderson on the Laggan road, Delaine impatiently awaited the arrival of the morning mail from Laggan. When it came, he recognised Anderson's handwriting on one of the envelopes put into his hand. Elizabeth, having kept him company at breakfast, had gone up to sit with Philip. Nevertheless, he took the precaution of carrying the letter out of doors to read it.

It ran as follows:

> "DEAR MR. DELAINE—You were rightly informed, and the man you saw is my father. I was intentionally deceived ten years ago by a false report of his death. Into that, however, I need not enter. If you talked with him, as I understand you did, for half an hour, you will, I think, have gathered that his life has been unfortunately of little advantage either to himself or others. But that also is my personal affair—and his. And although in a moment of caprice, and for reasons not yet plain to me, he revealed himself to you, he appears still to wish to preserve the assumed name and identity that he set up shortly after leaving Manitoba, seventeen years ago. As far as I am concerned, I am inclined to indulge him. But you will, of course, take your own line, and will no doubt communicate it to me. I do not imagine that my private affairs or my father's can be of any interest to you, but perhaps I may say that he is at present for a few days in the doctor's hands and that I propose as soon as his health is re-established to arrange for his return to the States, where his home has been for so long. I am, of course, ready to make any arrangements for his benefit that seem wise, and that he will accept. I hope to come up to Lake Louise to-morrow, and shall bring with me one or two things that Lady Merton asked me to get for her. Next week I hope she may be able and inclined to take one or two of the usual excursions from the hotel, if Mr. Gaddesden goes on as well as we all expect.

I could easily make the necessary arrangements for ponies, guides, &c.

"Yours faithfully,

"GEORGE ANDERSON."

"Upon my word, a cool hand! a very cool hand!" muttered Delaine in some perplexity, as he thrust the letter into his pocket, and strolled on toward the lake. His mind went back to the strange nocturnal encounter which had led to the development of this most annoying relation between himself and Anderson. He recalled the repulsive old man, his uneducated speech, the signs about him of low cunning and drunken living, his rambling embittered charges against his son, who, according to him, had turned his father out of the Manitoba farm in consequence of a family quarrel, and had never cared since to find out whether he was alive or dead. "Sorry to trouble you, sir, I'm sure—a genelman like you"—obsequious old ruffian!—"but my sons were always kittle-cattle, and George the worst of 'em all. If you would be so kind, sir, as to gie 'im a word o' preparation—"

Delaine could hear his own impatient reply: "I have nothing whatever, sir, to do with your business! Approach Mr. Anderson yourself if you have any claim to make." Whereupon a half-sly, half-threatening hint from the old fellow that he might be disagreeable unless well handled; that perhaps "the lady" would listen to him and plead for him with his son.

Lady Merton! Good heavens! Delaine had been immediately ready to promise anything in order to protect her.

Yet even now the situation was extremely annoying and improper. Here was this man, Anderson, still coming up to the hotel, on the most friendly terms with Lady Merton and her brother, managing for them, laying them under obligations, and all the time, unknown to Elizabeth, with this drunken old scamp of a father in the background, who had already half-threatened to molest her, and would be quite capable, if thwarted, of blackmailing his son through his English friends!

"What can I do?" he said to himself, in disgust. "I have no right whatever to betray this man's private affairs; at the same time I should never forgive myself—Mrs. Gaddesden would never forgive me—if I were to allow Lady Merton to run any risk of some sordid scandal which might get into the papers. Of course this young man ought to take himself off! If he had any proper feeling whatever he would see how altogether unfitting it is that he, with his antecedents, should be associating in this very friendly way with such persons as Elizabeth Merton and her brother!"

Unfortunately the "association" had included the rescue of Philip from the water of Lake Louise, and the provision of help to Elizabeth, in a strange country, which she could have ill done without. Philip's unlucky tumble had been, certainly, doubly unlucky, if it was to be the means of entangling his sister further in an intimacy which ought never to have been begun.

And yet how to break through this spider's web? Delaine racked his brain, and could think of nothing better than delay and a pusillanimous waiting on Providence. Who knew what mad view Elizabeth might take of the whole thing, in this overstrained sentimental mood which had possessed her throughout this Canadian journey? The young man's troubles might positively recommend him in her eyes!

No! there was nothing for it but to stay on as an old friend and watchdog, responsible, at least—if Elizabeth would have none of his counsels—to her mother and kinsfolk at home, who had so clearly approved his advances in the winter, and would certainly blame Elizabeth, on her return, for the fact that his long journey had been fruitless. He magnanimously resolved that Lady Merton should not be blamed if he could help it, by anyone except himself. And he had no intention at all of playing the rejected lover. The proud, well-born, fastidious Englishman stiffened as he walked. It was wounding to his self-love to stay where he was; since it was quite plain that Elizabeth could do without him, and would not regret his departure; but it was no less wounding to be dismissed, as it were, by Anderson. He would not be dismissed; he would hold his own. He too would go with them to Vancouver; and not till they were safely in charge of the Lieutenant-Governor at Victoria, would he desert his post.

As to any further communication to Elizabeth, he realised that the hints into which he had been so far betrayed had profited neither himself nor her. She had resented them, and it was most unlikely that she would ask him for any further explanations; and that being so he had better henceforward hold his peace. Unless of course any further annoyance were threatened.

The hotel cart going down to Laggan for supplies at midday brought Anderson his answer:

> "DEAR MR. ANDERSON—Your letter gave me great concern. I deeply sympathise with your situation. As far as I am concerned, I must necessarily look at the matter entirely from the point of view of my fellow-travellers. Lady Merton must not be distressed or molested. So long, however, as this is secured, I shall not feel myself at liberty to reveal a private matter which has accidentally come to my knowledge. I understand, of course, that your father will not attempt any further communication with me, and I propose to treat the interview as though it had not happened.
>
> "I will give Lady Merton your message. It seems to me doubtful whether she will be ready for excursions next week. But you are no doubt aware that the hotel makes what are apparently very excellent and complete arrangements for such things. I am sure Lady Merton would be sorry to give you avoidable trouble. However, we shall see you to-morrow, and shall of course be very glad of your counsels.
>
> "Yours faithfully,
>
> "ARTHUR MANDEVILLE DELAINE."

Anderson's fair skin flushed scarlet as he read this letter. He thrust it into his pocket and continued to pace up and down in the patch of half-cleared ground at the back of the Ginnells' house. He perfectly understood that Delaine's letter was meant to warn him not to be too officious in Lady Merton's service. "Don't suppose yourself indispensable—and don't at any time forget your undesirable antecedents, and compromising situation. On those conditions, I hold my tongue."

"Pompous ass!" Anderson found it a hard task to keep his own pride in check. It was of a different variety from Delaine's, but not a whit less clamorous. Yet for Lady Merton's sake it was desirable, perhaps imperative, that he should keep on civil terms with this member of her party. A hot impulse swept through him to tell her everything, to have done with secrecy. But he stifled it. What right had he to intrude his personal history upon her?—least of all this ugly and unsavoury development of it? Pride spoke again, and self-respect. If it humiliated him to feel himself in Delaine's power, he must bear it. The only other alternatives were either to cut himself off at once from his English friends—that, of course, was what Delaine wished—or to appeal to Lady Merton's sympathy and pity. Well, he would do neither—and Delaine might go hang!

Mrs. Ginnell, with her apron over her head to shield her from a blazing sun, appeared at the corner of the house.

"You're wanted, sir!" Her tone was sulky.

"Anything wrong?" Anderson turned apprehensively.

"Nothing more than 'is temper, sir. He won't let yer rest, do what you will for 'im."

Anderson went into the house. His father was sitting up in bed. Mrs. Ginnell had been endeavouring during the past hour to make her patient clean and comfortable, and to tidy his room; but had been at last obliged to desist, owing to the mixture of ill-humour and bad language with which he assailed her.

"Can I do anything for you?" Anderson inquired, standing beside him.

"Get me out of this blasted hole as soon as possible! That's about all you can do! I've told that woman to get me my things, and help me into the other room—but she's in your pay, I suppose. She won't do anything I tell her, drat her!"

"The doctor left orders you were to keep quiet to-day."

McEwen vowed he would do nothing of the kind. He had no time to be lolling in bed like a fine lady. He had business to do, and must get home.

"If you get up, with this fever on you, and the leg in that state, you will have blood-poisoning," said Anderson quietly, "which will either kill you or detain you here for weeks. You say you want to talk business with me. Well, here I am. In an hour's time I must go to Calgary for an appointment. Suppose you take this opportunity."

McEwen stared at his son. His blue eyes, frowning in their wrinkled sockets, gave little or no index, however, to the mind behind them. The straggling white locks falling round his blotched and feverish face caught Anderson's attention. Looking back thirty years he could remember his father vividly—a handsome man, solidly built, with a shock of fair hair. As a little lad he had been proud to sit high-perched beside him on the wagon which in summer drove them, every other Sunday, to a meeting-house fifteen miles away. He could see his mother at the back of the wagon with the little girls, her grey alpaca dress and cotton gloves, her patient look. His throat swelled. Nor was the pang of intolerable pity for his mother only. Deep in the melancholy of his nature and strengthened by that hateful tie of blood from which he could not escape, was a bitter, silent compassion for this outcast also. All the machinery of life set in motion and maintaining itself in the clash of circumstance for seventy years to produce *this*, at the end! Dismal questionings ran through his mind. Ought he to have acted as he had done seventeen years before? How would his mother have judged him? Was he not in some small degree responsible?

Meanwhile his father began to talk fast and querulously, with plentiful oaths from time to time, and using a local miner's slang which was not always intelligible to Anderson. It seemed it was a question of an old silver mine on a mountainside in Idaho, deserted some ten years before when the river gravels had been exhausted, and now to be reopened, like many others in the same neighbourhood, with improved methods and machinery, tunnelling instead of washing. Silver enough to pave Montreal! Ten thousand dollars for plant, five thousand for the claim, and the thing was done.

He became incoherently eloquent, spoke of the ease and rapidity with which the thing could be resold to a syndicate at an enormous profit, should his "pardners" and he not care to develop it themselves. If George would find the money—why, George should make his fortune, like the rest, though he had behaved so scurvily all these years.

Anderson watched the speaker intently. Presently he began to put questions—close, technical questions. His father's eyes—till then eager and greedy—began to flicker. Anderson perceived an unwelcome surprise—annoyance—

"You knew, of course, that I was a mining engineer?" he said at last, pulling up in his examination.

"Well, I heard of you that onst at Dawson City," was the slow reply. "I supposed you were nosin' round like the rest."

"Why, I didn't go as a mere prospector! I'd had my training at Montreal." And Anderson resumed his questions.

But McEwen presently took no pains to answer them. He grew indeed less and less communicative. The exact locality of the mine, the names of the partners, the precise machinery required—Anderson, in the end, could get at neither the one nor the other. And before many more minutes had passed he had convinced himself that he was wasting his time. That there was some swindling plot in his father's mind he was certain; he was probably the tool of some shrewder confederates, who had no doubt sent him to Montreal after his legacy, and would fleece him on his return.

"By the way, Aunt Sykes's money, how much was it?" Anderson asked him suddenly. "I suppose you could draw on that?"

McEwen could not be got to give a plain answer. It wasn't near enough, anyhow; not near. The evasion seemed to Anderson purposeless; the mere shifting and doubling that comes of long years of dishonest living. And again the question stabbed his consciousness—were his children justified in casting him so inexorably adrift?

"Well, I'd better run down and have a look," he said at last. "If it's a good thing I dare say I can find you the dollars."

"Run down—where?" asked McEwen sharply.

"To the mine, of course. I might spare the time next week."

"No need to trouble yourself. My pardners wouldn't thank me for betraying their secrets."

"Well, you couldn't expect me to provide the money without knowing a bit more about the property, could you?—without a regular survey?" said Anderson, with a laugh.

"You trust me with three or four thousand dollars," said McEwen doggedly—"because I'm your father and I give you my word. And if not, you can let it alone. I don't want any prying into my affairs."

Anderson was silent a moment.

Then he raised his eyes.

"Are you sure it's all square?" The tone had sharpened.

"Square? Of course it is. What are you aiming at? You'll believe any villainy of your old father, I suppose, just the same as you always used to. I've not had your opportunities, George. I'm not a fine gentleman—on the trail with a parcel of English swells. I'm a poor old broken-down miner, who wants to hole-up somewhere, and get comfortable for his old age; and if you had a heart in your body, you'd lend a helping hand. When I saw you at Winnipeg"—the tone became a trifle plaintive and slippery—"I ses to myself, George used to be a nice chap, with a good heart. If there's anyone ought to help me it's my own son. And so I boarded that train. But I'm a broken man, George, and you've used me hard."

"Better not talk like that," interrupted Anderson in a clear, resolute voice. "It won't do any good. Look here, father! Suppose you give up this kind of life, and settle down. I'm ready to give you an allowance, and look after you. Your health is bad. To speak the truth, this mine business sounds to me pretty shady. Cut it all! I'll put you with decent people, who'll look after you."

The eyes of the two men met; Anderson's insistently bright, McEwen's wavering and frowning. The June sunshine came into the small room through a striped and battered blind, illuminating the rough planks of which it was built, the "cuts" from illustrated papers that were pinned upon them, the scanty furniture, and the untidy bed. Anderson's head and shoulders were in a full mellowed light; he held himself with an unconscious energy, answering to a certain force of feeling within; a proud strength and sincerity expressed itself through every detail of attitude and gesture; yet perhaps the delicacy, or rather sensibility, mingling with the pride, would have been no less evident to a seeing eye. There was Highland blood in him, and a touch therefore of the Celtic responsiveness, the Celtic magnetism. The old man opposite to him in shadow, with his back to the light, had a crouching dangerous look. It was as though he recognised something in his son for ever lost to himself; and repulsed it, half enviously, half malignantly.

But he did not apparently resent Anderson's proposal. He said sulkily: "Oh, I dessay you'd like to put me away. But I'm not doddering yet."

All the same he listened in silence to the plan that Anderson developed, puffing the while at the pipe which he had made Mrs. Ginnell give him.

"I shan't stay on this side," he said, at last, decidedly. "There's a thing or two that might turn up agin me—and fellows as 'ud do me a bad turn if they come across me—dudes, as I used to know in Dawson City. I shan't stay in Canada. You can make up your mind to that. Besides, the winter'ud kill me!"

Anderson accordingly proposed San Francisco, or Los Angeles. Would his father go for a time to a Salvation Army colony near Los

Angeles? Anderson knew the chief officials—capital men, with no cant about them. Fruit farming—a beautiful climate—care in sickness—no drink—as much work or as little as he liked—and all expenses paid.

McEwen laughed out—a short sharp laugh—at the mention of the Salvation Army. But he listened patiently, and at the end even professed to think there might be something in it. As to his own scheme, he dropped all mention of it. Yet Anderson was under no illusion; there it lay sparkling, as it were, at the back of his sly wolfish eyes.

"How in blazes could you take me down?" muttered McEwen— "Thought you was took up with these English swells."

"I'm not taken up with anything that would prevent my looking after you," said Anderson rising. "You let Mrs. Ginnell attend to you—get the leg well—and we'll see."

McEwen eyed him—his good looks and his dress, his gentleman's refinement; and the shaggy white brows of the old miner drew closer together.

"What did you cast me off like that for, George?" he asked.

Anderson turned away.

"Don't rake up the past. Better not."

"Where are my other sons, George?"

"In Montreal, doing well." Anderson gave the details of their appointments and salaries.

"And never a thought of their old father, I'll be bound!" said McEwen, at the end, with slow vindictiveness.

"You forget that it was your own doing; we believed you dead."

"Aye!—you hadn't left a man much to come home for!—and all for an accident!—a thing as might ha' happened to any man."

The speaker's voice had grown louder. He stared sombrely, defiantly at his companion.

Anderson stood with his hands on his sides, looking through the further window. Then slowly he put his hand into his pocket and withdrew from it a large pocket-book. Out of the pocket-book he took a delicately made leather case, holding it in his hand a moment, and glancing uncertainly at the figure in the bed.

"What ha' you got there?" growled McEwen.

Anderson crossed the room. His own face had lost its colour. As he reached his father, he touched a spring, and held out his hand with the case lying open within it.

It contained a miniature—of a young woman in the midst of a group of children.

"Do you remember that photograph that was done of them—in a tent—when you took us all into Winnipeg for the first agricultural show?" he said hoarsely. "I had a copy—that wasn't burnt. At Montreal, there was a French artist one year, that did these things. I got him to do this."

McEwen stared at the miniature—the sweet-faced Scotch woman, the bunch of children. Then with a brusque movement he turned his face to the wall, and closed his eyes.

Anderson's lips opened once or twice as though to speak. Some imperious emotion seemed to be trying to force its way. But he could not find words; and at last he returned the miniature to his pocket, walked quietly to the door, and went out of the room.

The sound of the closing door brought immense relief to McEwen. He turned again in bed, and relit his pipe, shaking off the impression left by the miniature as quickly as possible. What business had George to upset him like that? He was down enough on his luck as it was.

He smoked away, gloomily thinking over the conversation. It didn't look like getting any money out of this close-fisted Puritanical son of his. Survey indeed! McEwen found himself shaken by a kind of internal convulsion as he thought of the revelations that would come out. George was a fool.

In his feverish reverie, many lines of thought crossed and danced in his brain; and every now and then he was tormented by the craving for alcohol. The Salvation Army proposal half amused, half infuriated him. He knew all about their colonies. Trust him! Your own master for seventeen years—mixed up in a lot of jobs it wouldn't do to go blabbing to the Mounted Police—and then to finish up with those hymn-singing fellows!—George was most certainly a fool! Yet dollars ought to be screwed out of him—somehow.

Presently, to get rid of some unpleasant reflections, the old man stretched out his hand for a copy of the *Vancouver Sentinel* that was lying on the bed, and began to read it idly. As he did so, a paragraph drew his attention. He gripped the paper, and, springing up in bed, read it twice, peering into it, his features quivering with eagerness. The passage described the "hold up" of a Northern Pacific train, at a point between Seattle and the Canadian border. By the help of masks, and a few sticks of dynamite, the thing had been very smartly done—a whole train terrorised, the mail van broken open and a large "swag" captured. Billy Symonds, the notorious train robber from Montana, was suspected, and there was a hue and cry through the whole border after him and his accomplices, amongst whom, so it was said, was a band from the Canadian side—foreign miners mixed up in some of the acts of violence which had marked the strike of the year before.

Bill Symonds!—McEwen threw himself excitedly from side to side, unable to keep still. *He* knew Symonds—a chap and a half! Why didn't he come and try it on this side of the line? Heaps of money going backwards and forwards over the railway! All these thousands of dollars paid out in wages week by week to these construction camps—must come from somewhere in cash—Winnipeg or Montreal. He began to play with the notion, elaborating and refining it; till presently a whole epic of attack and capture was rushing through his half-crazy brain.

He had dropped the paper, and was staring abstractedly through the foot of open window close beside him, which the torn blind did not cover. Outside, through the clearing with its stumps of jack-pine, ran a path, a short cut, connecting the station at Laggan with a section-house further up the line.

As McEwen's eyes followed it, he began to be aware of a group of men emerging from the trees on the Laggan side, and walking in single file along the path. Navvies apparently—carrying bundles and picks. The path came within a few yards of the window, and of the little stream that supplied the house with water.

Suddenly, McEwen sprang up in bed. The two foremost men paused beside the water, mopped their hot faces, and taking drinking cups out of their pockets stooped down to the stream. The old man in the cabin bed watched them with fierce intentness; and as they straightened themselves and were about to follow their companions who were already out of sight, he gave a low call.

The two started and looked round them. Their hands went to their pockets. McEwen swung himself round so as to reach the window better, and repeated his call—this time with a different inflection. The men exchanged a few hurried words. Carefully scrutinising the house, they noticed a newspaper waving cautiously in an open window. One of them came forward, the other remained by the stream bathing his feet and ankles in the water.

No one else was in sight. Mrs. Ginnell was cooking on the other side of the house. Anderson had gone off to catch his train. For twenty minutes, the man outside leant against the window-sash apparently lounging and smoking. Nothing could be seen from the path, but a battered blind flapping in the June breeze, and a dark space of room beyond.

CHAPTER X

The days passed on. Philip in the comfortable hotel at Lake Louise was recovering steadily, though not rapidly, from the general shock of immersion. Elizabeth, while nursing him tenderly, could yet find time to walk and climb, plunging spirit and sense in the beauty of the Rockies.

On these excursions Delaine generally accompanied her; and she bore it well. Secretly she cherished some astonishment and chagrin that Anderson could be with them so little on these bright afternoons among the forest trails and upper lakes, although she generally found that the plans of the day had been suggested and organised by him, by telephone from Laggan, to the kind and competent Scotch lady who was the manager of the hotel. It seemed to her that he had promised his company; whereas, as a rule, now he withheld it; and her pride was put to it, on her own part, not to betray any sign of discontent. He spoke vaguely of "business," and on one occasion, apparently had gone off for three days to Saskatchewan on matters connected with the coming general election.

From the newspaper, or the talk of visitors in the hotel, or the railway officials who occasionally found their way to Lake Louise to make courteous inquiries after the English party, Elizabeth became, indeed, more and more fully aware of the estimation in which Anderson was beginning to be held. He was already a personage in the Northwest; was said to be sure of success in his contest at Donaldminster, and of an immediate Parliamentary career at Ottawa. These prophecies seemed to depend more upon the man's character than his actual achievements; though, indeed, the story of the great strike, as she had gathered it once or twice from the lips of eye-witnesses, was a fine one. For weeks he had carried his life in his hand among thousands of infuriated navvies and miners—since the miners had made common cause with the railwaymen—with a cheerfulness, daring, and resource which in the end had wrung success from an apparently hopeless situation; a success attended, when all was over, by an amazing effusion of good will among both masters and men, especially towards Anderson himself, and a general improvement in the industrial temper and atmosphere of the Northwest.

The recital of these things stirred Elizabeth's pulses. But why did she never hear them from himself? Surely he had offered her friendship, and the rights of friendship. How else could he justify the scene at Field, when he had so brusquely probed her secret anxieties for Philip? Her pride rebelled when she thought of it, when she recalled her wet eyes, her outstretched hand. Mere humiliation!—in the case of a casual or indifferent acquaintance. No; on that day, certainly, he had claimed the utmost privileges, had even strained the rights, of a friend, a real friend. But his behaviour since had almost revived her first natural resentment.

Thoughts like these ran in her mind, and occasionally affected her manner when they did meet. Anderson found her more reserved, and noticed that she did not so often ask him for small services as of old. He suffered under the change; but it was, he knew, his own doing, and he did not alter his course.

Whenever he did come, he sat mostly with Philip, over whom he had gradually established a remarkable influence, not by any definite acts or speeches, but rather by the stoicism of his own mode of life, coupled with a proud or laughing contempt for certain vices and self-indulgences to which it was evident that he himself felt no temptation. As soon as Philip felt himself sufficiently at home with the Canadian to begin to jibe at his teetotalism, Anderson seldom took the trouble to defend himself; yet the passion of moral independence in his nature, of loathing for any habit that weakens and enslaves the will, infected the English lad whether he would or no. "There's lots of things he's stick-stock mad on," Philip would say impatiently to his sister. But the madness told. And the madman was all the while consolingly rich in other, and, to Philip, more attractive kinds of madness—the follies of the hunter and climber, of the man who holds his neck as dross in comparison with the satisfaction of certain wild instincts that the Rockies excite in him. Anderson had enjoyed his full share of adventures with goat and bear. Such things are the customary amusements, it seemed, of a young engineer in the Rockies. Beside them, English covert-shooting is a sport for babes;

Lady Merton: Colonist

and Philip ceased to boast of his own prowess in that direction. He would listen, indeed, open-mouthed, to Anderson's yarns, lying on his long chair on the verandah—a graceful languid figure—with a coyote rug heaped about him. It was clear to Elizabeth that Anderson on his side had become very fond of the boy. There was no trouble he would not take for him. And gradually, silently, proudly, she allowed him to take less and less for herself.

Once or twice Arthur Delaine's clumsy hints occurred to her. Was there, indeed, some private matter weighing on the young man's mind? She would not allow herself to speculate upon it; though she could not help watching the relation between the two men with some curiosity. It was polite enough; but there was certainly no cordiality in it; and once or twice she suspected a hidden understanding.

Delaine meanwhile felt a kind of dull satisfaction in the turn of events. The intimacy between Anderson and Lady Merton had clearly been checked, or was at least not advancing. Whether it was due to his own hints to Elizabeth, or to Anderson's chivalrous feeling, he did not know. But he wrote every mail to Mrs. Gaddesden, discreetly, yet not without giving her some significant information; he did whatever small services were possible in the case of a man who went about Canada as a Johnny Head-in-air, with his mind in another hemisphere; and it was understood that he was to leave them at Vancouver. In the forced association of their walks and rides, Elizabeth showed herself gay, kind, companionable; although often, and generally for no reason that he could discover, something sharp and icy in her would momentarily make itself felt, and he would find himself driven back within bounds that he had perhaps been tempted to transgress. And the result of it all was that he fell day by day more tormentingly in love with her. Those placid matrimonial ambitions with which he had left England had been all swept away; and as he followed her—she on pony-back, he on foot—along the mountain trails, watching the lightness of her small figure against the splendid background of peak and pine, he became a troubled, introspective person; concentrating upon himself and his disagreeable plight the attention he had hitherto given to a delightful outer world, sown with the *caches* of antiquity, in order to amuse him.

Meanwhile the situation in the cabin at Laggan appeared to be steadily improving. McEwen had abruptly ceased to be a rebellious and difficult patient. The doctor's orders had been obeyed; the leg had healed rapidly; and he no longer threatened or cajoled Mrs. Ginnell on the subject of liquor. As far as Anderson was concerned, he was generally sulky and uncommunicative. But Anderson got enough out of him by degrees to be able to form a fairly complete idea of his father's course of life since the false report of his death in the Yukon. He realised an existence on the fringe of civilisation, with its strokes of luck neutralised by drink, and its desperate, and probably criminal, moments. And as soon as his father got well enough to limp along the trails of the Laggan valley, the son noticed incidents which appeared to show that the old man, while playing the part of the helpless stranger, was by no means without acquaintance among the motley host of workmen that were constantly passing through. The links of international trades unionism no doubt accounted for it. But in McEwen's case, the fraternity to which he belonged seemed to apply only to the looser and more disreputable elements among the emigrant throng.

But at the same time he had shown surprising docility in the matter of Anderson's counsels. All talk of the Idaho mine had dropped between them, as though by common consent. Anderson had laid hands upon a young man, a Salvation Army officer in Vancouver, with whom his father consented to lodge for the next six weeks; and further arrangements were to be postponed till the end of that period. Anderson hoped, indeed, to get his father settled there before Lady Merton moved from Lake Louise. For in a few days now, the private car was to return from the coast, in order to take up the English party.

McEwen's unexpected complaisance led to a great softening in Anderson's feeling towards his father. All those inner compunctions that haunt a just and scrupulous nature came freely into play. And his evangelical religion—for he was a devout though liberal-minded Presbyterian—also entered in. Was it possible that he might be the agent of his father's redemption? The idea, the hope, produced in him occasional hidden exaltations—flights of prayer—mystical memories of his mother—which lightened what was otherwise a time of bitter renunciation, and determined wrestling with himself.

During the latter days of this fortnight, indeed, he could not do enough for his father. He had made all the Vancouver arrangements; he had supplied him amply with clothes and other personal necessaries; and he came home early at night in order to sit and smoke with him. Mrs. Ginnell, looking in of an evening, beheld what seemed to her a touching sight, though one far beyond the deserts of such creatures as McEwen—the son reading the newspaper aloud, or playing dominoes with his father, or just smoking and chatting. Her hard common sense as a working-woman suggested to her that Anderson was nursing illusions; and she scornfully though silently hoped that the "old rip" would soon, one way or another, be off his shoulders.

But the illusions, for the moment, were Anderson's sustenance. His imagination, denied a more personal and passionate food, gave itself with fire to the redeeming of an outlaw, and the paying of a spiritual debt.

It was Wednesday. After a couple of drizzling days the weather was again fair. The trains rolling through the pass began with these early days of July to bring a first crop of holiday-makers from Eastern Canada and the States; the hotels were filling up. On the morrow McEwen was to start for Vancouver. And a letter from Philip Gaddesden, delivered at Laggan in the morning, had bitterly reproached Anderson for neglecting them, and leaving him, in particular, to be bored to death by glaciers and tourists.

Early in the afternoon Anderson took his way up the mountain road to Lake Louise. He found the English travellers established among the pines by the lake-side, Philip half asleep in a hammock strung between two pines, while Delaine was reading to Elizabeth from an article in an archæological review on "Some Fresh Light on the Cippus of Palestrina."

Lady Merton: Colonist

Lady Merton was embroidering; it seemed to Anderson that she was tired or depressed. Delaine's booming voice, and the frequent Latin passages interspersed with stammering translations of his own, in which he appeared to be interminably tangled, would be enough—the Canadian thought—to account for a subdued demeanour; and there was, moreover, a sudden thunderous heat in the afternoon.

Elizabeth received him a little stiffly, and Philip roused himself from sleep only to complain: "You've been four mortal days without coming near us!"

"I had to go away. I have been to Regina."

"On politics?" asked Delaine.

"Yes. We had a couple of meetings and a row."

"Jolly for you!" grumbled Philip. "But we've had a beastly time. Ask Elizabeth."

"Nothing but the weather!" said Elizabeth carelessly. "We couldn't even see the mountains."

But why, as she spoke, should the delicate cheek change colour, suddenly and brightly? The answering blood leapt in Anderson. She *had* missed him, though she would not show it.

Delaine began to question him about Saskatchewan. The Englishman's forms of conversation were apt to be tediously inquisitive, and Anderson had often resented them. To-day, however, he let himself be catechised patiently enough, while all the time conscious, from head to foot, of one person only—one near and yet distant person.

Elizabeth wore a dress of white linen, and a broad hat of soft blue. The combination of the white and blue with her brown hair, and the pale refinement of her face, seemed to him ravishing, enchanting. So were the movements of her hands at work, and all the devices of her light self-command; more attractive, infinitely, to his mature sense than the involuntary tremor of girlhood.

"Hallo! What does Stewart want?" said Philip, raising himself in his hammock. The hunter who had been the companion of his first unlucky attempt at fishing was coming towards them. The boy sprang to the ground, and, vowing that he would fish the following morning whatever Elizabeth might say, went off to consult.

She looked after him with a smile and a sigh.

"Better give him his head!" laughed Anderson. Then, from where he stood, he studied her a moment, unseen, except by Delaine, who was sitting among the moss a few yards away, and had temporarily forgotten the Cippus of Palestrina.

Suddenly the Canadian came forward.

"Have you explored that path yet, over the shoulder?" he said to Lady Merton, pointing to the fine promontory of purple piny rock which jutted out in front of the glacier on the southern side of the lake.

She shook her head; but was it not still too early and too hot to walk? Anderson persisted. The path was in shade, and would repay climbing. She hesitated—and yielded; making a show of asking Delaine to come with them. Delaine also hesitated, and refrained; making a show of preferring the "Archaeological Review." He was left to watch them mount the first stretches of the trail; while Philip strolled along the lake with his companion in the slouch hat and leggings, deep in tales of bass and trout.

Elizabeth and Anderson climbed a long sloping ascent through the pines. The air was warm and scented; the heat of the sun on the moistened earth was releasing all its virtues and fragrances, overpowering in the open places, and stealing even through the shadows. When the trees broke or receded, the full splendour of the glacier was upon them to their left; and then for a space they must divine it as a presence behind the actual, faintly gleaming and flashing through the serried ranks of the forest. There were heaths and mosses under the pines; but otherwise for a while the path was flowerless; and Elizabeth discontentedly remarked it. Anderson smiled.

"Wait a little—or you'll have to apologise to the Rockies."

He looked down upon her, and saw that her small face had bloomed into a vivacity and charm that startled him. Was it only the physical effort and pleasure of the climb? As for himself, it took all the power of a strong will to check the happy tumult in his heart.

Elizabeth asked him of his Saskatchewan journey. He described to her the growing town he hoped to represent—the rush of its new life.

"On one Sunday morning there was nothing—the bare prairie; by the next—so to speak—there was a town all complete, with a hotel, an elevator, a bank, and a church. That was ten years ago. Then the railway came; I saw the first train come in, garlanded and wreathed with flowers. Now there are eight thousand people. They have reserved land for a park along the river, and sent for a landscape gardener from England to lay it out; they have made trees grow on the prairie; they have built a high school and a concert hall; the municipality is full of ambitions; and all round the town, settlers are pouring in. On market day you find yourself in a crowd of men, talking cattle and crops, the last thing in binders and threshers, as farmers do all over the world. But yet you couldn't match that crowd in the old world."

"Which you don't know," put in Elizabeth, with her sly smile.

"Which I don't know," repeated Anderson meekly. "But I guess. And I am thinking of sayings of yours. Where in Europe can you match the sense of *boundlessness* we have here—boundless space, boundless opportunity? It often makes fools of us: it intoxicates, turns our heads. There is a germ of madness in this Northwest. I have seen men destroyed by it. But it is Nature who is the witch. She brews the cup."

"All very well for the men," Elizabeth said, musing—"and the strong men. About the women in this country I can't make up my mind."

"You think of the drudgery, the domestic hardships?"

"There are some ladies in the hotel, from British Columbia. They are in easy circumstances—and the daughter is dying of overwork! The husband has a large fruit farm, but they can get no service; the fruit rots on the ground; and the two women are worn to death."

"Aye," said Anderson gravely. "This country breeds life, but it also devours it."

"I asked these two women—Englishwomen—if they wanted to go home, and give it up. They fell upon me with scorn."

"And you?"

Elizabeth sighed.

"I admired them. But could I imitate them? I thought of the house at home; of the old servants; how it runs on wheels; how pretty and—and dignified it all is; everybody at their post; no drudgery, no disorder."

"It is a dignity that costs you dear," said Anderson almost roughly, and with a change of countenance. "You sacrifice to it things a thousand times more real, more human."

"Do we?" said Elizabeth; and then, with a drop in her voice: "Dear, dear England!" She paused to take breath, and as she leant resting against a tree he saw her expression change, as though a struggle passed through her.

The trees had opened behind them, and they looked back over the lake, the hotel, and the wide Laggan valley beyond. In all that valley, not a sign of human life, but the line of the railway. Not a house, not a village to be seen; and at this distance the forest appeared continuous, till it died against the rock and snow of the higher peaks.

For the first time, Elizabeth was home-sick; for the first time she shrank from a raw, untamed land where the House of Life is only now rearing its walls and its roof-timbers, and all its warm furnishings, its ornaments and hangings are still to add. She thought of the English landscapes, of the woods and uplands round her Cumberland home; of the old church, the embowered cottages, the lichened farms; the generations of lives that have died into the soil, like the summer leaves of the trees; of the ghosts to be felt in the air—ghosts of squire and labourer and farmer, alive still in men and women of the present, as they too will live in the unborn. Her heart went out to England; fled back to it over the seas, as though renewing, in penitence, an allegiance that had wavered. And Anderson divined it, in the yearning of her just-parted lips, in the quivering, restrained sweetness of her look.

His own heart sank. They resumed their walk, and presently the path grew steeper. Some of it was rough-hewn in the rock, and encumbered by roots of trees. Anderson held out a helping hand; her fingers slipped willingly into it; her light weight hung upon him, and every step was to him a mingled delight and bitterness.

"Hard work!" he said presently, with his encouraging smile; "but you'll be paid."

The pines grew closer, and then suddenly lightened. A few more steps, and Elizabeth gave a cry of pleasure. They were on the edge of an alpine meadow, encircled by dense forest, and sloping down beneath their feet to a lake that lay half in black shadow, half blazing in the afternoon sun. Beyond was a tossed wilderness of peaks to west and south. Light masses of cumulus cloud were rushing over the sky, and driving waves of blue and purple colour across the mountain masses and the forest slopes. Golden was the sinking light and the sunlit half of the lake; golden the western faces and edges of the mountain world; while beyond the valley, where ran the white smoke of a train, there hung in the northern sky a dream-world of undiscovered snows, range, it seemed, beyond range, remote, ethereal; a Valhalla of the old gods of this vast land, where one might guess them still throned at bay, majestic, inviolate.

But it was the flowers that held Elizabeth mute. Anderson had brought her to a wild garden of incredible beauty. Scarlet and blue, purple and pearl and opal, rose-pink and lavender-grey the flower-field ran about her, as though Persephone herself had just risen from the shadow of this nameless northern lake, and the new earth had broken into eager flame at her feet. Painter's brush, harebell, speedwell, golden-brown gaillardias, silvery hawkweed, columbines yellow and blue, heaths, and lush grasses—Elizabeth sank down among them in speechless joy. Anderson gathered handfuls of columbine and vetch, of harebell and heath, and filled her lap with them, till she gently stopped him.

"No! Let me only look!"

And with her hands around her knees she sat motionless and still. Anderson threw himself down beside her. Fragrance, colour, warmth; the stir of an endless self-sufficient life; the fruitfulness and bounty of the earth; these things wove their ancient spells about them. Every little rush of the breeze seemed an invitation and a caress.

Presently she thanked him for having brought her there, and said something of remembering it in England.

"As one who will never see it again?" He turned and faced her smiling. But behind his frank, pleasant look there was something from which she shrank.

"I shall hardly see it, again," she said hesitating. "Perhaps that makes it the more—the more touching. One clings to it the more—the impression—because it is so fugitive—will be so soon gone."

He was silent a moment, then said abruptly:

"And the upshot of all this is, that you could not imagine living in Canada?"

She started.

"I never said so. Of course I could imagine living in Canada!"

"But you think, for women, the life up here—in the Northwest—is too hard."

She looked at him timidly.

"That's because I look at it from my English point of view. I am afraid English life makes weaklings of us."

"No—not of you!" he said, almost scornfully. "Any life that seemed to you worth while would find you strong enough for it. I am sure of that."

Elizabeth smiled and shrugged her shoulders. He went on—almost as though pleading with her.

"And as to our Western life—which you will soon have left so far behind—it strains and tests the women—true—but it rewards them. They have a great place among us. It is like the women of the early races. We listen to them in the house, and on the land; we depend on them indoors and out; their husbands and their sons worship them!"

Elizabeth flushed involuntarily; but she met him gaily.

"In England too! Come and see!"

"I shall probably be in England next spring."

Elizabeth made a sudden movement.

"I thought you would be in political life here!"

"I have had an offer—an exciting and flattering offer. May I tell you?"

He turned to her eagerly; and she smiled her sympathy, her curiosity. Whereupon he took a letter from his pocket—a letter from the Dominion Prime Minister, offering him a mission of inquiry to England, on some important matters connected with labour and emigration. The letter was remarkable, addressed to a man so young, and on the threshold of his political career.

Elizabeth congratulated him warmly.

"Of course you will come to stay with us!"

It was his turn to redden.

"You are very kind," he said formally. "As you know, I shall have everything to learn."

"I will show you *our* farms!" cried Elizabeth, "and all our dear decrepit life—our little chessboard of an England."

"How proud you are, you Englishwomen!" he said, half frowning. "You run yourselves down—and at bottom there is a pride like Lucifer's."

"But it is not my pride," she said, hurt, "any more than yours. We are yours—and you are ours. One state—one country."

"No, don't let us sentimentalise. We have our own future. It is not yours."

"But you are loyal!" The note was one of pain.

"Are we? Foolish word! Yes, we are loyal, as you are—loyal to a common ideal, a common mission in the world."

"To blood also—and to history?" Her voice was almost entreating. What he had said seemed to jar with other and earlier sayings of his, which had stirred in her a patriotic pleasure.

He smiled at her emotion—her implied reproach.

"Yes, we stand together. We march together. But Canada will have her own history; and you must not try to make it for her."

Their eyes met; in hers exaltion, in his a touch of sternness, a moment's revelation of the Covenanter in his soul.

Then as the delightful vision of her among the flowers, in her white dress, the mountains behind and around her, imprinted itself on his senses, he was conscious of a moment of intolerable pain. Between her and him—as it were—the abyss opened. The trembling waves of colour in the grass, the noble procession of the clouds, the gleaming of the snows, the shadow of the valleys—they were all wiped out. He saw instead a small unsavoury room—the cunning eyes and coarse mouth of his father. He saw his own future as it must now be; weighted with this burden, this secret; if indeed it were still to be a secret; if it were not rather the wiser and the manlier plan to have done with secrecy.

Elizabeth rose with a little shiver. The wind had begun to blow cold from the northwest.

"How soon can we run down? I hope Mr. Arthur will have sent Philip indoors."

Anderson left Lake Louise about eight o'clock, and hurried down the Laggan road. His mind was divided between the bitter-sweet of these last hours with Elizabeth Merton, and anxieties, small practical anxieties, about his father. There were arrangements still to make. He was not himself going to Vancouver. McEwen had lately shown a strong and petulant wish to preserve his incognito, or what was left of it. He would not have his son's escort. George might come and see him at Vancouver; and that would be time enough to settle up for the winter.

So Ginnell, owner of the boarding house, a stalwart Irishman of six foot three, had been appointed to see him through his journey, settle him with his new protectors, and pay all necessary expenses.

Anderson knocked at his father's door and was allowed to enter. He found McEwen walking up and down his room, with the aid of a stick, irritably pushing chairs and clothes out of his way. The room was in squalid disorder, and its inmate had a flushed, exasperated look that did not escape Anderson's notice. He thought it probable that his father was already repenting his consent to go to Vancouver, and he avoided general conversation as much as possible.

McEwen complained of having been left alone; abused Mrs. Ginnell; vowed she had starved and ill-treated him; and then, to Anderson's surprise, broke out against his son for having refused to provide him with the money he wanted for the mine, and so ruined his last chance. Anderson hardly replied; but what he did say was as soothing as possible; and at last the old man flung himself on his bed, excitement dying away in a sulky taciturnity.

Before Anderson left his room, Ginnell came in, bringing his accounts for certain small expenses. Anderson, standing with his back to his father, took out a pocketbook full of bills. At Calgary the day before a friend had repaid him a loan of a thousand dollars. He gave Ginnell a certain sum; talked to him in a low voice for a time, thinking his father had dropped asleep; and then dismissed him, putting the money in his pocket.

"Good night, father," he said, standing beside the bed.

McEwen opened his eyes.

"Eh?"

The eyes into which Anderson looked had no sleep in them. They were wild and bloodshot, and again Anderson felt a pang of helpless pity for a dishonoured and miserable old age.

"I'm sure you'll get on at Vancouver, father," he said gently. "And I shall be there next week."

His father growled some unintelligible answer. As Anderson went to the door he again called after him angrily: "You were a d—— fool, George, not to find those dibs."

"What, for the mine?" Anderson laughed. "Oh, we'll go into that again at Vancouver."

McEwen made no reply, and Anderson left him.

Anderson woke before seven. The long evening had passed into the dawn with scarcely any darkness, and the sun was now high. He sprang up, and dressed hastily. Going into the passage he saw to his astonishment that while the door of the Ginnells' room was still closed, his father's was wide open. He walked in. The room and the bed were empty. The contents of a box carefully packed by Ginnell—mostly with new clothes—the night before, were lying strewn about the room. But McEwen's old clothes were gone, his gun and revolver, also his pipes and tobacco.

Anderson roused Ginnell, and they searched the house and its neighbourhood in vain. On going back into his own room, Anderson noticed an open drawer. He had placed his pocketbook there the night before, but without locking the drawer. It was gone, and in its place was a dirty scrap of paper.

"Don't you try chivvying me, George, for you won't get any good of it. You let me alone, and I'll let you. You were a stingy fellow about that money, so I've took some of it. Good-bye."

Sick at heart, Anderson resumed the search, further afield. He sent Ginnell along the line to make confidential inquiries. He telegraphed to persons known to him at Golden, Revelstoke, Kamloops, Ashcroft, all to no purpose. Twenty-four—thirty-six hours passed and nothing had been heard of the fugitive.

He felt himself baffled and tricked, with certain deep instincts and yearnings wounded to the death. The brutal manner of his father's escape—the robbery—the letter—had struck him hard.

When Friday night came, and still no news, Anderson found himself at the C.P.R. Hotel at Field. He was stupid with fatigue and depression. But he had been in telephonic communication all the afternoon with Delaine and Lady Merton at Lake Louise, as to their departure for the Pacific. They knew nothing and should know nothing of his own catastrophe; their plans should not suffer.

He went out into the summer night to take breath, and commune with himself. The night was balmy; the stars glorious. On a siding near the hotel stood the private car which had arrived that evening from Vancouver, and was to go to Laggan the following morning to fetch the English party. They were to pick him up, on the return, at Field.

He had failed to save his father, and his honest effort had been made in vain. Humiliation and disappointment overshadowed him. Passionately, his whole soul turned to Elizabeth. He did not yet grasp all the bearings of what had happened. But he began to count the hours to the time when he should see her.

CHAPTER XI

A day of showers and breaking clouds—of sudden sunlight, and broad clefts of blue; a day when shreds of mist are lightly looped and meshed about the higher peaks of the Rockies and the Selkirks, dividing the forest world from the ice world above....

The car was slowly descending the Kicking Horse Pass, at the rear of a heavy train. Elizabeth, on her platform, was feasting her eyes once more on the great savage landscape, on these peaks and valleys that have never till now known man, save as the hunter, treading them once or twice perhaps in a century. Dreamily her mind contrasted them with the Alps, where from all time man has laboured and sheltered, blending his life, his births and deaths, his loves and hates with the glaciers and the forests, wresting his food from the valleys, creeping height over height to the snow line, writing his will on the country, so that in our thought of it he stands first, and Nature second. The Swiss mountains and streams breathe a "mighty voice," lent to them by the free passion and aspiration of man; they are interfused and interwoven forever with human fate. But in the Rockies and the Selkirks man counts for nothing in their past; and, except as wayfarer and playfellow, it is probable that he will count for nothing in their future. They will never be the familiar companions of his work and prayer and love; a couple of railways, indeed, will soon be driving through them, linking the life of the prairies to the life of the Pacific; but, except for this conquest of them as barriers in his path, when his summer camps in them are struck, they, sheeted in a winter inaccessible and superb, know him and his puny deeds no more, till again the lakes melt and the trees bud. This it is that gives them their strange majesty, and clothes their brief summer, their laughing fields of flowers, their thickets of red raspberry and slopes of strawberry, their infinity of gleaming lakes and foaming rivers—rivers that turn no mill and light no town—with a charm, half magical, half mocking.

And yet, though the travelled intelligence made comparisons of this kind, it was not with the mountains that Elizabeth's deepest mind was busy. She took really keener note of the railway itself, and its appurtenances. For here man had expressed himself; had pitched his battle with a fierce nature and won it; as no doubt he will win other similar battles in the coming years. Through Anderson this battle had become real to her. She looked eagerly at the construction camps in the pass; at the new line that is soon to supersede the old; at the bridges and tunnels and snow-sheds, by which contriving man had made his purpose prevail over the physical forces of this wild world. The great railway spoke to her in terms of human life; and because she had known Anderson she understood its message.

Secretly and sorely her thoughts clung to him. Just as, insensibly, her vision of Canada had changed, so had her vision of Anderson. Canada was no longer mere fairy tale and romance; Anderson was no longer merely its picturesque exponent or representative. She had come to realise him as a man, with a man's cares and passions; and her feelings about him had begun to change her life.

Arthur Delaine, she supposed, had meant to warn her that Mr. Anderson was falling in love with her and that she had no right to encourage it. Her thoughts went back intently over the last fortnight—Anderson's absences—his partial withdrawal from the intimacy which had grown up between himself and her—their last walk at Lake Louise. The delight of that walk was still in her veins, and at last she was frank with herself about it! In his attitude towards her, now that she forced herself to face the truth, she must needs recognise a passionate eagerness, restrained no less passionately; a profound impulse, strongly felt, and strongly held back. By mere despair of attainment?—or by the scruple of an honourable self-control?

Could she—*could* she marry a Canadian? There was the central question, out at last!—irrevocable!—writ large on the mountains and the forests, as she sped through them. Could she, possessed by inheritance of all that is most desirable and delightful in English society, linked with its great interests and its dominant class, and through them with the rich cosmopolitan life of cultivated Europe— could she tear herself from that old soil, and that dear familiar environment? Had the plant vitality enough to bear transplanting?

She did not put her question in these terms; but that was what her sudden tumult and distress of mind really meant.

Looking up, she saw Delaine beside her. Well, there was Europe, and at her feet! For the last month she had been occupied in scorning it. English country-house life, artistic society and pursuits, London in the season, Paris and Rome in the spring, English social and political influence—there they were beside her. She had only to stretch out her hand.

A chill, uncomfortable laughter seemed to fill the inner mind through which the debate passed, while all the time she was apparently looking at the landscape, and chatting with her brother or Delaine. She fell into an angry contempt for that mood of imaginative delight in which she had journeyed through Canada so far. What! treat a great nation in the birth as though it were there for her mere pleasure and entertainment? Make of it a mere spectacle and pageant, and turn with disgust from the notion that you, too, could ever throw in your lot with it, fight as a foot-soldier in its ranks, on equal terms, for life and death!

She despised herself. And yet—and yet! She thought of her mother— her frail, refined, artistic mother; of a hundred subtleties and charms and claims, in that world she understood, in which she had been reared; of all that she must leave behind, were she asked, and did she consent, to share the life of a Canadian of Anderson's type. What would it be to fail in such a venture! To dare it, and then to find life sinking in sands of cowardice and weakness! Very often, and sometimes as though by design, Anderson had spoken to her of the part to be played by women in Canada; not in the defensive, optimistic tone of their last walk together, but forbiddingly, with a kind of rough insistence. Substantial comfort, a large amount of applied science—that could be got. But the elegancies and refinements of English rich life in a prairie farm—impossible! A woman who marries a Canadian farmer, large or small, must put her own hands to the drudgery of life, to the cooking, sewing, baking, that keep man—animal man—alive. A certain amount of rude service money can command in the Northwest; but it is a service which only the housewife's personal coöperation can make tolerable.

Life returns, in fact, to the old primitive pattern; and a woman counts on the prairie according as "she looketh well to the ways of her household and eateth not the bread of idleness."

Suddenly Elizabeth perceived her own hands lying on her lap. Useless bejewelled things! When had they ever fed a man or nursed a child?

Under her gauze veil she coloured fiercely. If the housewife, in her primitive meaning and office, is vital to Canada, still more is the house-mother. "Bear me sons and daughters; people my wastes!" seems to be the cry of the land itself. Deep in Elizabeth's being there stirred instincts and yearnings which life had so far stifled in her. She shivered as though some voice, passionate and yet austere, spoke to her from this great spectacle of mountain and water through which she was passing.

"There he is!" cried Philip, craning his head to look ahead along the train.

Anderson stood waiting for them on the Field platform. Very soon he was seated beside her, outside the car, while Philip lounged in the doorway, and Delaine inside, having done his duty to the Kicking Horse Pass, was devoting himself to a belated number of the "Athenæum" which had just reached him.

Philip had stored up a string of questions as to the hunting of goat in the Rockies, and impatiently produced them. Anderson replied, but, as Elizabeth immediately perceived, with a complete lack of his usual animation. He spoke with effort, occasionally stumbling over his words. She could not help looking at him curiously, and presently even Philip noticed something wrong.

"I say, Anderson!—what have you been doing to yourself? You look as though you had been knocking up."

"I have been a bit driven this week," said Anderson, with a start. "Oh, nothing! You must look at this piece of line."

And as they ran down the long ravine from Field to Golden, beside a river which all the way seems to threaten the gliding train by the savage force of its descent, he played the showman. The epic of the C.P.R.—no one knew it better, and no one could recite it more vividly than he.

So also, as they left the Rockies behind; as they sped along the Columbia between the Rockies to their right and the Selkirks to their left; or as they turned away from the Columbia, and, on the flanks of the Selkirks, began to mount that forest valley which leads to Roger's Pass, he talked freely and well, exerting himself to the utmost. The hopes and despairs, the endurances and ambitions of the first explorers who ever broke into that fierce solitude, he could reproduce them; for, though himself of a younger generation, yet by sympathy he had lived them. And if he had not been one of the builders of the line, in the incessant guardianship which preserves it from day to day, he had at one time played a prominent part, battling with Nature for it, summer and winter.

Delaine, at last, came out to listen. Philip in the grip of his first hero-worship, lay silent and absorbed, watching the face and gestures of the speaker. Elizabeth sat with her eyes turned away from Anderson towards the wild valley, as they rose and rose above it. She listened; but her heart was full of new anxieties. What had happened to him? She felt him changed. He was talking for their pleasure, by a strong effort of will; that she realised. When could she get him alone?—her friend!—who was clearly in distress.

They approached the famous bridges on the long ascent. Yerkes came running through the car to point out with pride the place where the Grand Duchess had fainted beneath the terrors of the line. With only the railing of their little platform between them and the abyss, they ran over ravines hundreds of feet deep—the valley, a thousand feet sheer, below. And in that valley, not a sign of house, of path; only black impenetrable forest—huge cedars and Douglas pines, filling up the bottoms, choking the river with their débris, climbing up the further sides, towards the gleaming line of peaks.

"It is a nightmare!" said Delaine involuntarily, looking round him.

Elizabeth laughed, a bright colour in her cheeks. Again the wilderness ran through her blood, answering the challenge of Nature. Faint!—she was more inclined to sing or shout. And with the exhilaration, physical and mental, that stole upon her, there mingled secretly, the first thrill of passion she had ever known. Anderson sat beside her, once more silent after his burst of talk. She was vividly conscious of him—of his bare curly head—of certain lines of fatigue and suffering in the bronzed face. And it was conveyed to her that, although he was clearly preoccupied and sad, he was yet conscious of her in the same way. Once, as they were passing the highest bridge of all, where, carried on a great steel arch, that has replaced the older trestles, the rails run naked and gleaming, without the smallest shred of wall or parapet, across a gash in the mountain up which they were creeping, and at a terrific height above the valley, Elizabeth, who was sitting with her back to the engine, bent suddenly to one side, leaning over the little railing and looking ahead—that she might if possible get a clearer sight of Mount Macdonald, the giant at whose feet lies Roger's Pass. Suddenly, as her weight pressed against the ironwork where only that morning a fastening had been mended, she felt a grip on her arm. She drew back, startled.

"I beg your pardon!" said Anderson, smiling, but a trifle paler than before. "I'm not troubled with nerves for myself, but—"

He did not complete the sentence, and Elizabeth, could find nothing to say.

"Why, Elizabeth's not afraid!" cried Philip, scornfully.

"This is Roger's Pass, and here we are at the top of the Selkirks," said Anderson, rising. "The train will wait here some twenty minutes. Perhaps you would like to walk about."

They descended, all but Philip, who grumbled at the cold, wrapped himself in a rug inside the car, and summoned Yerkes to bring him a cup of coffee.

On this height indeed, and beneath the precipices of Mount Macdonald, which rise some five thousand feet perpendicularly above the railway, the air was chill and the clouds had gathered. On the right, ran a line of glacier-laden peaks, calling to their fellows across the pass. The ravine itself, darkly magnificent, made a gulf of shadow out of which rose glacier and snow slope, now veiled and now revealed by scudding cloud. Heavy rain had not long since fallen on the pass; the small stream, winding and looping through the narrow strip of desolate ground which marks the summit, roared in flood through marshy growths of dank weed and stunted shrub; and the noise reverberated from the mountain walls, pressing straight and close on either hand.

"Hark!" cried Elizabeth, standing still, her face and her light dress beaten by the wind.

A sound which was neither thunder nor the voice of the stream rose and swelled and filled the pass. Another followed it. Anderson pointed to the snowy crags of Mount Macdonald, and there, leaping from ledge to ledge, they saw the summer avalanches descend, roaring as they came, till they sank engulfed in a vaporous whirl of snow.

Delaine tried to persuade Elizabeth to return to the car—in vain. He himself returned thither for a warmer coat, and she and Anderson walked on alone.

"The Rockies were fine!—but the Selkirks are superb!"

She smiled at him as she spoke, as though she thanked him personally for the grandeur round them. Her slender form seemed to have grown in stature and in energy. The mountain rain was on her fresh cheek and her hair; a blue veil eddying round her head and face framed the brilliance of her eyes. Those who had known Elizabeth in Europe would hardly have recognised her here. The spirit of earth's wild and virgin places had mingled with her spirit, and as she had grown in sympathy, so also she had grown in beauty. Anderson looked at her from time to time in enchantment, grudging every minute that passed. The temptation strengthened to tell her his trouble. But how, or when?

As he turned to her he saw that she, too, was gazing at him with an anxious, wistful expression, her lips parted as though to speak.

He bent over her.

"What was that?" exclaimed Elizabeth, looking round her.

They had passed beyond the station where the train was at rest. But the sound of shouts pursued them. Anderson distinguished his own name. A couple of railway officials had left the station and were hurrying towards them.

A sudden thought struck Anderson. He held up his hand with a gesture as though to ask Lady Merton not to follow, and himself ran back to the station.

Elizabeth, from where she stood, saw the passengers all pouring out of the train on to the platform. Even Philip emerged and waved to her. She slowly returned, and meanwhile Anderson had disappeared.

She found an excited crowd of travellers and a babel of noise. Delaine hurried to her.

It appeared that an extraordinary thing had happened. The train immediately in front of them, carrying mail and express cars but no passengers, had been "held up" by a gang of train-robbers, at a spot between Sicamous junction and Kamloops. In order to break open the mail van the robbers had employed a charge of dynamite, which had wrecked the car and caused some damage to the line; enough to block the permanent way for some hours.

"And Philip has just opened this telegram for you."

Delaine handed it to her. It was from the District Superintendent, expressing great regret for the interruption to their journey, and suggesting that they should spend the night at the hotel at Glacier.

"Which I understand is only four miles off, the other side of the pass," said Delaine. "Was there ever anything more annoying!"

Elizabeth's face expressed an utter bewilderment.

"A train held up in Canada—and on the C.P.R.—impossible!"

An elderly man in front of her heard what she said, and turned upon her a face purple with wrath.

"You may well say that, madam! We are a law-abiding nation. We don't put up with the pranks they play in Montana. They say the scoundrels have got off. If we don't catch them, Canada's disgraced."

"I say, Elizabeth," cried Philip, pushing his way to her through the crowd, "there's been a lot of shooting. There's some Mounted Police here, we picked up at Revelstoke, on their way to help catch these fellows. I've been talking to them. The police from Kamloops came upon them just as they were making off with a pretty pile—boxes full of money for some of the banks in Vancouver. The police fired, so did the robbers. One of the police was killed, and one of the thieves. Then the rest got off. I say, let's go and help hunt them!"

The boy's eyes danced with the joy of adventure.

"If they've any sense they'll send bloodhounds after them," said the elderly man, fiercely. "I helped catch a murderer with my own hands that way, last summer, near the Arrow Lakes."

"Where is Mr. Anderson?"

The question escaped Elizabeth involuntarily. She had not meant to put it. But it was curious that he should have left them in the lurch at this particular moment.

"Take your seats!" cried the station-master, making his way through the crowded platform. "This train goes as far as Sicamous Junction only. Any passenger who wishes to break his journey will find accommodation at Glacier—next station."

The English travellers were hurried back into their car. Still no sign of Anderson. Yerkes was only able to tell them that he had seen Anderson go into the station-master's private room with a couple of the Mounted Police. He might have come out again, or he might not. Yerkes had been too well occupied in exciting gossip with all his many acquaintances in the train and the station to notice.

Lady Merton: Colonist

The conductor went along through the train. Yerkes, standing on the inside platform, called to him:

"Have you seen Mr. Anderson?"

The man shook his head, but another standing by, evidently an official of some kind, looked round and ran up to the car.

"I'm sorry, madam," he said, addressing Elizabeth, who was standing in the doorway, "but Mr. Anderson isn't at liberty just now. He'll be travelling with the police."

And as he spoke a door in the station building opened, and Anderson came out, accompanied by two constables of the Mounted Police and two or three officials. They walked hurriedly along the train and got into an empty compartment together. Immediately afterwards the train moved off.

"Well, I wonder what's up now!" said Philip in astonishment. "Do you suppose Anderson's got some clue to the men?"

Delaine looked uncomfortably at Elizabeth. As an old adviser and servant of the railway, extensively acquainted moreover with the population—settled or occasional—of the district it was very natural that Anderson should be consulted on such an event. And yet—Delaine had caught a glimpse of his aspect on his way along the platform, and had noticed that he never looked towards the car. Some odd conjectures ran through his mind.

Elizabeth sat silent, looking back on the grim defile the train was just leaving. It was evident that they had passed the water-shed, and the train was descending. In a few minutes they would be at Glacier.

She roused herself to hold a rapid consultation over plans.

They must of course do as they were advised, and spend the night at Glacier.

The train drew up.

"Well, of all the nuisances!"—cried Philip, disgusted, as they prepared to leave the car.

Yerkes, like the showman that he was, began to descant volubly on the advantages and charms of the hotel, its Swiss guides, and the distinguished travellers who stayed there; dragging rugs and bags meanwhile out of the car. Nobody listened to him. Everybody in the little party, as they stood forlornly on the platform, was in truth searching for Anderson.

And at last he came—hurrying along towards them. His face, set, strained, and colourless, bore the stamp of calamity. But he gave them no time to question him.

"I am going on," he said hastily to Elizabeth; "they will look after you here. I will arrange everything for you as soon as possible, and if we don't meet before, perhaps—in Vancouver—"

"I say, are you going to hunt the robbers?" asked Philip, catching his arm.

Anderson made no reply. He turned to Delaine, drew him aside a moment, and put a letter into his hand.

"My father was one of them," he said, without emotion, "and is dead. I have asked you to tell Lady Merton."

There was a call for him. The train was already moving. He jumped into it, and was gone.

CHAPTER XII

The station and hotel at Sicamous Junction, overlooking the lovely Mara lake, were full of people—busy officials of different kinds, or excited on-lookers—when Anderson reached them. The long summer day was just passing into a night that was rather twilight than darkness, and in the lower country the heat was great. Far away to the north stretched the wide and straggling waters of another and larger lake. Woods of poplar and cottonwood grew along its swampy shore, and hills, forest clad, held it in a shallow cup flooded with the mingled light of sunset and moonlight.

Anderson was met by a district superintendent, of the name of Dixon, as he descended from the train. The young man, with whom he was slightly acquainted, looked at him with excitement.

"This is a precious bad business! If you can throw any light upon it, Mr. Anderson, we shall be uncommonly obliged to you—"

Anderson interrupted him.

"Is the inquest to be held here?"

"Certainly. The bodies were brought in a few hours ago."

His companion pointed to a shed beyond the station. They walked thither, the Superintendent describing in detail the attack on the train and the measures taken for the capture of the marauders, Anderson listening in silence. The affair had taken place early that morning, but the telegraph wires had been cut in several places on both sides of the damaged line, so that no precise news of what had happened had reached either Vancouver on the west, or Golden on the east, till the afternoon. The whole countryside was now in movement, and a vigorous man-hunt was proceeding on both sides of the line.

"There is no doubt the whole thing was planned by a couple of men from Montana, one of whom was certainly concerned in the hold-up there a few months ago and got clean away. But there were six or seven of them altogether and most of the rest—we suspect—from this side of the boundary. The old man who was killed"—Anderson raised his eyes abruptly to the speaker—"seems to have come from Nevada. There were some cuttings from a Nevada newspaper found upon him, besides the envelope addressed to you, of which I sent you word at Roger's Pass. Could you recognise anything in my description of the man? There was one thing I forgot to say. He had evidently been in the doctor's hands lately. There is a surgical bandage on the right ankle."

"Was there nothing in the envelope?" asked Anderson, putting the question aside, in spite of the evident eagerness of the questioner.

"Nothing."

"And where is it?"

"It was given to the Kamloops coroner, who has just arrived." Anderson said nothing more. They had reached the shed, which his companion unlocked. Inside were two rough tables on trestles and lying on them two sheeted forms.

Dixon uncovered the first, and Anderson looked steadily down at the face underneath. Death had wrought its strange ironic miracle once more, and out of the face of an outcast had made the face of a sage. There was little disfigurement; the eyes were closed with dignity; the mouth seemed to have unlearnt its coarseness. Silently the tension of Anderson's inner being gave way; he was conscious of a passionate acceptance of the mere stillness and dumbness of death.

"Where was the wound?" he asked, stooping over the body.

"Ah, that was the strange thing! He didn't die of his wound at all! It was a mere graze on the arm." The Superintendent pointed to a rent on the coat-sleeve. "He died of something quite different—perhaps excitement and a weak heart. There may have to be a post-mortem."

"I doubt whether that will be necessary," said Anderson.

The other looked at him with undisguised curiosity.

"Then you do recognise him?"

"I will tell the coroner what I know."

Anderson drew back from his close examination of the dead face, and began in his turn to question the Superintendent. Was it certain that this man had been himself concerned in the hold-up and in the struggle with the police?

Dixon could not see how there could be any doubt of it. The constables who had rushed in upon the gang while they were still looting the express car—the brakesman having managed to get away and convey the alarm to Kamloops—remembered seeing an old man with white hair, apparently lame, at the rear of the more active thieves, and posted as sentinel. He had been the first to give warning of the police approach, and had levelled his revolver at the foremost constable but had missed his shot. In the free firing which had followed nobody exactly knew what had happened. One of the attacking force, Constable Brown, had fallen, and while his comrades were attempting to save him, the thieves had dropped down the steep bank of the river close by, into a boat waiting for them, and got off. The constable was left dead upon the ground, and not far from him lay the old man, also lifeless. But when they came to examine the bodies, while the constable was shot through the head, the other had received nothing but the trifling wound Dixon had already pointed out.

Anderson listened to the story in silence. Then with a last long look at the rigid features below him, he replaced the covering. Passing on to the other table, he raised the sheet from the face of a splendid young Englishman, whom he had last seen the week before at Regina; an English public-school boy of the manliest type, full of hope for himself, and of enthusiasm, both for Canada and for the fine body of men in which he had been just promoted. For the first time a stifled groan escaped from Anderson's lips. What hand had done this murder?

They left the shed. Anderson inquired what doctor had been sent for. He recognised the name given as that of a Kamloops man whom he knew and respected; and he went on to look for him at the hotel.

For some time he and the doctor paced a trail beside the line together. Among other facts that Anderson got from this conversation, he learnt that the American authorities had been telegraphed to, and that a couple of deputy sheriffs were coming to assist the Canadian police. They were expected the following morning, when also the coroner's inquest would be held.

As to Anderson's own share in the interview, when the two men parted, with a silent grasp of the hand, the Doctor had nothing to say to the bystanders, except that Mr. Anderson would have some evidence to give on the morrow, and that, for himself, he was not at liberty to divulge what had passed between them.

It was by this time late. Anderson shut himself up in his room at the hotel; but among the groups lounging at the bar or in the neighbourhood of the station excitement and discussion ran high. The envelope addressed to Anderson, Anderson's own demeanour since his arrival on the scene—with the meaning of both conjecture was busy.

Towards midnight a train arrived from Field. A messenger from the station knocked at Anderson's door with a train letter. Anderson locked the door again behind the man who had brought it, and stood looking at it a moment in silence. It was from Lady Merton. He opened it slowly, took it to the small deal table, which held a paraffin lamp, and sat down to read it.

> "Dear Mr. Anderson—Mr. Delaine has given me your message and read me some of your letter to him. He has also told me what he knew before this happened—we understood that you wished it. Oh! I cannot say how very sorry we are, Philip and I, for your great trouble. It makes me sore at heart to think that all the time you have been looking after us so kindly, taking this infinite pains for us, you have had this heavy anxiety on your mind. Oh, why didn't you tell me! I thought we were to be friends. And now this tragedy! It is terrible—terrible! Your father has been his own worst enemy—and at last death has come,—and he has

escaped himself. Is there not some comfort in that? And you tried to save him. I can imagine all that you have been doing and planning for him. It is not lost, dear Mr. Anderson. No love and pity are ever lost. They are undying—for they are God's life in us. They are the pledge—the sign—to which He is eternally bound. He will surely, surely, redeem—and fulfil.

"I write incoherently, for they are waiting for my letter. I want you to write to me, if you will. And when will you come back to us? We shall, I think, be two or three days here, for Philip has made friends with a man we have met here—a surveyor, who has been camping high up, and shooting wild goat. He is determined to go for an expedition with him, and I had to telegraph to the Lieutenant-Governor to ask him not to expect us till Thursday. So if you were to come back here before then you would still find us. I don't know that I could be of any use to you, or any consolation to you. But, indeed, I would try.

"To-morrow I am told will be the inquest. My thoughts will be with you constantly. By now you will have determined on your line of action. I only know that it will be noble and upright—like yourself.

"I remain, yours most sincerely"

"ELIZABETH MERTON."

Anderson pressed the letter to his lips. Its tender philosophising found no echo in his own mind. But it soothed, because it came from her.

He lay dressed and wakeful on his bed through the night, and at nine next morning the inquest opened, in the coffee-room of the hotel.

The body of the young constable was first identified. As to the hand which had fired the shot that killed him, there was no certain evidence; one of the police had seen the lame man with the white hair level his revolver again after the first miss; but there was much shooting going on, and no one could be sure from what quarter the fatal bullet had come.

The court then proceeded to the identification of the dead robber. The coroner, a rancher who bred the best horses in the district, called first upon two strangers in plain clothes, who had arrived by the first train from the South that morning. They proved to be the two officers from Nevada. They had already examined the body, and they gave clear and unhesitating evidence, identifying the old man as one Alexander McEwen, well known to the police of the silver-mining State as a lawless and dangerous character. He had been twice in jail, and had been the associate of the notorious Bill Symonds in one or two criminal affairs connected with "faked" claims and the like. The elder of the two officers in particular drew a vivid and damning picture of the man's life and personality, of the cunning with which he had evaded the law, and the ruthlessness with which he had avenged one or two private grudges.

"We have reason to suppose," said the American officer finally, "that McEwen was not originally a native of the States. We believe that he came from Dawson City or the neighbourhood about ten years ago, and that he crossed the border in consequence of a mysterious affair—which has never been cleared up—in which a rich German gentleman, Baron von Aeschenbach, disappeared, and has not been heard of since. Of that, however, we have no proof, and we cannot supply the court with any information as to the man's real origin and early history. But we are prepared to swear that the body we have seen this morning is that of Alexander McEwen, who for some years past has been well known to us, now in one camp, now in another, of the Comstock district."

The American police officer resumed his seat. George Anderson, who was to the right of the coroner, had sat, all through this witness's evidence, bending forward, his eyes on the ground, his hands clasped between his knees. There was something in the rigidity of his attitude, which gradually compelled the attention of the onlookers, as though the perception gained ground that here—in that stillness—those bowed shoulders—lay the real interest of this sordid outrage, which had so affronted the pride of Canada's great railway.

The coroner rose. He briefly expressed the thanks of the court to the Nevada State authorities for having so promptly supplied the information in their possession in regard to this man McEwen. He would now ask Mr. George Anderson, of the C.P.R., whether he could in any way assist the court in this investigation. An empty envelope, fully addressed to Mr. George Anderson, Ginnell's Boarding House, Laggan, Alberta, had, strangely enough, been found in McEwen's pocket. Could Mr. Anderson throw any light upon the matter?

Anderson stood up as the coroner handed him the envelope. He took it, looked at it, and slowly put it down on the table before him. He was perfectly composed, but there was that in his aspect which instantly hushed all sounds in the crowded room, and drew the eyes of everybody in it upon him. The Kamloops doctor looked at him from a distance with a sudden twitching smile—the smile of a reticent man in whom strong feeling must somehow find a physical expression. Dixon, the young Superintendent, bent forward eagerly. At the back of the room a group of Japanese railway workers, with their round, yellow faces and half-opened eyes stared impassively at the tall figure of the fair-haired Canadian; and through windows and doors, thrown open to the heat, shimmered lake and forest, the eternal background of Canada.

"Mr. Coroner," said Anderson, straightening himself to his full height, "the name of the man into whose death you are inquiring is not Alexander McEwen. He came from Scotland to Manitoba in 1869. His real name was Robert Anderson, and I—am his son."

The coroner gave an involuntary "Ah!" of amazement, which was echoed, it seemed, throughout the room.

On one of the small deal tables belonging to the coffee-room, which had been pushed aside to make room for the sitting of the court, lay the newspapers of the morning—the *Vancouver Sentinel* and the *Montreal Star*. Both contained short and flattering articles on the important Commission entrusted to Mr. George Anderson by the Prime Minister. "A great compliment to so young a man," said the *Star*, "but one amply deserved by Mr. Anderson's record. We look forward on his behalf to a brilliant career, honourable both to himself and to Canada."

Several persons had already knocked at Anderson's door early that morning in order to congratulate him; but without finding him. And this honoured and fortunate person—?

Men pushed each other forward in their eagerness not to lose a word, or a shade of expression on the pale face which confronted them.

Anderson, after a short pause, as though to collect himself, gave the outlines of his father's early history, of the farm in Manitoba, the fire and its consequences, the breach between Robert Anderson and his sons. He described the struggle of the three boys on the farm, their migration to Montreal in search of education, and his own later sojourn in the Yukon, with the evidence which had convinced him of his father's death.

"Then, only a fortnight ago, he appeared at Laggan and made himself known to me, having followed me apparently from Winnipeg. He seemed to be in great poverty, and in bad health. If he had wished it, I was prepared to acknowledge him; but he seemed not to wish it; there were no doubt reasons why he preferred to keep his assumed name. I did what I could for him, and arrangements had been made to put him with decent people at Vancouver. But last Wednesday night he disappeared from the boarding house where he and I were both lodging, and various persons here will know"—he glanced at one or two faces in the ring before him—"that I have been making inquiries since, with no result. As to what or who led him into this horrible business, I know nothing. The Nevada deputies have told you that he was acquainted with Symonds—a fact unknown to me—and I noticed on one or two occasions that he seemed to have acquaintances among the men tramping west to the Kootenay district. I can only imagine that after his success in Montana last year, Symonds made up his mind to try the same game on the C.P.R., and that during the last fortnight he came somehow into communication with my father. My father must have been aware of Symonds's plans—and may have been unable at the last to resist the temptation to join in the scheme. As to all that I am entirely in the dark."

He paused, and then, looking down, he added, under his breath, as though involuntarily—"I pray—that he may not have been concerned in the murder of poor Brown. But there is—I think—no evidence to connect him with it. I shall be glad to answer to the best of my power any questions that the court may wish to put."

He sat down heavily, very pale, but entirely collected. The room watched him a moment, and then a friendly, encouraging murmur seemed to rise from the crowd—to pass from them to Anderson.

The coroner, who was an old friend of Anderson's, fidgeted a little and in silence. He took off his glasses and put them on again. His tanned face, long and slightly twisted, with square harsh brows, and powerful jaw set in a white fringe of whisker, showed an unusual amount of disturbance. At last he said, clearing his throat: "We are much obliged to you, Mr. Anderson, for your frankness towards this court. There's not a man here that don't feel for you, and don't wish to offer you his respectful sympathy. We know you—and I reckon we know what to think about you. Gentlemen," he spoke with nasal deliberation, looking round the court, "I think that's so?"

A shout of consent—the shout of men deeply moved—went up. Anderson, who had resumed his former attitude, appeared to take no notice, and the coroner resumed.

"I will now call on Mrs. Ginnell to give her evidence."

The Irishwoman rose with alacrity—what she had to say held the audience. The surly yet good-hearted creature was divided between her wish to do justice to the demerits of McEwen, whom she had detested, and her fear of hurting Anderson's feelings in public. Beneath her rough exterior, she carried some of the delicacies of Celtic feeling, and she had no sooner given some fact that showed the coarse dishonesty of the father, than she veered off in haste to describe the pathetic efforts of the son. Her homely talk told; the picture grew.

Meanwhile Anderson sat impatient or benumbed, annoyed with Mrs. Ginnell's garrulity, and longing for the whole thing to end. He had a letter to write to Ottawa before post-time.

When the verdicts had been given, the doctor and he walked away from the court together. The necessary formalities were carried through, a coffin ordered, and provision made for the burial of Robert Anderson. As the two men passed once or twice through the groups now lounging and smoking as before outside the hotel, all conversation ceased, and all eyes followed Anderson. Sincere pity was felt for him; and at the same time men asked each other anxiously how the revelation would affect his political and other chances.

Late in the same evening the burial of McEwen took place. A congregational minister at the graveside said a prayer for mercy on the sinner. Anderson had not asked him to do it, and felt a dull resentment of the man's officiousness, and the unctious length of his prayer. Half an hour later he was on the platform, waiting for the train to Glacier.

He arrived there in the first glorious dawn of a summer morning. Over the vast Illecillowaet glacier rosy feather-clouds were floating in a crystal air, beneath a dome of pale blue. Light mists rose from the forests and the course of the river, and above them shone the dazzling snows, the hanging glaciers, and glistening rock faces, ledge piled on ledge, of the Selkirk giants—Hermit and Tupper, Avalanche and Sir Donald—with that cleft of the pass between.

The pleasant hotel, built to offer as much shelter and comfort as possible to the tired traveller and climber, was scarcely awake. A sleepy-eyed Japanese showed Anderson to his room. He threw himself on the bed, longing for sleep, yet incapable of it. He was once more under the same roof with Elizabeth Merton—and for the last time! He longed for her presence, her look, her touch; and yet with equal intensity he shrank from seeing her. That very morning through the length of Canada and the States would go out the news of the train-robbery on the main line of the C.P.R., and with it the "dramatic" story of himself and his father, made more dramatic by a score of reporters. And as the news of his appointment, in the papers of the day before, had made him a public person, and had been no doubt telegraphed to London and Europe, so also would it be with the news of the "hold-up," and his own connection with it; partly because it had happened on the C.P.R.; still more because of the prominence given to his name the day before.

He felt himself a disgraced man; and he had already put from him all thought of a public career. Yet he wondered, not without self-contempt, as he lay there in the broadening light, what it was in truth that made the enormous difference between this Monday and the Monday before. His father was dead, and had died in the very commission of a criminal act. But all or nearly all that Anderson knew now about his character he had known before this happened. The details given by the Nevada officers were indeed new to him; but he had shrewdly suspected all along that the record, did he know it, would be something like that. If such a parentage in itself involves stain and degradation, the stain and degradation had been always there, and the situation, looked at philosophically, was no worse for the catastrophe which had intervened between this week and last.

And yet it was of course immeasurably worse! Such is the "bubble reputation"—the difference between the known and the unknown.

At nine o'clock a note was brought to his room:

"Will you breakfast with me in half an hour? You will find me alone.

"E.M."

Before the clock struck the half-hour, Elizabeth was already waiting for her guest, listening for every sound. She too had been awake half the night.

When he came in she went up to him, with her quick-tripping step, holding out both her hands; and he saw that her eyes were full of tears.

"I am so—so sorry!" was all she could say. He looked into her eyes, and as her hands lay in his he stooped suddenly and kissed them. There was a great piteousness in his expression, and she felt through every nerve the humiliation and the moral weariness which oppressed him. Suddenly she recalled that first moment of intimacy between them when he had so brusquely warned her about Philip, and she had been wounded by his mere strength and fearlessness; and it hurt her to realise the contrast between that strength and this weakness.

She made him sit down beside her in the broad window of her little sitting-room, which over-looked the winding valley with the famous loops of the descending railway, and the moving light and shade on the forest; and very gently and tenderly she made him tell her all the story from first to last.

His shrinking passed away, soothed by her sweetness, her restrained emotion, and after a little he talked with freedom, gradually recovering his normal steadiness and clearness of mind.

At the same time she perceived some great change in him. The hidden spring of melancholy in his nature, which, amid all his practical energies and activities, she had always discerned, seemed to have overleaped its barriers, and to be invading the landmarks of character.

At the end of his narrative he said something in a hurried, low voice which gave her a clue.

"I did what I could to help him—but my father hated me. He died hating me. Nothing I could do altered him. Had he reason? When my brother and I in our anger thought we were avenging our mother's death, were we in truth destroying him also—driving him into wickedness beyond hope? Were we—was I—for I was the eldest—responsible? Does his death, moral and physical, lie at my door?"

He raised his eyes to her—his tired appealing eyes—and Elizabeth realised sharply how deep a hold such questionings take on such a man. She tried to argue with and comfort him—and he seemed to absorb, to listen—but in the middle of it, he said abruptly, as though to change the subject:

"And I confess the publicity has hit me hard. It may be cowardly, but I can't face it for a while. I think I told you I owned some land in Saskatchewan. I shall go and settle down on it at once."

"And give up your appointment—your public life?" she cried in dismay.

He smiled at her faintly, as though trying to console her.

"Yes; I shan't be missed, and I shall do better by myself. I understand the wheat and the land. They are friends that don't fail one."

Elizabeth flushed.

"Mr. Anderson!—you mustn't give up your work. Canada asks it of you."

"I shall only be changing my work. A man can do nothing better for Canada than break up land."

"You can do that—and other things besides. Please—please—do nothing rash!"

She bent over to him, her brown eyes full of entreaty, her hand laid gently, timidly on his.

He could not bear to distress her—but he must.

"I sent in my resignation yesterday to the Prime Minister."

The delicate face beside him clouded.

"He won't accept it."

Anderson shook his head. "I think he must."

Elizabeth looked at him in despair.

"Oh! no. You oughtn't to do this—indeed, indeed you oughtn't. It is cowardly—forgive me!—unworthy of you. Oh! can't you see how the sympathy of everybody who knows—everybody whose opinion you care for—"

She stopped a moment, colouring deeply, checked indeed by the thought of a conversation between herself and Philip of the night before. Anderson interrupted her:

"The sympathy of one person," he said hoarsely, "is very precious to me. But even for her—"

She held out her hands to him again imploringly—

"Even for her?—"

But instead of taking the hands he rose and went out on the balcony a moment, as though to look at the great view. Then he returned, and stood over her.

"Lady Merton, I am afraid—it's no use. We are not—we can't be—friends."

"Not friends?" she said, her lip quivering. "I thought I—"

He looked down steadily on her upturned face. His own spoke eloquently enough. Turning her head away, with fluttering breath, she began to speak fast and brokenly:

"I, too, have been very lonely. I want a friend whom I might help—who would help me. Why should you refuse? We are not either of us quite young; what we undertook we could carry through. Since my husband's death I—I have been playing at life. I have always been hungry, dissatisfied, discontented. There were such splendid things going on in the world, and I—I was just marking time. Nothing to do!—as much money as I could possibly want—society of course—travelling—and visiting—and amusing myself—but oh! so tired all the time. And somehow Canada has been a great revelation of real, strong, living things—this great Northwest—and you, who seemed to explain it to me—"

"Dear Lady Merton!" His tone was low and full of emotion. And this time it was he who stooped and took her unresisting hands in his. She went on in the same soft, pleading tone—

"I felt what it might be—to help in the building up a better human life—in this vast new country. God has given to you this task—such a noble task!—and through your friendship, I too seemed to have a little part in it, if only by sympathy. Oh, no! you mustn't turn back— you mustn't shrink—because of what has happened to you. And let me, from a distance, watch and help. It will ennoble my life, too. Let me!"—she smiled—"I shall make a good friend, you'll see. I shall write very often. I shall argue—and criticise—and want a great deal of explaining. And you'll come over to us, and do splendid work, and make many English friends. Your strength will all come back to you."

He pressed the hands he held more closely.

"It is like you to say all this—but—don't let us deceive ourselves. I could not be your friend, Lady Merton. I must not come and see you."

She was silent, very pale, her eyes on his—and he went on:

"It is strange to say it in this way, at such a moment; but it seems as though I had better say it. I have had the audacity, you see—to fall in love with you. And if it was audacity a week ago, you can guess what it is now—now when—Ask your mother and brother what they would think of it!" he said abruptly, almost fiercely.

There was a moment's silence. All consciousness, all feeling in each of these two human beings had come to be—with the irrevocable swiftness of love—a consciousness of the other. Under the sombre renouncing passion of his look, her own eyes filled slowly— beautifully—with tears. And through all his perplexity and pain there shot a thrill of joy, of triumph even, sharp and wonderful. He understood. All this might have been his—this delicate beauty, this quick will, this rare intelligence—and yet the surrender in her aspect was not the simple surrender of love; he knew before she spoke that she did not pretend to ignore the obstacles between them; that she was not going to throw herself upon his renunciation, trying vehemently to break it down, in a mere blind girlish impulsiveness. He realised at once her heart, and her common sense; and was grateful to her for both.

Gently she drew herself away, drawing a long breath. "My mother and brother would not decide those things for me—oh, *never!*—I should decide them for myself. But we are not going to talk of them to-day. We are not going to make any—any rash promises to each other. It is you we must think for—your future—your life. And then—if you won't give me a friend's right to speak—you will be unkind—and I shall respect you less."

She threw back her little head with vivacity. In the gesture he saw the strength of her will and his own wavered.

"How can it be unkind?" he protested. "You ought not to be troubled with me any more."

"Let me be judge of that. If you will persist in giving up this appointment, promise me at least to come to England. That will break this spell of this—this terrible thing, and give you courage—again. Promise me!"

"No, no!—you are too good to me—too good;—let it end here. It is much, much better so."

Then she broke down a little.

She looked round her, like some hurt creature seeking a means of escape. Her lips trembled. She gave a low cry. "And I have loved Canada so! I have been so happy here."

"And now I have hurt you?—I have spoilt everything?"

"It is your unhappiness does that—and that you will spoil your life. Promise me only this one thing—to come to England! Promise me!"

He sat down in a quiet despair that she would urge him so. A long argument followed between them, and at last she wore him down. She dared say nothing more of the Commissionership; but he promised her to come to England some time in the following winter; and with that she had to be content.

Then she gave him breakfast. During their conversation, which Elizabeth guided as far as possible to indifferent topics, the name of Mariette was mentioned. He was still, it seemed, at Vancouver. Elizabeth gave Anderson a sudden look, and casually, without his noticing, she possessed herself of the name of Mariette's hotel.

At breakfast also she described, with a smile and sigh, her brother's first and last attempt to shoot wild goat in the Rockies, an expedition which had ended in a wetting and a chill—"luckily nothing much; but poor Philip won't be out of his room to-day."

"I will go and see him," said Anderson, rising.

Elizabeth looked up, her colour fluttering.

"Mr. Anderson, Philip is only a boy, and sometimes a foolish boy—"

"I understand," said Anderson quietly, after a moment. "Philip thinks his sister has been running risks. Who warned him?"

Elizabeth shrugged her shoulders without replying. He saw a touch of scorn in her face that was new to him.

"I think I guess," he said. "Why not? It was the natural thing. So Mr. Delaine is still here?"

"Till to-morrow."

"I am glad. I shall like to assure him that his name was not mentioned—he was not involved at all!"

Elizabeth's lip curled a little, but she said nothing. During the preceding forty-eight hours there had been passages between herself and Delaine that she did not intend Anderson to know anything about. In his finical repugnance to soiling his hands with matters so distasteful, Delaine had carried out the embassy which Anderson had perforce entrusted to him in such a manner as to rouse in Elizabeth a maximum of pride on her own account, and of indignation on Anderson's. She was not even sorry for him any more; being, of course, therein a little unjust to him, as was natural to a high-spirited and warm-hearted woman.

Anderson, meanwhile, went off to knock at Philip's door, and Philip's sister was left behind to wonder nervously how Philip would behave and what he would say. She was still smarting under the boy's furious outburst of the night before when, through a calculated indiscretion of Delaine's, the notion that Anderson had presumed and might still presume to set his ambitions on Elizabeth had been presented to him for the first time.

"My sister marry a mining engineer!—with a drunken old robber for a father! By Jove! Anybody talking nonsense of that kind will jolly well have to reckon with me! Elizabeth!—you may say what you like, but I am the head of the family!"

Anderson found the head of the family in bed, surrounded by novels, and a dozen books on big-game shooting in the Rockies. Philip received him with an evident and ungracious embarrassment.

"I am awfully sorry—beastly business. Hard lines on you, of course—very. Hope they'll get the men."

"Thank you. They are doing their best."

Anderson sat down beside the lad. The fragility of his look struck him painfully, and the pathetic contrast between it and the fretting spirit—the books of travel and adventure heaped round him.

"Have you been ill again?" he asked in his kind, deep voice.

"Oh, just a beastly chill. Elizabeth would make me take too many wraps. Everyone knows you oughtn't to get overheated walking."

"Do you want to stay on here longer?"

"Not I! What do I care about glaciers and mountains and that sort of stuff if I can't hunt? But Elizabeth's got at the doctor somehow, and he won't let me go for three or four days unless I kick over the traces. I daresay I shall."

"No you won't—for your sister's sake. I'll see all arrangements are made."

Philip made no direct reply. He lay staring at the ceiling—till at last he said—

"Delaine's going. He's going to-morrow. He gets on Elizabeth's nerves."

"Did he say anything to you about me?" said Anderson.

Philip flushed.

"Well, I daresay he did."

"Make your mind easy, Gaddesden. A man with my story is not going to ask your sister to marry him."

Philip looked up. Anderson sat composedly erect, the traces of his nights of sleeplessness and revolt marked on every feature, but as much master of himself and his life—so Gaddesden intuitively felt—as he had ever been. A movement of remorse and affection stirred in the young man mingled with the strength of other inherited things.

"Awfully sorry, you know," he said clumsily, but this time sincerely. "I don't suppose it makes any difference to you that your father—well, I'd better not talk about it. But you see—Elizabeth might marry anybody. She might have married heaps of times since Merton died, if she hadn't been such an icicle. She's got lots of money, and—well, I don't want to be snobbish—but at home—we—our family—"

"I understand," said Anderson, perhaps a little impatiently—"you are great people. I understood that all along."

Family pride cried out in Philip. "Then why the deuce—" But he said aloud in some confusion, "I suppose that sounded disgusting"—then floundering deeper—"but you see—well, I'm very fond of Elizabeth!"

Anderson rose and walked to the window which commanded a view of the railway line.

"I see the car outside. I'll go and have a few words with Yerkes."

The boy let him go in silence—conscious on the one hand that he had himself played a mean part in their conversation, and on the other that Anderson, under this onset of sordid misfortune, was somehow more of a hero in his eyes, and no doubt in other people's, than ever.

On his way downstairs Anderson ran into Delaine, who was ascending with an armful of books and pamphlets.

"Oh, how do you do? Had only just heard you were here. May I have a word with you?"

Anderson remounted the stairs in silence, and the two men paused, seeing no one in sight, in the corridor beyond.

"I have just read the report of the inquest, and should like to offer you my sincere sympathy and congratulations on your very straightforward behaviour—" Anderson made a movement. Delaine went on hurriedly—

"I should like also to thank you for having kept my name out of it."

"There was no need to bring it in," said Anderson coldly.

"No of course not—of course not! I have also seen the news of your appointment. I trust nothing will interfere with that."

Anderson turned towards the stairs again. He was conscious of a keen antipathy—the antipathy of tired nerves—to the speaker's mere aspect, his long hair, his too picturesque dress, the antique on his little finger, the effeminate stammer in his voice.

"Are you going to-day? What train?" he said, in a careless voice as he moved away.

Delaine drew back, made a curt reply, and the two men parted.

"Oh, he'll get over it; there will very likely be nothing to get over," Delaine reflected tartly, as he made his way to his room. "A new country like this can't be too particular." He was thankful, at any rate, that he would have an opportunity before long—for he was going straight home and to Cumberland—of putting Mrs. Gaddesden on her guard. "I may be thought officious; Lady Merton let me see very plainly that she thinks me so—but I shall do my duty nevertheless."

And as he stood over his packing, bewildering his valet with a number of precise and old-maidish directions, his sore mind ran alternately on the fiasco of his own journey and on the incredible folly of nice women.

Delaine departed; and for two days Elizabeth ministered to Anderson. She herself went strangely through it, feeling between them, as it were, the bared sword of his ascetic will—no less than her own terrors and hesitations. But she set herself to lift him from the depths; and as they walked about the mountains and the forests, in a glory of summer sunshine, the sanity and sweetness of her nature made for him a spiritual atmosphere akin in its healing power to the influence of pine and glacier upon his physical weariness.

On the second evening, Mariette walked into the hotel. Anderson, who had just concluded all arrangements for the departure of the car with its party within forty-eight hours, received him with astonishment.

"What brings you here?"

Mariette's harsh face smiled at him gravely.

"The conviction that if I didn't come, you would be committing a folly."

"What do you mean?"

"Giving up your Commissionership, or some nonsense of that sort."

"I have given it up."

"H'm! Anything from Ottawa yet?"

It was impossible, Anderson pointed out, that there should be any letter for another three days. But he had written finally and did not mean to be over-persuaded.

Mariette at once carried him off for a walk and attacked him vigorously. "Your private affairs have nothing whatever to do with your public work. Canada wants you—you must go."

"Canada can easily get hold of a Commissioner who would do her more credit," was the bitter reply. "A man's personal circumstances are part of his equipment. They must not be such as to injure his mission."

Mariette argued in vain.

As they were both dining in the evening with Elizabeth and Philip, a telegram was brought in for Anderson from the Prime Minister. It contained a peremptory and flattering refusal to accept his resignation. "Nothing has occurred which affects your public or private character. My confidence quite unchanged. Work is best for yourself, and the public expects it of you. Take time to consider, and wire me in two days."

Anderson thrust it into his pocket, and was only with difficulty persuaded to show it to Mariette.

But in the course of the evening many letters arrived—letters of sympathy from old friends in Quebec and Manitoba, from colleagues and officials, from navvies and railwaymen, even, on the C.P.R., from his future constituents in Saskatchewan—drawn out by the newspaper reports of the inquest and of Anderson's evidence. For once the world rallied to a good man in distress! and Anderson was strangely touched and overwhelmed by it.

He passed an almost sleepless night, and in the morning as he met Elizabeth on her balcony he said to her, half reproachfully, pointing to Mariette below—

"It was you sent for him."

Elizabeth smiled.

"A woman knows her limitations! It is harder to refuse two than one."

For twenty-four hours the issue remained uncertain. Letters continued to pour in; Mariette applied the plain-spoken, half-scornful arguments natural to a man holding a purely spiritual standard of life; and Elizabeth pleaded more by look and manner than by words.

Anderson held out as long as he could. He was assaulted by that dark midway hour of manhood, that distrust of life and his own powers, which disables so many of the world's best men in these heightened, hurrying days. But in the end his two friends saved him—as by fire.

Mariette himself dictated the telegram to the Prime Minister in which Anderson withdrew his resignation; and then, while Anderson, with a fallen countenance, carried it to the post, the French Canadian and Elizabeth looked at each other—in a common exhaustion and relief.

"I feel a wreck," said Elizabeth. "Monsieur, you are an excellent ally." And she held out her hand to her colleague. Mariette took it, and bowed over it with the air of a *grand seigneur* of 1680.

"The next step must be yours, madam—if you really take an interest in our friend."

Elizabeth rather nervously inquired what it might be.

"Find him a wife!—a good wife. He was not made to live alone."

His penetrating eyes in his ugly well-bred face searched the features of his companion. Elizabeth bore it smiling, without flinching.

A fortnight passed—and Elizabeth and Philip were on their way home through the heat of July. Once more the railway which had become their kind familiar friend sped them through the prairies, already whitening to the harvest, through the Ontarian forests and the Ottawa valley. The wheat was standing thick on the illimitable earth; the plains in their green or golden dress seemed to laugh and sing under the hot dome of sky. Again the great Canadian spectacle unrolled itself from west to east, and the heart Elizabeth brought to it was no longer the heart of a stranger. The teeming Canadian life had become interwoven with her life; and when Anderson came to bid her a hurried farewell on the platform at Regina, she carried the passionate memory of his face with her, as the embodiment and symbol of all that she had seen and felt.

Then her thoughts turned to England, and the struggle before her. She braced herself against the Old World as against an enemy. But her spirit failed her when she remembered that in Anderson himself she was like to find her chiefest foe.

CHAPTER XIII

"What about the shooters, Wilson? I suppose they'll be in directly?"

"They're just finishing the last beat, ma'am. Shall I bring in tea?"

Mrs. Gaddesden assented, and then leaving her seat by the fire she moved to the window to see if she could discover any signs in the wintry landscape outside of Philip and his shooting party. As she did so she heard a rattle of distant shots coming from a point to her right beyond the girdling trees of the garden. But she saw none of the shooters—only two persons, walking up and down the stone terrace outside, in the glow of the November sunset. One was Elizabeth, the other a tall, ungainly, yet remarkable figure, was a Canadian friend of Elizabeth's, who had only arrived that forenoon—M. Félix Mariette, of Quebec. According to Elizabeth, he had come over to attend a Catholic Congress in London. Mrs. Gaddesden understood that he was an Ultramontane, and that she was not to mention to him the word "Empire." She knew also that Elizabeth had made arrangements with a neighbouring landowner, who was also a Catholic, that he should be motored fifteen miles to Mass on the following morning, which was Sunday; and her own easy-going Anglican temper, which carried her to the parish church about twelve times a year, had been thereby a good deal impressed.

How well those furs became Elizabeth! It was a chill frosty evening, and Elizabeth's slight form was wrapped in the sables which had been one of poor Merton's earliest gifts to her. The mother's eye dwelt with an habitual pride on the daughter's grace of movement and carriage. "She is always so distinguished," she thought, and then checked herself by the remembrance that she was applying to Elizabeth an adjective that Elizabeth particularly disliked. Nevertheless, Mrs. Gaddesden knew very well what she herself meant by it. She meant something—some quality in Elizabeth, which was always provoking in her mother's mind despairing comparisons between what she might make of her life and what she was actually making, or threatening to make of it.

Alas, for that Canadian journey—that disastrous Canadian journey! Mrs. Gaddesden's thoughts, as she watched the two strollers outside, were carried back to the moment in early August when Arthur Delaine had reappeared in her drawing-room, three weeks before Elizabeth's return, and she had gathered from his cautious and stammering revelations what kind of man it was who seemed to have established this strange hold on her daughter. Delaine, she thought, had spoken most generously of Elizabeth and his own disappointment, and most kindly of this Mr. Anderson.

"I know nothing against him personally—nothing! No doubt a very estimable young fellow, with just the kind of ability that will help him in Canada. Lady Merton, I imagine, will have told you of the sad events in which we found him involved?"

Mrs. Gaddesden had replied that certainly Elizabeth had told her the whole story, so far as it concerned Mr. Anderson. She pointed to the letters beside her.

"But you cannot suppose," had been her further indignant remark, "that Elizabeth would ever dream of marrying him!"

"That, my dear old friend, is for her mother to find out," Delaine had replied, not without a touch of venom. "I can certainly assure you that Lady Merton is deeply interested in this young man, and he in her."

"Elizabeth—exiling herself in Canada—burying herself on the prairies—when she might have everything here—the best of everything—at her feet. It is inconceivable!"

Delaine had agreed that it was inconceivable, and they had mourned together over the grotesque possibilities of life. "But you will save her," he had said at last. "You will save her! You will point out to her all she would be giving up—the absurdity, the really criminal waste of it!"

On which he had gloomily taken his departure for an archæological congress at Berlin, and an autumn in Italy; and a few weeks later she had recovered her darling Elizabeth, paler and thinner than before—and quite, quite incomprehensible!

As for "saving" her, Mrs. Gaddesden had not been allowed to attempt it. In the first place, Elizabeth had stoutly denied that there was anything to save her from. "Don't believe anything at all, dear Mummy, that Arthur Delaine may have said to you! I have made a great friend—of a very interesting man; and I am going to correspond with him. He is coming to London in November, and I have asked him to stay here. And you must be *very* kind to him, darling—just as kind as you can be—for he has had a hard time—he saved Philip's life—and he is an uncommonly fine fellow!"

And with that—great readiness to talk about everything except just what Mrs. Gaddesden most wanted to know. Elizabeth sitting on her mother's bed at night, crooning about Canada—her soft brown hair over her shoulders, and her eyes sparkling with patriotic enthusiasm, was a charming figure. But let Mrs. Gaddesden attempt to probe and penetrate beyond a certain point, and the way was resolutely barred. Elizabeth would kiss her mother tenderly—it was as though her own reticence hurt her—but would say nothing. Mrs. Gaddesden could only feel sorely that a great change had come over the being she loved best in the world, and that she was not to know the whys and wherefores of it.

And Philip—alack! had been of very little use to her in the matter!

"Don't you bother your head, Mother! Anderson's an awfully good chap—but he's not going to marry Elizabeth. Told me he knew he wasn't the kind. And of course he isn't—must draw the line somewhere—hang it! But he's an awfully decent fellow. He's not going to push himself in where he isn't wanted. You let Elizabeth alone, Mummy—it'll work off. And of course we must be civil to him when he comes over—I should jolly well think we must—considering he saved my life!"

Certainly they must be civil! News of Anderson's sailing and arrival had been anxiously looked for. He had reached London three days before this date, had presented his credentials at the Board of Trade and the Colonial Office, and after various preliminary interviews with ministers, was now coming down to Martindale for a week-end before the assembling of the small conference of English and colonial representatives to which he had been sent.

Mrs. Gaddesden saw from the various notices of his arrival in the English papers that even in England, among the initiated he was understood to be a man of mark. She was all impatience to see him, and had shown it outwardly much more plainly than Elizabeth. How quiet Elizabeth had been these last days! moving about the house so silently, with vaguely smiling eyes, like one husbanding her strength before an ordeal.

What was going to happen? Mrs. Gaddesden was conscious in her own mind of a strained hush of expectation. But she had never ventured to say a word to Elizabeth. In half an hour—or less—he would be here. A motor had been sent to meet the express train at the country town fifteen miles off. Mrs. Gaddesden looked round her in the warm dusk, as though trying to forecast how Martindale and its inmates would look to the new-comer. She saw a room of medium size, which from the end of the sixteenth century had been known as the Red Drawing Room—a room panelled in stamped Cordovan leather, and filled with rare and beautiful things; with ebony cabinets, and fine lacquer; with the rarest of oriental carpets, with carved chairs, and luxurious sofas. Set here and there, sparingly, among the shadows, as though in scorn of any vulgar profusion, the eye caught the gleam of old silver, or rock crystal, or agate; *bibelots* collected a hundred and fifty years ago by a Gaddesden of taste, and still in their original places. Overhead, the uneven stucco ceiling showed a pattern of Tudor roses; opposite to Mrs. Gaddesden the wall was divided between a round mirror, in whose depths she saw herself reflected and a fine Holbein portrait of a man, in a flat velvet hat on a green background. Over the carved mantelpiece with its date of 1586, there reigned a Romney portrait—one of the most famous in existence—of a young girl in black. Elizabeth Merton bore a curious resemblance to it. Chrysanthemums, white, yellow and purple, gleamed amid the richness of the room; while the light of the solitary lamp beside which Mrs. Gaddesden had been sitting with her embroidery, blended with the orange glow from outside now streaming in through the unshuttered windows, to deepen a colour effect of extraordinary beauty, produced partly by time, partly by the conscious effort of a dozen generations.

And from the window, under the winter sunset, Mrs. Gaddesden could see, at right angles to her on either side, the northern and southern wings of the great house; the sloping lawns; the river winding through the park; the ivy-grown church among the trees; the distant woods and plantations; the purple outlines of the fells. Just as in the room within, so the scene without was fused into a perfect harmony and keeping by the mellowing light. There was in it not a jarring note, a ragged line—age and dignity, wealth and undisputed place: Martindale expressed them all. The Gaddesdens had twice refused a peerage; and with contempt. In their belief, to be Mr. Gaddesden of Martindale was enough; a dukedom could not have bettered it. And the whole country-side in which they had been rooted for centuries agreed with them. There had even been a certain disapproval of the financial successes of Philip Gaddesden's father. It was true that the Gaddesden rents had gone down. But the country, however commercialised itself, looked with jealousy on any intrusion of "commercialism" into the guarded and venerable precincts of Martindale.

The little lady who was now, till Philip's majority and marriage, mistress of Martindale, was a small, soft, tremulous person, without the intelligence of her daughter, but by no means without character. Secretly she had often felt oppressed by her surroundings. Whenever Philip married, she would find it no hardship at all to retire to the dower house at the edge of the park. Meanwhile she did her best to uphold the ancient ways. But if *she* sometimes found Martindale oppressive—too old, too large, too rich, too perfect—how was it going to strike a young Canadian, fresh from the prairies, who had never been in England before?

A sudden sound of many footsteps in the hall. The drawing-room door was thrown open by Philip, and a troop of men entered. A fresh-coloured man with grizzled hair led the van.

"Well, Mrs. Gaddesden, here we all are. Philip has given us a capital day!"

A group of men followed him; the agent of the property, two small neighbouring squires, a broad-browed burly man in knickerbockers, who was apparently a clergyman, to judge from his white tie, the adjutant of the local regiment, and a couple of good-looking youths, Etonian friends of Philip. Elizabeth and Mariette came in from the garden, and a young cousin of the Gaddesdens, a Miss Lucas, slipped into the room under Elizabeth's wing. She was a pretty girl, dressed in an elaborate demi-toilette of white chiffon, and the younger men of the party in their shooting dress—with Philip at their head—were presently clustered thick about her, like bees after pollen. It was clear, indeed, that Philip was paying her considerable attention, and as he laughed and sparred with her, the transient colour that exercise had given him disappeared, and a pale look of excitement took its place.

Mariette glanced from one to another with a scarcely disguised curiosity. This was only his third visit to England and he felt himself in a foreign country. That was a *pasteur* he supposed, in the gaiters— grotesque! And why was the young lady in evening dress, while Lady Merton, now that she had thrown off her furs, appeared in the severest of tweed coats and skirts? The rosy old fellow beside Mrs. Gaddesden was, he understood from Lady Merton, the Lord Lieutenant of the county.

But at that moment his hostess laid hands upon him to present him to her neighbour. "Monsieur Mariette—Lord Waynflete."

"Delighted to see you," said the great man affably, holding out his hand. "What a fine place Canada is getting! I am thinking of sending my third son there."

Mariette bowed.

"There will be room for him."

"I am afraid he hasn't brains enough to do much here—but perhaps in a new country—"

"He will not require them? Yes, it is a common opinion," said Mariette, with composure. Lord Waynflete stared a little, and returned to his hostess. Mariette betook himself to Elizabeth for tea, and she introduced him to the girl in white, who looked at him with enthusiasm, and at once threw over her bevy of young men, in favour of the spectacled and lean-faced stranger.

"You are a Catholic, Monsieur?" she asked him, fervently. "How I envy you! I *adore* the Oratory! When we are in town I always go there to Benediction—unless Mamma wants me at home to pour out tea. Do you know Cardinal C— —?"

She named a Cardinal Archbishop, then presiding over the diocese of Westminster.

"Yes, mademoiselle, I know him quite well. I have just been staying with him."

She clasped her hands eagerly.

"How *very* interesting! I know him a little. *Isn't* he nice?"

"No," said Mariette resolutely. "He is magnificent—a saint—a scholar—everything—but not nice!"

The girl looked a little puzzled, then angry, and after a few minutes' more conversation she returned to her young men, conspicuously turning her back on Mariette.

He threw a deprecating, half-penitent look at Elizabeth, whose faced twitched with amusement, and sat down in a corner behind her that he might observe without talking. His quick intelligence sorted the people about him almost at once—the two yeoman-squires, who were not quite at home in Mrs. Gaddesden's drawing-room, were awkward with their tea-cups, and talked to each other in subdued voices, till Elizabeth found them out, summoned them to her side, and made them happy; the agent who was helping Lady Merton with tea, making himself generally useful; Philip and another gilded youth, the son, he understood, of a neighbouring peer, who were flirting with the girl in white; and yet a third fastidious Etonian, who was clearly bored by the ladies, and was amusing himself with the adjutant and a cigarette in a distant corner. His eyes came back at last to the *pasteur*. An able face after all; cool, shrewd, and not unspiritual. Very soon, he, the parson—whose name was Everett—and Elizabeth were drawn into conversation, and Marietta under Everett's good-humoured glance found himself observed as well as observer.

"You are trying to decipher us?" said Everett, at last, with a smile. "Well, we are not easy."

"Could you be a great nation if you were?"

"Perhaps not. England just now is a palimpsest—the new writing everywhere on top of the old. Yet it is the same parchment, and the old is there. Now *you* are writing on a fresh skin."

"But with the old ideas!" said Mariette, a flash in his dark eyes. "Church—State—family!—there is nothing else to write with."

The two men drew closer together, and plunged into conversation. Elizabeth was left solitary a moment, behind the tea-things. The buzz of the room, the hearty laugh of the Lord Lieutenant, reached the outer ear. But every deeper sense was strained to catch a voice—a step—that must soon be here. And presently across the room, her eyes met her mother's, and their two expectancies touched.

"Mother!—here is Mr. Anderson!"

Philip entered joyously, escorting his guest.

To Anderson's half-dazzled sight, the room, which was now fully lit by lamplight and fire, seemed crowded. He found himself greeted by a gentle grey-haired lady of fifty-five, with a strong likeness to a face he knew; and then his hand touched Elizabeth's. Various commonplaces passed between him and her, as to his journey, the new motor which had brought him to the house, the frosty evening. Mariette gave him a nod and smile, and he was introduced to various men who bowed without any change of expression, and to a girl, who smiled carelessly, and turned immediately towards Philip, hanging over the back of her chair.

Elizabeth pointed to a seat beside her, and gave him tea. They talked of London a little, and his first impressions. All the time he was trying to grasp the identity of the woman speaking with the woman he had parted from in Canada. Something surely had gone? This restrained and rather cold person was not the Elizabeth of the Rockies. He watched her when she turned from him to her other guests; her light impersonal manner towards the younger men, with its occasional touch of satire; the friendly relation between her and the parson; the kindly deference she showed the old Lord Lieutenant. Evidently she was mistress here, much more than her mother. Everything seemed to be referred to her, to circle round her.

Presently there was a stir in the room. Lord Waynflete asked for his carriage.

"Don't forget, my dear lady, that you open the new Town Hall next Wednesday," he said, as he made his way to Elizabeth.

She shrugged her shoulders.

"But you make the speech!"

"Not at all. They only want to hear you. And there'll be a great crowd."

"Elizabeth can't speak worth a cent!" said Philip, with brotherly candour. "Can you, Lisa?"

"I don't believe it," said Lord Waynflete, "but it don't matter. All they want is that a Gaddesden should say something. Ah, Mrs. Gaddesden—how glorious the Romney looks to-night!" He turned to the fireplace, admiring the illuminated picture, his hands on his sides.

"Is it an ancestress?" Mariette addressed the question to Elizabeth.

"Yes. She had three husbands, and is supposed to have murdered the fourth," said Elizabeth drily.

"All the same she's an extremely handsome woman," put in Lord Waynflete. "And as you're the image of her, Lady Merton, you'd better not run her down." Elizabeth joined in the laugh against herself and the speaker turned to Anderson.

"You'll find this place a perfect treasure-house, Mr. Anderson, and I advise you to study it—for the Radicals won't leave any of us anything, before many years are out. You're from Manitoba? Ah, you're not troubled with any of these Socialist fellows yet! But you'll get 'em—you'll get 'em—like rats in the corn. They'll pull the old flag down if they can. But you'll help us to keep it flying. The Colonies are our hope—we look to the Colonies!"

The handsome old man raised an oratorical hand, and looked round on his audience, like one to whom public speaking was second nature.

Anderson made a gesture of assent; he was not really expected to say anything. Mariette in the background observed the speaker with an amused and critical detachment.

"Your carriage will be round directly, Lord Waynflete," said Philip, "but I don't see why you should go."

"My dear fellow—I have to catch the night train. There is a most important debate in the House of Lords to-morrow." He turned to the Canadian politely. "Of course you know there is an autumn session on. With these Radical Governments we shall soon have one every year."

"What! the Education Bill again to-morrow?" said Everett. "What are you going to do with it?"

Lord Waynflete looked at the speaker with some distaste. He did not much approve of sporting parsons, and Everett's opinions were too Liberal to please him. But he let himself be drawn, and soon the whole room was in eager debate on some of the old hot issues between Church and Dissent. Lord Waynflete ceased to be merely fatuous and kindly. His talk became shrewd, statesmanlike even; he was the typical English aristocrat and Anglican Churchman, discussing topics with which he had been familiar from his cradle, and in a manner and tone which every man in the room—save the two Canadians—accepted without question. He was the natural leader of these men of the land-owning or military class; they liked to hear him harangue; and harangue he did, till the striking of a clock suddenly checked him.

"I must be off! Well, Mrs. Gaddesden, it's the *Church*—the Church we have to think of!—the Church we have to fight for! What would England be without the Church—let's ask ourselves that. Good-bye—good-bye!"

"Is he talking of the Anglican establishment?" muttered Mariette. *"Quel drôle de vieillard!"*

The parson heard him, and, with a twinkle in his eyes, turned and proposed to show the French Canadian the famous library of the house.

The party melted away. Even Elizabeth had been summoned for some last word with Lord Waynflete on the subject of the opening of the Town Hall. Anderson was left alone.

He looked around him, at the room, the pictures, the panelled walls, and then moving to the window which was still unshuttered, he gazed out into the starlit dusk, and the dim, stately landscape. There were lights in the church showing the stained glass of the perpendicular windows, and a flight of rooks was circling round the old tower.

As he stood there, somebody came back into the room. It was the adjutant, looking for his hat.

"Jolly old place, isn't it?" said the young man civilly, seeing that the stranger was studying the view. "It's to be hoped that Philip will keep it up properly."

"He seems fond of it," said Anderson.

"Oh, yes! But you've got to be a big man to fill the position. However, there's money enough. They're all rich—and they marry money."

Anderson murmured something inaudible, and the young man departed.

A little later Anderson and Elizabeth were seated together in the Red Drawing Room. Mrs. Gaddesden, after a little perfunctory conversation with the new-comer, had disappeared on the plea of letters to write. The girl in white, the centre of a large party in the hall, was flirting to her heart's content. Philip would have dearly liked to stay and flirt with her himself; but his mother, terrified by his pallor and fatigue after the exertion of the shoot, had hurried him off to take a warm bath and rest before dinner. So that Anderson and Elizabeth were alone.

Conversation between them did not move easily. Elizabeth was conscious of an oppression against which it seemed vain to fight. Up to the moment of his sailing from Canada his letters had been frank and full, the letters of a deeply attached friend, though with no trace in them of the language of love. What change was it that the touch of English ground—the sight of Martindale—had wrought? He talked with some readiness of the early stages of his mission—of the kindness shown to him by English public men, and the impressions of a first night in the House of Commons. But his manner was constrained; anything that he said might have been heard by all the world; and as their talk progressed, Elizabeth felt a miserable paralysis descending on her own will. She grew whiter and whiter. This old house in which they sat, with its splendours and treasures, this environment of the past all about them seemed to engulf and entomb them both. She had looked forward with a girlish pleasure—and yet with a certain tremor—to showing Anderson her old home, the things she loved and had inherited. And now it was as though she were vulgarly conscious of wealth and ancestry as dividing her from him. The wildness within her which found its scope and its voice in Canada was here like an imprisoned stream, chafing in caverns underground. Ah! it had been easy to defy the Old World in Canada, its myriad voices and claims—the many-fingered magic with which an old society plays on those born into it!

"I shall be here perhaps a month," said Anderson, "but then I shall be wanted at Ottawa."

And he began to describe a new matter in which he had been lately engaged—a large development scheme applying to some of the great Peace River region north of Edmonton. And as he told her of his August journey through this noble country, with its superb rivers, its shining lakes and forests, and its scattered settlers, waiting for a Government which was their servant and not their tyrant, to come and help their first steps in ordered civilisation; to bring steamers to their waters, railways to link their settlements, and fresh settlers to let loose the fertile forces of their earth—she suddenly saw in him his old self—the Anderson who had sat beside her in the crossing of the prairies, who had looked into her eyes the day of Roger's Pass. He had grown older and thinner; his hair was even lightly touched with grey. But the traces in him of endurance and of pain were like the weathering of a fine building; mellowing had come, and strength had not been lost.

Yet still no word of feeling, of intimacy even. Her soul cried out within her, but there was no answer. Then, when it was time to dress, and she led him through the hall, to the inlaid staircase with its famous balustrading—early English ironwork of extraordinary delicacy—and through the endless corridors upstairs, old and dim, but crowded with portraits and fine furniture, Anderson looked round him in amazement.

"What a wonderful place!"

"It is too old!" cried Elizabeth, petulantly; then with a touch of repentance—"Yet of course we love it. We are not so stifled here as you would be."

He smiled and did not reply.

"Confess you have been stifled—ever since you came to England."

He drew a long breath, throwing back his head with a gesture which made Elizabeth smile. He smiled in return.

"It was you who warned me how small it would all seem. Such little fields—such little rivers—such tiny journeys! And these immense towns treading on each other's heels. Don't you feel crowded up?"

"You are home-sick already?"

He laughed—"No, no!" But the gleam in his eyes admitted it. And Elizabeth's heart sank—down and down.

A few more guests arrived for Sunday—a couple of politicians, a journalist, a poet, one or two agreeable women, a young Lord S., who had just succeeded to one of the oldest of English marquisates, and so on.

Elizabeth had chosen the party to give Anderson pleasure, and as a guest he did not disappoint her pride in him. He talked well and modestly, and the feeling towards Canada and the Canadians in English society had been of late years so friendly that although there was often colossal ignorance, there was no coolness in the atmosphere about him. Lord S. confused Lake Superior with Lake Ontario, and was of opinion that the Mackenzie River flowed into the Ottawa. But he was kind enough to say that he would far sooner go to Canada than any of "those beastly places abroad"—and as he was just a simple handsome youth, Anderson took to him, as he had taken to Philip at Lake Louise, and by the afternoon of Sunday was talking sport and big game in a manner to hold the smoking-room enthralled.

Only unfortunately Philip was not there to hear. He had been overtired by the shoot, and had caught a chill beside. The doctor was in the house, and Mrs. Gaddesden had very little mind to give to her Sunday party. Elizabeth felt a thrill of something like comfort as she noticed how in the course of the day Anderson unconsciously slipped back into the old Canadian position; sitting with Philip, amusing him and "chaffing" him; inducing him to obey his doctor; cheering his mother, and in general producing in Martindale itself the same impression of masculine help and support which he had produced on Elizabeth, five months before, in a Canadian hotel.

By Sunday evening Mrs. Gaddesden, instead of a watchful enemy, had become his firm friend; and in her timid, confused way she asked him to come for a walk with her in the November dusk. Then, to his astonishment, she poured out her heart to him about her son, whose health, together with his recklessness, his determination to live like other and sound men, was making the two women who loved him more and more anxious. Anderson was very sorry for the little lady, and genuinely alarmed himself with regard to Philip, whose physical condition seemed to him to have changed considerably for the worse since the Canadian journey. His kindness, his real concern, melted Mrs. Gaddesden's heart.

"I hope we shall find you in town when we come up!" she said, eagerly, as they turned back to the house, forgetting, in her maternal egotism, everything but her boy. "Our man here wants a consultation. We shall go up next week for a short time before Christmas."

Anderson hesitated a moment.

"Yes," he said, slowly, but in a changed voice, "Yes, I shall still be there."

Whereupon, with perturbation, Mrs. Gaddesden at last remembered there were other lions in the path. They had not said a single word—however conventional—of Elizabeth. But she quickly consoled herself by the reflection that he must have seen by now, poor fellow, how hopeless it was; and that being so, what was there to be said against admitting him to their circle, as a real friend of all the family—Philip's friend, Elizabeth's, and her own?

That night Mrs. Gaddesden was awakened by her maid between twelve and one. Mr. Gaddesden wanted a certain medicine that he thought was in his mother's room. Mrs. Gaddesden threw on her dressing-gown and looked for it anxiously in vain. Perhaps Elizabeth might remember where it was last seen. She hurried to her. Elizabeth had a sitting-room and bedroom at the end of the corridor, and Mrs. Gaddesden went into the sitting-room first, as quietly as possible, so as not to startle her daughter.

She had hardly entered and closed the door behind her, guided by the light of a still flickering fire, when a sound from the inner room arrested her.

Elizabeth—Elizabeth in distress?

The mother stood rooted to the spot, in a sudden anguish. Elizabeth—sobbing? Only once in her life had Mrs. Gaddesden heard that sound before—the night that the news of Francis Merton's death reached Martindale, and Elizabeth had wept, as her mother believed, more for what her young husband might have been to her, than for what he had been. Elizabeth's eyes filled readily with tears answering to pity or high feeling; but this fierce stifled emotion—this abandonment of pain!

Mrs. Gaddesden stood trembling and motionless, the tears on her own cheeks. Conjecture hurried through her mind. She seemed to be learning her daughter, her gay and tender Elizabeth, afresh. At last she turned and crept out of the room, noiselessly shutting the door. After lingering a while in the passage, she knocked, with an uncertain hand, and waited till Elizabeth came—Elizabeth, hardly visible in the firelight, her brown hair falling like a veil round her face.

CHAPTER XIV

A few days later the Gaddesdens were in town, settled in a house in Portman Square. Philip was increasingly ill, and moreover shrouded in a bitterness of spirit which wrung his mother's heart. She suspected a new cause for it in the fancy that he had lately taken for Alice Lucas, the girl in the white chiffon, who had piped to Mariette in vain. Not that he ever now wanted to see her. He had passed into a phase indeed of refusing all society—except that of George Anderson. A floor of the Portman Square house was given up to him. Various treatments were being tried, and as soon as he was strong enough his mother was to take him to the South. Meanwhile his only pleasure seemed to lie in Anderson's visits, which however could not be frequent, for the business of the Conference was heavy, and after the daily sittings were over, the interviews and correspondence connected with them took much time.

On these occasions, whether early in the morning before the business of the day began, or in the hour before dinner—sometimes even late at night—Anderson after his chat with the invalid would descend from Philip's room to the drawing-room below, only allowing himself a few minutes, and glancing always with a quickening of the pulse through the shadows of the large room, to see whether it held two persons or one. Mrs. Gaddesden was invariably there; a small, faded woman in trailing lace dresses, who would sit waiting for him, her embroidery on her knee, and when he appeared would hurry across the floor to meet him, dropping silks, scissors, handkerchief on the way. This dropping of all her incidental possessions—a performance repeated night after night, and followed always by her soft fluttering apologies—soon came to be symbolic, in Anderson's eyes. She moved on the impulse of the moment, without thinking what she might scatter by the way. Yet the impulse was always a loving impulse—and the regrets were sincere.

As to the relation to Anderson, Philip was here the pivot of the situation exactly as he had been in Canada. Just as his physical weakness, and the demands he founded upon it had bound the Canadian to their chariot wheels in the Rockies, so now—*mutatis mutandis*—in London. Mrs. Gaddesden before a week was over had become pitifully dependent upon him, simply because Philip was pleased to desire his society, and showed a flicker of cheerfulness whenever he appeared. She was torn indeed between her memory of Elizabeth's sobbing, and her hunger to give Philip the moon out of the sky, should he happen to want it. Sons must come first, daughters second; such has been the philosophy of mothers from the beginning. She feared—desperately feared—that Elizabeth had given her heart away. And as she agreed with Philip that it would not be a seemly or tolerable marriage for Elizabeth, she would, in the natural course of things, both for Elizabeth's sake and the family's, have tried to keep the unseemly suitor at a distance. But here he was, planted somehow in the very midst of their life, and she, making feeble efforts day after day to induce him to root himself there still more firmly. Sometimes indeed she would try to press alternatives on Philip. But Philip would not have them. What with the physical and moral force that seemed to radiate from Anderson, and bring stimulus with them to the weaker life—and what with the lad's sick alienation for the moment from his ordinary friends and occupations, Anderson reigned supreme, often clearly to his own trouble and embarrassment. Had it not been for Philip, Portman Square would have seen him but seldom. That Elizabeth knew with a sharp certainty, dim though it might be to her mother. But as it was, the boy's tragic clinging to his new friend governed all else, simply because at the bottom of each heart, unrecognised and unexpressed, lurked the same foreboding, the same fear of fears.

The tragic clinging was also, alack, a tragic selfishness. Philip had a substantial share of that quick perception which in Elizabeth became something exquisite and impersonal, the source of all high emotions. When Delaine had first suggested to him "an attachment" between Anderson and his sister, a hundred impressions of his own had emerged to verify the statement and aggravate his wrath; and when Anderson had said "a man of my history is not going to ask your sister to marry him," Philip perfectly understood that but for the history the attempt would have been made. Anderson was therefore—most unreasonably and presumptuously—in love with Elizabeth; and as to Elizabeth, the indications here also were not lost upon Philip. It was all very amazing, and he wished, to use his phrase to his mother, that it would "work off." But whether or no, he could not do without Anderson—if Anderson was to be had. He threw him and Elizabeth together, recklessly; trusting to Anderson's word, and unable to resist his own craving for comfort and distraction.

The days passed on, days so charged with feeling for Elizabeth that they could only be met at all by a kind of resolute stillness and self-control. Philip was very dependent on the gossip his mother and sister brought him from the world outside. Elizabeth therefore, to please him, went into society as usual, and forgot her heartaches, for her brother and for herself, as best she could. Outwardly she was much occupied in doing all that could be done—socially and even politically—for Anderson and Mariette. She had power and she used it. The two friends found themselves the object of one of those sudden cordialities that open all doors, even the most difficult, and run like a warm wave through London society. Mariette remained throughout the ironic spectator—friendly on his own terms, but entirely rejecting, often, the terms offered him tacitly or openly, by his English acquaintance.

"Your ways are not mine—your ideals are not mine, God forbid they should be!"—he seemed to be constantly saying. "But we happen to be oxen bound under the same yoke, and dragging the same plough. No gush, please—but at the same time no ill-will! Loyal?—to your loyalties? Oh yes—quite sufficiently—so long as you don't ask us to let it interfere with our loyalty to our own! Don't be such fools as to expect us to take much interest in your Imperial orgies. But we're all right! Only let us alone—we're all right!"

Such seemed to be the voice of this queer, kindly, satiric personality. London generally falls into the arms of those who flout her; and Mariette, with his militant Catholicism, and his contempt for our governing ideals, became the fashion. As for Anderson, the contact with English Ministers and men of affairs had but carried on the generous process of development that Nature had designed for a strong man. Whereas in Mariette the vigorous, self-confident English world—based on the Protestant idea—produced a bitter and profound irritation, Anderson seemed to find in that world something ripening and favouring that brought out all the powers—the intellectual powers at least—of his nature. He did his work admirably; left the impression of a "coming man" on a great many leading persons interested in the relations between England and Canada; and when as often happened Elizabeth and he found themselves at the same dinner-table, she would watch the changes in him that a larger experience was bringing about, with a heart half proud, half miserable. As for his story, which was very commonly known, in general society, it only added to his attractions. Mothers who were under no anxieties lest he might want to marry their daughters, murmured the facts of his unlucky *provenance* to each other, and then the more eagerly asked him to dinner.

Meanwhile, for Elizabeth life was one long debate, which left her often at night exhausted and spiritless. The shock of their first meeting at Martindale, when all her pent-up yearning and vague expectation had been met and crushed by the silent force of the man's unaltered will, had passed away. She understood him better. The woman who is beloved penetrates to the fact through all the disguises that a lover may attempt. Elizabeth knew well that Anderson had tones and expressions for her that no other woman could win from him; and looking back to their conversation at the Glacier House, she realised, night after night, in the silence of wakeful hours, the fulness of his confession, together with the strength of his recoil from any pretension to marry her.

Yes, he loved her, and his mere anxiety—now, and as things stood—to avoid any extension or even repetition of their short-lived intimacy, only betrayed the fact the more eloquently. Moreover, he had reason, good reason, to think, as she often passionately reminded herself, that he had touched her heart, and that had the course been clear, he might have won her.

But—the course was not clear. From many signs, she understood how deeply the humiliation of the scene at Sicamous had entered into a proud man's blood. Others might forget; he remembered. Moreover, that sense of responsibility—partial responsibility at least—for his father's guilt and degradation, of which he had spoken to her at Glacier, had, she perceived, gone deep with him. It had strengthened a stern and melancholy view of life, inclining him to turn away from personal joy, to an exclusive concern with public duties and responsibilities.

And this whole temper had no doubt been increased by his perception of the Gaddesdens' place in English society. He dared not—he would not—ask a woman so reared in the best that England had to give, now that he understood what that best might be, to renounce it all in favour of what he had to offer. He realised that there was a generous weakness in her own heart on which he might have played. But he would not play; his fixed intention was to disappear as soon as possible from her life; and it was his honest hope that she would marry in her own world and forget him. In fact he was the prey of a kind of moral terror that here also, as in the case of his father, he might make some ghastly mistake, pursuing his own will under the guise of love, as he had once pursued it under the guise of retribution—to Elizabeth's hurt and his own remorse.

All this Elizabeth understood, more or less plainly. Then came the question—granted the situation, how was she to deal with it? Just as he surmised that he could win her if he would, she too believed that were she merely to set herself to prove her own love and evoke his, she could probably break down his resistance. A woman knows her own power. Feverishly, Elizabeth was sometimes on the point of putting it out, of so provoking and appealing to the passion she divined, as to bring him, whether he would or no, to her feet.

But she hesitated. She too felt the responsibility of his life, as of hers. Could she really do this thing—not only begin it, but carry it through without repentance, and without recoil?

She made herself look steadily at this English spectacle with its luxurious complexity, its concentration within a small space of all the delicacies of sense and soul, its command of a rich European tradition, in which art and literature are living streams springing from fathomless depths of life. Could she, whose every fibre responded so perfectly to the stimulus of this environment, who up till now—but for moments of revolt—had been so happy and at ease in it, could she wrench herself from it—put it behind her—and adapt herself to quite another, without, so to speak, losing herself, and half her value, whatever that might be, as a human being?

As we know, she had already asked herself the question in some fashion, under the shadow of the Rockies. But to handle it in London was a more pressing and poignant affair. It was partly the characteristic question of the modern woman, jealous, as women have never been before in the world's history, on behalf of her own individuality. But Elizabeth put it still more in the interests of her pure and passionate feeling for Anderson. He must not—he should not—run any risks in loving her!

On a certain night early in December, Elizabeth had been dining at one of the great houses of London. Anderson too had been there. The dinner party, held in a famous room panelled with full-length Vandycks, had been of the kind that only London can show; since only in England is society at once homogeneous enough and open enough to provide it. In this house, also, the best traditions of an older regime still prevailed, and its gatherings recalled—not without some conscious effort on the part of the hostess—the days of Holland House, and Lady Palmerston. To its smaller dinner parties, which were the object of so many social ambitions, nobody was admitted who could not bring a personal contribution. Dukes had no more claim than other people, but as most of the twenty-eight were blood-relations of the house, and some Dukes are agreeable, they took their turn. Cabinet Ministers, Viceroys, Ambassadors, mingled with the men of letters and affairs. There was indeed a certain old-fashioned measure in it all. To be merely notorious—even though you were amusing—was not passport enough. The hostess—a beautiful tall woman, with the brow of a child, a quick intellect, and an amazing experience of life—created round her an atmosphere that was really the expression of her own personality; fastidious, and yet eager; cold, and yet steeped in intellectual curiosities and passions. Under the mingled stimulus and restraint of it, men and women brought out the best that was in them. The talk was good, and nothing—neither the last violinist, nor the latest *danseuse*—was allowed to interfere with it. And while the dress and jewels of the women were generally what a luxurious capital expects and provides, you might often find some little girl in a dyed frock—with courage, charm and breeding—the centre of the scene.

Elizabeth in white, and wearing some fine jewels which had been her mother's, had found herself placed on the left of her host, with an ex-Viceroy of India on her other hand. Anderson, who was on the opposite side of the table, watched her animation, and the homage that was eagerly paid her by the men around her. Those indeed who had known her of old were of opinion that whereas she had always been an agreeable companion, Lady Merton had now for some mysterious reason blossomed into a beauty. Some kindling change had passed over the small features. Delicacy and reserve were still there, but interfused now with a shimmering and transforming brightness, as though some flame within leapt intermittently to sight.

Elizabeth more than held her own with the ex-Viceroy, who was a person of brilliant parts, accustomed to be flattered by women. She did not flatter him, and he was reduced in the end to making those efforts for himself, which he generally expected other people to make for him. Elizabeth's success with him drew the attention of several other persons at the table besides Anderson. The ex-Viceroy was a bachelor, and one of the great *partis* of the day. What could be more fitting than that Elizabeth Merton should carry him off, to the discomfiture of innumerable intriguers?

After dinner, Elizabeth waited for Anderson in the magnificent gallery upstairs where the guests of the evening party were beginning to gather, and the musicians were arriving. When he came she played her usual fairy godmother's part; introducing him to this person and that, creating an interest in him and in his work, wherever it might be useful to him. It was understood that she had met him in Canada, and that he had been useful to the poor delicate brother. No other idea entered in. That she could have any interest in him for herself would have seemed incredible to this world looking on.

"I must slip away," said Anderson, presently, in her ear; "I promised to look in on Philip if possible. And to-morrow I fear I shall be too busy."

And he went on to tell her his own news of the day—that the Conference would be over sooner than he supposed, and that he must get back to Ottawa without delay to report to the Canadian Ministry. That afternoon he had written to take his passage for the following week.

It seemed to her that he faltered in telling her; and, as for her, the crowd of uniformed or jewelled figures around them became to her, as he spoke, a mere meaningless confusion. She was only conscious of him, and of the emotion which at last he could not hide.

She quietly said that she would soon follow him to Portman Square, and he went away. A few minutes afterwards, Elizabeth said goodnight to her hostess, and emerged upon the gallery running round the fine Italianate hall which occupied the centre of the house. Hundreds of people were hanging over the balustrading of the gallery, watching the guests coming and going on the marble staircase which occupied the centre of the hall.

Elizabeth's slight figure slowly descended.

"Pretty creature!" said one old General, looking down upon her. "You remember—she was a Gaddesden of Martindale. She has been a widow a long time now. Why doesn't someone carry her off?"

Meanwhile Elizabeth, as she went down, dreamily, from step to step, her eyes bent apparently upon the crowd which filled all the spaces of the great pictorial house, was conscious of one of those transforming impressions which represent the sudden uprush and consummation in the mind of some obscure and long-continued process.

One moment, she saw the restless scene below her, the diamonds, the uniforms, the blaze of electric light, the tapestries on the walls, the handsome faces of men and women; the next, it had been wiped out; the prairies unrolled before her; she beheld a green, boundless land invaded by a mirage of sunny water; scattered through it, the white farms; above it, a vast dome of sky, with summer clouds in glistening ranks climbing the steep of blue; and at the horizon's edge, a line of snow-peaks. Her soul leapt within her. It was as though she felt the freshness of the prairie wind upon her cheek, while the call of that distant land—Anderson's country—its simpler life, its undetermined fates, beat through her heart.

And as she answered to it, there was no sense of renunciation. She was denying no old affection, deserting no ancient loyalty. Old and new; she seemed to be the child of both—gathering them both to her breast.

Yet, practically, what was going to happen to her, she did not know. She did not say to herself, "It is all clear, and I am going to marry George Anderson!" But what she knew at last was that there was no dull hindrance in herself, no cowardice in her own will; she was ready, when life and Anderson should call her.

At the foot of the stairs Mariette's gaunt and spectacled face broke in upon her trance. He had just arrived as she was departing.

"You are off—so early?" he asked her, reproachfully.

"I want to see Philip before he settles for the night."

"Anderson, too, meant to look in upon your brother."

"Yes?" said Elizabeth vaguely, conscious of her own reddening, and of Mariette's glance.

"You have heard his news?" He drew her a little apart into the shelter of a stand of flowers. "We both go next week. You—Lady Merton—have been our good angel—our providence. Has he been saying that to you? All the same—*ma collègue*—I am disappointed in you!"

Elizabeth's eye wavered under his.

"We agreed, did we not—at Glacier—on what was to be done next to our friend? Oh! don't dispute! I laid it down—and you accepted it. As for me, I have done nothing but pursue that object ever since—in my own way. And you, Madam?"

As he stood over her, a lean Don Quixotish figure, his long arms akimbo, Elizabeth's fluttering laugh broke out.

"Inquisitor! Good night!"

"Good night—but—just a word! Anderson has done well here. Your public men say agreeable things of him. He will play your English game—your English Imperialist game—which I can't play. But only, if he is happy—if the fire in him is fed. Consider! Is it not a patriotic duty to feed it?"

And grasping her hand, he looked at her with a gentle mockery that passed immediately into that sudden seriousness—that unconscious air of command—of which the man of interior life holds the secret. In his jests even, he is still, by natural gift, the confessor, the director, since he sees everything as the mystic sees it, *sub specie æternitatis.*

Elizabeth's soft colour came and went. But she made no reply—except it were through an imperceptible pressure of the hand holding her own.

At that moment the ex-Viceroy, resplendent in his ribbon of the Garter, who was passing through the hall, perceived her, pounced upon her, and insisted on seeing her to her carriage. Mariette, as he mounted the staircase, watched the two figures disappear—smiling to himself.

But on the way home the cloud of sisterly grief descended on Elizabeth. How could she think of herself—when Philip was ill—suffering—threatened? And how would he bear the news of Anderson's hastened departure?

As soon as she reached home, she was told by the sleepy butler that Mrs. Gaddesden was in the drawing-room, and that Mr. Anderson was still upstairs with Philip.

As she entered the drawing-room, her mother came running towards her with a stifled cry:

"Oh, Lisa, Lisa!"

In terror, Elizabeth caught her mother in her arms.

"Mother—is he worse?"

"No! At least Barnett declares to me there is no real change. But he has made up his mind, to-day, that he will never get better. He told me so this evening, just after you had gone; and Barnett could not satisfy him. He has sent for Mr. Robson." Robson was the family lawyer.

The two women looked at one another in a pale despair. They had reached the moment when, in dealing with a sick man, the fictions of love drop away, and the inexorable appears.

"And now he'll break his heart over Mr. Anderson's going!" murmured the mother, in an anguish. "I didn't want him to see Philip to-night—but Philip heard his ring—and sent down for him."

They sat looking at each other, hand in hand—waiting—and listening. Mrs. Gaddesden murmured a broken report of the few words of conversation which rose now, like a blank wall, between all the past, and this present; and Elizabeth listened, the diamonds in her hair and the folds of her satin dress glistening among the shadows of the half-lit room, the slow tears on her cheeks.

At last a step descended. Anderson entered the room.

"He wants you," he said, to Elizabeth, as the two women rose. "I am afraid you must go to him."

The electric light immediately above him showed his frowning, shaken look.

"He is so distressed by your going?" asked Elizabeth, trembling.

Anderson did not answer, except to repeat insistently—

"You must go to him. I don't myself think he is any worse—but—"

Elizabeth hurried away. Anderson sat down beside Mrs. Gaddesden, and began to talk to her.

When his sister entered his room, Philip was sitting up in an arm-chair near the fire; looking so hectic, so death-doomed, so young, that his sister ran to him in an agony—"Darling Philip—my precious Philip—why did you want me? Why aren't you asleep?"

She bent over him and kissed his forehead, and then taking his hand she laid it against her cheek, caressing it tenderly.

"I'm not asleep—because I've had to think of a great many things," said the boy in a firm tone. "Sit down, please, Elizabeth. For a few days past, I've been pretty certain about myself—and to-night I screwed it out of Barnett. I haven't said anything to you and mother, but—well, the long and short of it is, Lisa, I'm not going to recover— that's all nonsense—my heart's too dicky—I'm going to die."

She protested with tears, but he impatiently asked her to be calm. "I've got to say something—something important—and don't you make it harder, Elizabeth! I'm not going to get well, I tell you—and though I'm not of age—legally—yet I do represent father—I am the head of the family—and I have a right to think for you and mother. Haven't I?"

The contrast between the authoritative voice, the echo of things in him, ancestral and instinctive, and the poor lad's tremulous fragility, was moving indeed. But he would not let her caress him.

"Well, these last weeks, I've been thinking a great deal, I can tell you, and I wasn't going to say anything to you and mother till I'd got it straight. But now, all of a sudden, Anderson comes and says that he's going back. Look here, Elizabeth—I've just been speaking to Anderson. You know that he's in love with you—of course you do!"

With a great effort, Elizabeth controlled herself. She lifted her face to her brother's as she sat on a low chair beside him. "Yes, dear Philip, I know."

"And did you know too that he had promised me not to ask you to marry him?"

Elizabeth started.

"No—not exactly. But perhaps—I guessed."

"He did then!" said Philip, wearily. "Of course I told him what I thought of his wanting to marry you, in the Rockies; and he behaved awfully decently. He'd never have said a word, I think, without my leave. Well—now I've changed my mind!"

Elizabeth could not help smiling through her tears. With what merry scorn would she have met this assertion of the *patria potestas* from the mouth of a sound brother! Her poor Philip!

"Dear old boy!—what have you been saying to Mr. Anderson?"

"Well!"—the boy choked a little—"I've been telling him that—well, never mind!—he knows what I think about him. Perhaps if I'd known him years ago—I'd have been different. That don't matter. But I want to settle things up for you and him. Because you know, Elizabeth, you're pretty gone on him, too!"

Elizabeth hid her face against his knee—without speaking. The boy resumed:

"And so I've been telling him that now I thought differently—I hoped he would ask you to marry him—and I knew that you cared for him—but that he mustn't dream of taking you to Canada. That was all nonsense—couldn't be thought of! He must settle here. You've lots of money—and—well, when I'm gone—you'll have more. Of course Martindale will go away from us, and I know he will look after mother as well as you."

There was silence—till Elizabeth murmured—"And what did he say?"

The lad drew himself away from her with an angry movement.

"He refused!"

Elizabeth lifted herself, a gleam of something splendid and passionate lighting up her small face.

"And what else, dear Philip, did you expect?"

"I expected him to look at it reasonably!" cried the boy. "How can he ask a woman like you to go and live with him on the prairies? It's ridiculous! He can go into English politics, if he wants politics. Why shouldn't he live on your money? Everybody does it!"

"Did you really understand what you were asking him to do, Philip?"

"Of course I did! Why, what's Canada compared to England? Jolly good thing for him. Why he might be anything here! And as if I wouldn't rather be a dustman in England than a—"

"Philip, my dear boy! do rest—do go to bed," cried his mother imploringly, coming into the room with her soft hurrying step. "It's going on for one o'clock. Elizabeth mustn't keep you talking like this!"

She smiled at him with uplifted finger, trying to hide from him all traces of emotion.

But her son looked at her steadily.

"Mother, is Anderson gone?"

"No," said Mrs. Gaddesden, with hesitation. "But he doesn't want you to talk any more to-night—he begs you not. Please—Philip!"

"Ask him to come here!" said Philip, peremptorily. "I want to talk to him and Elizabeth."

Mrs. Gaddesden protested in vain. The mother and daughter looked at each other with flushed faces, holding a kind of mute dialogue. Then Elizabeth rose from her seat by the fire.

"I will call Mr. Anderson, Philip. But if we convince you that what you ask is quite impossible, will you promise to go quietly to bed and try to sleep? It breaks mother's heart, you know, to see you straining yourself like this."

Philip nodded—a crimson spot in each cheek, his frail hands twining and untwining as he tried to compose himself.

Elizabeth went half-way down the stairs and called. Anderson hurried out of the drawing-room, and saw her bending to him from the shadows, very white and calm.

"Will you come back to Philip a moment?" she said, gently. "Philip has told me what he proposed to you."

Anderson could not find a word to say. In a blind tumult of feeling he caught her hand, and pressed his lips to it, as though appealing to her dumbly to understand him.

She smiled at him.

"It will be all right," she whispered. "My poor Philip!" and she led him back to the sick room.

"George—I wanted you to come back, to talk this thing out," said Philip, turning to him as he entered, with the tyranny of weakness. "There's no time to waste. You know—everybody knows—I may get worse—and there'll be nothing settled. It's my duty to settle—"

Elizabeth interrupted him.

"Philip darling!—"

She was hanging over his chair, while Anderson stood a few feet away, leaning against the mantelpiece, his face turned from the brother and sister. The intimacy—solemnity almost—of the sick-room, the midnight hour, seemed to strike through Elizabeth's being, deepening and yet liberating emotion.

"Dear Philip! It is not for Mr. Anderson to answer you—it is for me. If he could give up his country—for happiness—even for love—I should never marry him—for—I should not love him any more."

Anderson turned to look at her. She had moved, and was now standing in front of Philip, her head thrown back a little, her hands lightly clasped in front of her. Her youth, her dress, her diamonds, combined strangely with the touch of high passion in her shining eyes, her resolute voice.

"You see, dear Philip, I love George Anderson—"

Anderson gave a low cry—and, moving to her side, he grasped her hand. She gave it to him, smiling—and went on:

"I love him—partly—because he is so true to his own people—because I saw him first—and knew him first—among them. No! dear Philip, he has his work to do in Canada—in that great, great nation that is to be. He has been trained for it—no one else can do it but he—and neither you nor I must tempt him from it."

The eyes of the brother and sister met. Elizabeth tried for a lighter tone.

"But as neither of us *could* tempt him from it—it is no use talking—is it?"

Philip looked from her to Anderson in a frowning silence. No one spoke for a little while. Then it seemed to them as though the young man recognised that his effort had failed, and his physical weakness shrank from renewing it. But he still resisted his mother's attempt to put an end to the scene.

"That's all very well, Lisa," he said at last, "but what are you going to do?"

Elizabeth withdrew her hand from Anderson's.

"What am I going to do? *Wait*—just that!"

But her lip trembled. And to hide it she sank down again in the low chair in front of her brother, propping her face in both hands.

"Wait?" repeated Philip, scornfully—"and what for?"

"Till you and mother—come to my way of thinking—and"—she faltered—"till Mr. Anderson—"

Her voice failed her a moment. Anderson stood motionless, bending towards her, hanging upon her every gesture and tone.

"Till Mr. Anderson—" she resumed, "is—well!—is brave enough to—trust a woman! and—oh! good Heavens!"—she dashed the tears from her eyes, half laughing, as her self-control broke down—"clever enough to save her from proposing to him in this abominable way!"

She sprang to her feet impatiently. Anderson would have caught her in his arms; but with a flashing look, she put him aside. A wail broke from Mrs. Gaddesden:

"Lisa—you won't leave us!"

"Never, darling—unless you send me!—or come with me! And now, don't you think, Philip dearest, you might let us all go to bed? You are really not worse, you know; and Mother and I are going to carry you off south—very, very soon."

She bent to him and kissed his brow. Philip's face gradually changed beneath her look, from the tension and gloom with which he had begun the scene to a kind of boyish relief—a touch of pleasure—of mischief even. His high, majestical pretensions vanished away; a light and volatile mind thought no more of them; and he turned eagerly to another idea.

"Elizabeth, do you know that you have proposed to Anderson?"

"If I have, it was your fault."

"He hasn't said Yes?"

Elizabeth was silent. Anderson came forward—but Philip stopped him with a gesture.

"He can't say Yes—till I give him back his promise," said the boy, triumphantly. "Well, George, I do give it you back—on one condition—that you put off going for a week, and that you come back as soon as you can. By Jove, I think you owe me that!"

Anderson's difficult smile answered him.

"And now you've got rid of your beastly Conference, you can come in, and talk business with me to-morrow—next day—every day!" Philip resumed, "can't he, Elizabeth? If you're going to be my brother, I'll jolly well get you to tackle the lawyers instead of me—boring old idiots! I say—I'm going to take it easy now!"

He settled himself in his chair with a long breath, and his eyelids fell. He was speaking, as they all knew, of the making of his will. Mrs.

Gaddesden stooped piteously and kissed him. Elizabeth's face quivered. She put her arm round her mother and led her away. Anderson went to summon Philip's servant.

A little later Anderson again descended the dark staircase, leaving Philip in high spirits and apparently much better.

In the doorway of the drawing-room, stood a white form. Then the man's passion, so long dyked and barriered, had its way. He sprang towards her. She retreated, catching her breath; and in the shadows of the empty room she sank into his arms. In the crucible of that embrace all things melted and changed. His hesitations and doubts, all that hampered his free will and purpose, whether it were the sorrows and humiliations of the past—or the compunctions and demurs of the present—dropped away from him, as unworthy not of himself, but of Elizabeth. She had made him master of herself, and her fate; and he boldly and loyally took up the part. He had refused to become the mere appanage of her life, because he was already pledged to that great idea he called his country. She loved him the more for it; and now he had only to abound in the same sense, in order to hold and keep the nature which had answered so finely to his own. He had so borne himself as to wipe out all the social and external inequalities between them. What she had given him, she had had to sue him to take. But now that he had taken it, she knew herself a weak woman on his breast, and she realised with a happy tremor that he would make her no more apologies for his love, or for his story. Rather, he stood upon that dignity she herself had given him—her lover, and the captain of her life!

EPILOGUE

About nine months later than the events told in the last chapter, the August sun, as it descended upon a lake in that middle region of the northern Rockies which is known as yet only to the Indian trapper, and—on certain tracks—to a handful of white explorers, shone on a boat containing two persons—Anderson and Elizabeth. It was but twenty-four hours since they had reached the lake, in the course of a long camping expedition involving the company of two guides, a couple of half-breed *voyageurs*, and a string of sixteen horses. No white foot had ever before trodden the slender beaches of the lake; its beauty of forest and water, of peak and crag, of sun and shadow, the terror of its storms, the loveliness of its summer—only some stray Indian hunter, once or twice in a century perhaps, throughout all the æons of human history, had ever beheld them.

But now, here were Anderson and Elizabeth!—first invaders of an inviolate nature, pioneers of a long future line of travellers and worshippers.

They had spent the day of summer sunshine in canoeing on the broad waters, exploring the green bays, and venturing a long way up a beautiful winding arm which seemed to lose itself in the bosom of superb forest-skirted mountains, whence glaciers descended, and cataracts leapt sheer into the glistening water. Now they were floating slowly towards the little promontory where their two guides had raised a couple of white tents, and the smoke of a fire was rising into the evening air.

Sunset was on the jagged and snow-clad heights that shut in the lake to the eastward. The rose of the sky had been caught by the water and interwoven with its own lustrous browns and cool blues; while fathom-deep beneath the shining web of colour gleamed the reflected snows and the forest slopes sliding downwards to infinity. A few bird-notes were in the air—the scream of an eagle, the note of a whip-poor-will, and far away across the lake a dense flight of wild duck rose above a reedy river-mouth, black against a pale band of sky.

They were close now to the shore, and to a spot where lightning and storm had ravaged the pines and left a few open spaces for the sun to work. Elizabeth, in delight, pointed to the beds of wild strawberries crimsoning the slopes, intermingled with stretches of bilberry, and streaks of blue and purple asters. But a wilder life was there. Far away the antlers of a swimming moose could be seen above the quiet lake. Anderson, sweeping the side with his field glass, pointed to the ripped tree-trunks, which showed where the brown bear or the grizzly had been, and to the tracks of lynx or fox on the firm yellow sand. And as they rounded the point of a little cove they came upon a group of deer that had come down to drink.

The gentle creatures were not alarmed at their approach; they raised their heads in the red light, seeing man perhaps for the first time, but they did not fly. Anderson stayed the boat—and he and Elizabeth watched them with enchantment—their slender bodies and proud necks, the bright sand at their feet, the brown water in front, the forest behind.

Elizabeth drew a long breath of joy—looking back again at the dying glory of the lake, and the great thunder-clouds piled above the forest.

"Where are we exactly?" she said. "Give me our bearings."

"We are about seventy miles north of the main line of the C.P.R., and about forty or fifty miles from the projected line of the Grand Trunk Pacific," said Anderson. "Make haste, dearest, and name your lake!—for where we come, others will follow."

So Elizabeth named it—Lake George—after her husband; seeing that it was his topographical divination, his tracking of the lake through the ingenious unravelling of a score of Indian clues which had led them at last to that Pisgah height whence the silver splendour of it had first been seen. But the name was so hotly repudiated by Anderson on the ground of there being already a famous and an historical Lake George on the American continent, that the probability is, when that noble sheet of water comes to be generally visited of mankind, it will be known rather as Lake Elizabeth; and so those early ambitions of Elizabeth which she had expressed to Philip in the first days of her Canadian journeying, will be fulfilled.

"LAKE ELIZABETH"

Alas!—poor Philip! Elizabeth's black serge dress, and the black ribbon on her white sun-hat were the outward tokens of a grief, cherished deep in her protesting, pitiful heart. Her brother had lived for some four months after her engagement to Anderson; always, in spite of encouraging doctors, under the same sharp premonition of death which had dictated his sudden change of attitude towards his Canadian friend. In the January of the new year, Anderson had joined them at Bordighera, and there, after many alternating hopes and fears, a sudden attack of pneumonia had slit the thin-spun life. A few weeks later, at Mrs. Gaddesden's urgent desire, and while she was in the care of a younger sister to whom she was tenderly attached, there had been a quiet wedding at Genoa, and a very pale and sad Elizabeth had been carried by her Anderson to some of the beloved Italian towns, where for so long she had reaped a yearly harvest of delight. In Rome, Florence, and Venice she must needs rouse herself, if only to show the keen novice eyes, beside her what to look at, and to grapple with the unexpected remarks which the spectacle evoked from Anderson. He looked in respectful silence at Bellini and Tintoret; but the industrial growth of the north, the strikes of *braccianti* on the central plains, and the poverty of Sicily and the south—in these problems he was soon deeply plunged, teaching himself Italian in order to understand them.

Then they had returned to Mrs. Gaddesden, and to the surrender of Martindale to its new master. For the estate went to a cousin, and when the beauty and the burden of it were finally gone, Philip's gentle ineffectual mother departed with relief to the moss-grown dower-house beside Bassenthwaite lake, there to sorrow for her only son, and to find in the expansion of Elizabeth's life, in Elizabeth's letters, and the prospects of Elizabeth's visits, the chief means left of courage and resignation. Philip's love for Anderson, his actual death in those strong arms, had strengthened immeasurably the latter's claim upon her; and in March she parted with him and Elizabeth, promising them boldly that she would come to them in the fall, and spend a Canadian winter with them.

Then Anderson and Elizabeth journeyed West in hot haste to face a general election. Anderson was returned, and during three or four months at Ottawa, Elizabeth was introduced to Canadian politics, and to the swing and beat of those young interests and developing national hopes which, even after London, and for the Londoner, lend romance and significance to the simpler life of Canada's nascent capital. But through it all both she and Anderson pined for the West, and when Parliament rose in early July, they fled first to their rising farm-buildings on one of the tributaries of the Saskatchewan, and then, till the homestead was ready, and the fall ploughing in sight, they had gone to the Rockies, in order that they might gratify a passionate wish of Elizabeth's—to get for once beyond beaten tracks, and surprise the unknown. She pleaded for it as their real honeymoon. It might never be possible again; for the toils of life would soon have snared them.

And so, after a month's wandering beyond all reach of civilisation, they were here in the wild heart of Manitou's wild land, and the red and white of Elizabeth's cheek, the fire in her eyes showed how the god's spell had worked....

The evening came. Their frugal meal, prepared by one of the Indian half-breeds, and eaten in a merry community among beds of orchids and vetch, was soon done; and the husband and wife pushed off again in the boat—for the densely wooded shores of the lake were impassable on foot—to watch the moon rise on this mysterious land.

And as they floated there, often hand in hand, talking a little, but dreaming more—Anderson's secret thoughts reviewed the past year, and the incredible fortune which had given him Elizabeth.

Deep in his nature was still the old pessimism, the old sadness. Could he make her happy? In the close contact of marriage he realised all that had gone to the making of her subtle and delicate being—the influences of a culture and tradition of which he was mostly ignorant, though her love was opening many gates to him. He felt himself in many respects her inferior—and there were dark moments when it seemed to him inevitable that she must tire of him. But whenever they overshadowed him, the natural reaction of a vigorous manhood was not far off. Patriotism and passion—a profound and simple pride—stood up and wrestled with his doubt. She was not less, but more, than he had imagined her. What was in truth his safeguard and hers, was the fact that, at the very root of her, Elizabeth was a poet! She had seen Canada and Anderson from the beginning in the light of imagination; and that light was not going to fail her now. For it sprang from the truth and glow of her own nature; by the help of it she *made* her world; and Canada and Anderson moved under it, nobly seen and nobly felt.

This he half shrinkingly understood, and he repaid her with adoration, and a wisely yielding mind. For her sake he was ready to do a hundred things he had never yet thought of, reading, inquiring, observing, in wider circles and over an ampler range. For as the New World, through Anderson, worked on Elizabeth—so Europe, through Elizabeth, worked on Anderson. And thus, from life to life, goes on the great interpenetrating, intermingling flux of things!

It seemed as though the golden light could not die from the lake, though midsummer was long past. And presently up into its midst floated the moon, and as they watched the changing of the light upon the northern snow-peaks, they talked of the vast undiscovered regions beyond, of the valleys and lakes that no survey has ever mapped, and the rivers that from the beginning of time have spread their pageant of beauty for the heavens alone; then, of that sudden stir and uproar of human life—prospectors, navvies, lumbermen—that is now beginning to be heard along that narrow strip where the new line of the Grand Trunk Pacific is soon to pierce the wilderness—yet another link in the girdling of the world. And further yet, their fancy followed, ever northward—solitude beyond solitude, desert beyond desert—till, in the Yukon, it lit upon gold-seeking man, dominating, at last, a terrible and hostile earth, which had starved and tortured and slain him in his thousands, before he could tame her to his will.

And last—by happy reaction—it was the prairies again—their fruitful infinity—and the emigrant rush from East and South.

"When we are old"—said Elizabeth softly, slipping her hand into Anderson's—"will all this courage die out of us? Now—nothing of all this vastness, this mystery frightens me. I feel a kind of insolent, superhuman strength!—as if I—even I—could guide a plough, reap corn, shoot rapids, 'catch a wild goat by the hair—and hurl my lances at the sun!'"

"With this hand?" said Anderson, looking at it with a face of amusement. But Elizabeth took no heed—except to slip the other hand after it—both into the same shelter.

She pursued her thought, murmuring the words, the white lids falling over her eyes:

"But when one is feeble and dying, will it all grow awful to me? Suddenly—shall I long to creep into some old, old corner of England or Italy—and feel round me close walls, and dim small rooms, and dear, stuffy, familiar streets that thousands and thousands of feet have worn before mine?"

Anderson smiled at her. He had guided their boat into a green cove where there was a little strip of open ground between the water and the forest. They made fast the boat, and Anderson found a mossy seat under a tall pine from which the lightning of a recent storm had stripped a great limb, leaving a crimson gash in the trunk. And there Elizabeth nestled to him, and he with his arm about her, and the intoxication of her slender beauty mastering his senses, tried to answer her as a plain man may. The commonplaces of passion—its foolish promises—its blind confidence—its trembling joy—there is no other path for love to travel by, and Elizabeth and Anderson trod it like their fellows.

Six months later on a clear winter evening Elizabeth was standing in the sitting-room of a Saskatchewan farmhouse. She looked out upon a dazzling world of snow, lying thinly under a pale greenish sky in which the sunset clouds were just beginning to gather. The land before her sloped to a broad frozen river up which a wagon and a team of horses was plodding its way—the steam rising in clouds round the bodies of the horses and men. On a track leading to the river a sledge was running—the bells jingling in the still, light air. To her left were the great barns of the homestead, and beyond, the long low cowshed, with a group of Shorthorns and Herefords standing beside the open door. Her eyes delighted in the whiteness of the snow, or the touches of orange and scarlet in the clumps of bush, in a note of crimson here and there, among the withered reeds pushing through the snow, or in the thin background of a few taller trees—the "shelter-belt" of the farm—rising brown and sharp against the blue.

Within the farmhouse sitting-room flamed a great wood fire, which shed its glow on the white walls, on the prints and photographs and books which were still Elizabeth's companions in the heart of the prairies, as they had been at Martindale. The room was simplicity itself, yet full of charm, with its blue druggetting, its pale green chairs and hangings. At its further end, a curtain half drawn aside showed another room, a dining-room, also firelit—with a long table spread for tea, a bare floor of polished woodblocks, and a few prints on the walls.

The wagon she had seen on the river approached the homestead. The man who was driving it—a strong-limbed, fair-haired fellow—

lifted his cap when he saw Elizabeth at the window. She nodded and smiled at him. He was Edward Tyson, one of the two engine-drivers who had taken her and Philip through the Kicking Horse Pass. His friend also could be seen standing among the cattle gathered in the farmyard. They had become Anderson's foremen and partners on his farm of twelve hundred acres, of which only some three hundred acres had been as yet brought under plough. The rest was still virgin prairie, pasturing a large mixed herd of cattle and horses. The two North-Countrymen had been managing it all in Anderson's Parliamentary absences, and were quite as determined as he to make it a centre of science and progress for a still remote and sparely peopled district. One of the kinsmen was married, and lived in a small frame house, a stone's throw from the main buildings of the farm. The other was the head of the "bothy" or boarding-house for hired men, a long low building, with cheerful white-curtained windows, which could be seen just beyond the cow-house.

As she looked over the broad whiteness of the farmlands, above which the sunset clouds were now tossing in climbing lines of crimson and gold, rising steeply to a zenith of splendour, and opening here and there, amid their tumult, to show a further heaven of untroubled blue—Elizabeth thought with lamentation that their days on the farm were almost done. The following week could see them at Ottawa for the opening of the session. Anderson was full of Parliamentary projects; important work for the Province had been entrusted to him; and in the general labour policy of the Dominion he would find himself driven to take a prominent part. But all the while his heart and Elizabeth's were in the land and its problems; for them the true, the entrancing Canada was in the wilds. And for Anderson, who through so many years, as an explorer and engineer, had met Nature face to face, his will against hers, in a direct and simple conflict, the tedious and tortuous methods of modern politics were not easy to learn. He must indeed learn them—he was learning them; and the future had probably great things in store for him, as a politician. But he came back to the Saskatchewan farm with joy, and he would leave it reluctantly.

"If only I wasn't so rich!" thought Elizabeth, with compunction. For she often looked with envy on her neighbours who had gone through the real hardships of the country; who had bought their Canadian citizenship with the toil and frugality of years. It seemed to her sometimes that she was step-child rather than daughter of the dear new land, in spite of her yearning towards it.

And yet money had brought its own romance. It had enabled Anderson to embark on this ample farm of nearly two square miles, to staff it with the best labour to be got, on a basis of copartnership, to bring herds of magnificent cattle into these park-like prairies, to set up horse-breeding, and to establish on the borders of the farm a large creamery which was already proving an attraction for settlers. It was going to put into Elizabeth's hands the power of helping the young University of Strathcona just across the Albertan border, and perhaps of founding in their own provincial capital of Regina a training college for farm-students—girls and boys—which might reproduce for the West the college of St. Anne's, that wonderful home of all the useful arts, which an ever-generous wealth has given to the Province of Quebec. Already she had in her mind a cottage hospital—sorely wanted—for the little town of Donaldminster, wherein the weaklings of this great emigrant army now pouring into the country might find help.

Her heart, indeed, was full of schemes for help. Here she was, a woman of high education, and much wealth, in the midst of this nascent community. Her thoughts pondered the life of these scattered farms—of the hard-working women in them—the lively rosy-cheeked children. It was her ambition so to live among them that they might love her—trust her—use her.

Meanwhile their own home was a "temple of industrious peace." Elizabeth was a prairie housewife like her neighbours. She had indeed brought out with her from Cumberland one of the Martindale gardeners and his young wife and sister; and the two North-Country women shared with the farm mistress the work of the house, till such time as Anderson should help the husband to a quarter-section of his own, and take someone else to train in his place. But the atmosphere of the house was one of friendly equality. Elizabeth—who had herself gone into training for a few weeks at St. Anne's—prided herself on her dairy, her bread, her poultry. One might have seen her, on this winter afternoon, in her black serge dress with white cap and apron, slipping into the kitchen behind the dining-room, testing the scones in the oven, looking to the preparations for dinner, putting away stores, and chatting to the two clear-eyed women who loved her, and would not for the world have let her try her strength too much! For she who was so eagerly planning the help of others must now be guarded and cherished herself—lest ill befall!

But now she was at the window watching for Anderson.

The trail from Donaldminster to Battleford passed in front of the house, dividing the farm. Presently there came slowly along it a covered wagon drawn by a pair of sorry horses and piled at the back with household possessions. In front sat a man of slouching carriage, and in the interior of the wagon another figure could be dimly seen. The whole turn-out gave an impression of poverty and misfortune; and Elizabeth looked at it curiously.

Suddenly, the wagon drew up with a jerk at the gate of the farm, and the man descended, with difficulty, his limbs being evidently numb with cold.

Elizabeth caught up a fur cloak and ran to the door.

"Could you give us a bit of shelter for the night?" said the man sheepishly. "We'd thought of getting on to Battleford, but the little un's bad—and the missus perished with cold. We'd give you no trouble if we might warm ourselves a bit."

And he looked under his eyebrows at Elizabeth, at the bright fire behind her, and all the comfort of the new farmhouse. Yet under his shuffling manner there was a certain note of confidence. He was appealing to that Homeric hospitality which prevails throughout the farms of the Northwest.

And in five minutes, the horses were in the barn, the man sitting by the kitchen fire, while Elizabeth was ministering to the woman and child. The new-comers made a forlorn trio. They came from a district some fifty miles further south, and were travelling north in order to take shelter for a time with relations. The mother was a girl of twenty, worn with hardship and privation. The father, an English labourer, had taken up free land, but in spite of much help from a paternal Government, had not been able to fulfil his statutory obligation, and had now forfeited his farm. There was a history of typhoid fever, and as Elizabeth soon suspected, an incipient history of drink. In the first two years of his Canadian life the man worked for a farmer during the summer, and loafed in Winnipeg during the winter. There demoralisation had begun, and as Elizabeth listened, the shadow of the Old World seemed to be creeping across the radiant Canadian landscape. The same woes?—the same weaknesses?—the same problems of an unsound urban life?

Her heart sank for a moment—only to provoke an instant reaction of cheerfulness. No!—in Canada the human will has still room to work, and is not yet choked by a jungle growth of interests.

She waited for Anderson to come in, and meanwhile she warmed and comforted the mother. The poor girl looked round her in amazement at the pretty spacious room, as she spread her hands, knotted and coarsened by work, to the blaze. Elizabeth held her sickly babe, rocking it and crooning to it, while upstairs one of kind-eyed Cumberland women was getting a warm bath ready, and lighting a fire in the guest-room.

"How old is it?" she asked.

"Thirteen months."

"You ought to give up nursing it. It would be better for you both."

"I tried giving it a bit o' what we had ourselves," said the mother, dully—"But I nearly lost her."

"I should think so!" laughed Elizabeth indignantly; and she began to preach rational ways of feeding and caring for the child, while the mother sat by, despondent, and too crushed and hopeless to take much notice. Presently Elizabeth gave her back the babe, and went to fetch hot tea and bread and butter.

"Shall I come and get it in the kitchen?" said the woman, rising.

"No, no—stay where you are!" cried Elizabeth. And she was just carrying back a laden tray from the dining-room when Anderson caught her.

"Darling!—that's too heavy for you!—what are you about?"

"There's a woman in there who's got to be fed—and there's a man in there"—she pointed to the kitchen—"who's got to be talked to. Hopeless case!—so you'd better go and see about it!"

She laughed happily in his face, and he snatched a kiss from her as he carried off the tray.

The woman by the fire rose again in amazement as she saw the broad-shouldered handsome man who was bringing in the tea. Anderson had been tramping through the thin-lying snow all day, inquiring into the water-supply of a distant portion of the farm. He was ruddy with exercise, and the physical strength that seemed to radiate from him intimidated the wanderer.

"Where are you bound to?" he said kindly, as he put down the tea beside her.

The woman, falteringly, told her story. Anderson frowned a little.

"Well, I'd better go and talk to your husband. Mrs. Anderson will look after you."

And Elizabeth held the baby, while the woman fed languidly—too tired and spiritless indeed to eat.

When she could be coaxed no further, Elizabeth took her and the babe upstairs.

"I never saw anything like this in these parts!" cried the girl, looking round her at the white-tiled bathroom.

"Oh, they're getting quite common!" laughed Elizabeth. "See how nice and warm the water is! Shall we bathe the baby?" And presently the child lay warm and swaddled in its mother's arms, dressed in some baby-clothes produced by Elizabeth from a kind of travellers' cupboard at the top of the stairs. Then the mother was induced to try a bath for herself, while Elizabeth tried her hand at spoon-feeding the baby; and in half an hour she had them both in bed, in the bright spare-room—the young mother's reddish hair unbound lying a splendid mass on the white pillows, and a strange expression—as of some long tension giving way—on her pinched face.

"We'll not know how to thank you"—she said brokenly. "We were just at the last. Tom wouldn't ask no one to help us before. But we'd only a few shillings left—we thought at Battleford, we'd sell our bits of things—perhaps that'd take us through." She looked piteously at Elizabeth, the tears gathering in her eyes.

"Oh! well, we'll see about that!" said Elizabeth, as she tucked the blankets round her. "Nobody need starve in this country! Mr. Anderson'll be able perhaps to think of something. Now you go to sleep, and we'll look after your husband."

Anderson joined his wife in the sitting-room, with a perplexed countenance. The man was a poor creature—and the beginnings of the drink-craving were evident.

"Give him a chance," said Elizabeth. "You want one more man in the bothy."

She sat down beside him, while Anderson pondered, his legs stretched to the fire. A train of thought ran through his mind, embittered by the memory of his father.

He was roused from it by the perception that Elizabeth was looking tired. Instantly he was all tenderness, and anxious misgiving. He made her lie down on the sofa by the fire, and brought her some important letters from Ottawa to read, and the English newspapers.

From the elementary human need with which their minds had just been busy, their talk passed on to National and Imperial affairs. They discussed them as equals and comrades, each bringing their own contribution.

"In a fortnight we shall be in Ottawa!" sighed Elizabeth, at last.

Anderson smiled at her plaintive voice.

"Darling!—is it such a tragedy?"

"No, I shall be as keen as anybody else when we get there. But—we are so happy here!"

"Is that really, really true?" asked Anderson, taking her hand and pressing it to his lips.

"Yes"—she murmured—"yes—but it will be truer still next year!"

They looked at each other tenderly. Anderson stooped and kissed her, long and closely.

He was called away to give some directions to his men, and Elizabeth lay dreaming in the firelight of the past and the future, her hands clasped on her breast, her eyes filling with soft tears. Upstairs, in the room above her, the emigrant mother and baby lay sleeping in the warmth and shelter gathered round them by Elizabeth. But in tending them, she had been also feeding her own yearning, quickening her own hope. She had given herself to a man whom she adored, and she carried his child on her heart. Many and various strands would have gone to the weaving of that little soul; she trembled sometimes to think of them. But no fear with her lasted long. It was soon lost in the deep poetic faith that Anderson's child in her arms would be the heir of two worlds, the pledge of a sympathy, a union, begun long before her marriage in the depths of the spirit, when her heart first went out to Canada—to the beauty of the Canadian land, and the freedom of the Canadian life.

THE END

CPSIA information can be obtained
at www.ICGtesting.com
Printed in the USA
FSHW011017270921
85044FS